Diary of a
Dying Woman

*A True-Life Love Story Dealing
with a Terminal Illness*

TIM AND SAVANNAH HELLER

PAGE PUBLISHING, INC.
Conneaut Lake, PA

First originally published by Page Publishing 2021

ISBN 978-1-6624-5446-2 (pbk)
ISBN 978-1-6624-5447-9 (digital)

Printed in the United States of America

Introduction

This is a tragic love story. It is a true story. This story starts oddly enough with me being drunk at the bar shooting pool with some friends. I was on a recent self-destructive path of booze and women. I was at a point of low self-esteem in my life. I had survived two divorces in a matter of a three-year span. In addition, I was providing food and shelter to my two teenage daughters (Michaela, nineteen, and Marinia, sixteen) and one grandchild (Keegan, six months old). I was working, checking in on my kids who seemed okay with me not being home watching them, and then going to the bar for three or four hours a night before repeating this routine the next day. It was a Saturday, and I had gotten drunk by early afternoon, and I was just tired and wanted to go home. I called Savannah. She and I had talked a couple of times, and she had watched my grandson one day as I took my daughters to an amusement park. I had hoped to get lucky with her, but she had spurned my advances, but I did trust her. She seemed genuine and honest to me. I did not want my teenage daughters to see me that drunk that early, so I reached out to her as a way of getting a safe ride home and a diversion to hide my drunkenness from my kids. I called her and asked her, "Can you come save me?" She gave me a ride home, and I convinced her to watch a movie with me and the kids. She was a single mom with two teenagers (Heaven, fifteen, and Gavin, thirteen), but that weekend, they were with her ex. She came and got me and agreed to watch a movie. I was so drunk that I fell asleep on her shoulder, and my grandson had fallen asleep on her other shoulder. The movie was the 2001 motion picture Moulin Rouge. I feel an ironic connection with the movie as I write these words. Two quotes from the movie stand out to me. Satine (the main female character) says to Christian, the male main character, as she is dying, "Tell our story Christian. That way, I'll…I'll always be with you." And I feel compelled to tell this story as a way of staying connected to the love of my life. And it is a positive message of love, as Christian later says in the film, "The greatest thing you'll ever learn is just to love and be loved in return." If people can understand this message from this story, then I feel that I have honored Savannah.

After this, we eventually started dating. She was not only beautiful but also a hard worker and a great mother, and we both shared a faith in God. My first night staying over, we prayed together and then prayed together every night after that. After six and a half weeks, we got married. We got married in her backyard, and our motto was, "Forever and a day." I moved my family into her house as I was a renter, and she was purchasing her house. We converted the dining room into a bedroom, and Savannah and I made a bedroom on the back porch. That night, Savannah and I had a reception at the bar with our friends. Our kids surprisingly got along, and we settled into working multiple jobs and raising teenagers in the same house. We surprisingly did okay despite a few heated arguments with our children at the times we allowed them to live long enough to graduate. Our kids moved out one by one, and we started to enjoy our time together. We went on trips, we went out every weekend, we golfed, and we enjoyed having grandchildren over. By this time, Marinia had her first child (Lincoln), and Heaven had her children (Emmett and Kalem). We were truly enjoying a golden age in our life. We continued to pay bills and got a little money ahead, and we got into a business opportunity to run a local wedding venue/ bar. It seemed as if we were both going to be able to live our happily ever after. This story takes you through the trials and tribulations of a couple and family dealing with a terminal illness, but more importantly it is a story of love and hope and beauty—everything Savannah was.

Chapter 1

Denial and Hospitalization

It was a typical day in late December. I had gotten off work and headed to SwaggerZ (our business) to help Savannah at the business. She had worked all day and was our day manager and made sure the ballroom and bar and bathrooms were clean. We had a huge New Year's Eve event in a couple of days, and we still had to decorate and make sure we had everything ready for the celebration. Savannah had a cold for a couple weeks, but we had a business to run. We both understood that in running your own business, there was no such thing as calling in sick. Besides, the weather had gotten colder, and we both smoked, so a seasonal cold was expected. I worked as a social worker for the hospice during the day to make sure we had health insurance and allow us time to build the business. I worked at the bar on weekends and occasionally on a weekday night. Savannah worked every day of the week and helped run tables and bartended on weekends as well. We were used to working and being tired. Still, we both noted she was getting winded easily and had to take more breaks than normal. I suggested she get checked out by the doctor, but she blew it off as nothing to be concerned about.

We held the New Year's Eve event at the venue, and we both looked forward to going back to a more normal routine of working six or seven days a week, but not as hard and going home earlier instead of decorating, ordering food, lining up entertainment, etc. We still had weddings and events at our venue, but the responsibility of decorating, food, entertainment, etc., was on the wedding or party planners. Several weeks went by, and her cold got worse. Finally, in February she went to the doctor. The initial diagnosis was pneumonia. They prescribed her antibiotics and steroids and for several weeks. She returned to work at the bar, but she was taking a long time to get better. Luckily, we had a friend who was a regular at a bar that helped her mop and clean things. We paid him with beer, and he was happy helping her and drinking each day for free. She continued to get weaker, and we had to hire employees to work some of her shift when she couldn't, but she had to train them. And of course, there were times when employees would call in or want a day off, and Savannah tried to work the shift anyway. On weekends, we had weddings, and I had to go in early and help set up tables and chairs. She would stock refrigerators and clean.

By April, the prescriptions for pneumonia had ended, and she was back to having difficulty breathing. I urged her to go back to the doctor, and eventually she agreed to go. This time, they were going to hospitalize her. After a few days of testing, we were informed that she did not have lung cancer. We both looked at each other and sighed a collective sigh of relieve. AND then…and then…we were told she had pulmonary hypertension and right heart failure. What the hell was that? It didn't sound good. We asked for a better explanation of it. The doctor informed us that Savannah had emphysema and her lungs were not working properly. This was causing her heart on the right side to pump harder trying to get blood flow into the lungs, and this was causing right heart failure. Fluid was building up around the sacs around her lungs, and this was making it hard for her to breath. They informed us she would need to go to Mayo Clinic to have consultation for treatment approaches, including heart and lung transplant. We were still confused. She had smoked since she was fifteen years old, but she was rarely sick. She had never had asthma or problems breathing or ever had an inhaler. The doctor told us her condition was terminal with a life expectancy of one to two years. Savannah's first reaction was to say, "I can't die. I got shit to do." This was the moment we remembered vividly when we started writing the book, and this comment by her was a title we thought about in naming the book. It summed up our shock and disbelief.

6

She had gotten so weak they had to be hospitalized, and they performed a pleural effusion. Savannah often referred to this as her lungs being tapped. In actuality, this was really a short version of a medical term called thoracentesis. Thoracentesis is a procedure to remove fluid from the space between the lining of the outside of the lungs (pleura) and the wall of the chest. Normally, very little fluid is present in this space. An accumulation of excess fluid between the layers of the pleura is called a pleural effusion. It is often referred to as pleural fluid aspiration, pleural tap, or thoracentesis. It involves a needle pushed through the back area into a sac around the lungs. A tube is attached to the needle, and suction draws the fluid out of this area. In some heart and lung patients, the fluid builds up in this area, putting pressure on the heart and lungs because the lungs can't fully expand. This makes it hard for them to breath. She was discharged, and we were expecting to go to Mayo in a couple of weeks. However, after a few days home, it was evident the fluids were building up around her again. They decided to take her to Mayo immediately by ambulance. I ran home and grabbed clothes and drove myself to the Mayo hospital.

As I was driving to Mayo, I couldn't believe what we were told and thought Mayo would give us a second opinion and we would get treatment or something and things would return to normal. Was I in denial? HELL YES, but when most people hear the word *denial*, they have negative ideas of people not realizing the reality of the situation. Also, people believe that denial is a stage people experience in the beginning of a terminal illness. I'm here to challenge these traditional views of denial. I suggest we look at it differently. Denial is a powerful coping method that allows you to keep moving when otherwise you'd want to curl up in a ball and die. Savannah lived in denial for over two years. It allowed her to continue to work at our business for months after being hospitalized. It allowed her to continue to cook and do housekeeping. It allowed her to plant flowers and start a garden. It allowed her to paint and do craft projects. Even in the last month of life, she was wanting to "get shit done." Additionally, denial allowed me to go to work every day. It allowed our kids to live their lives while she was dying. I remember one day at the hospice office. One of our nurses was talking about a family being in denial. I laughed as they asked me what I thought. I agreed. They were in denial. Hell, I was in denial. I was going to work every day with a wife with a severe terminal illness. How many times did I worry I would go home and find her fallen and unconscious or dead? We are all in some denial. Every day, we are closer to losing a loved one. Although it was over two years from her diagnosis to her death, denial was with us throughout the entire process. Even today I'm in denial and still have a hard time believing she is gone.

Once we got to Mayo, they put her on high oxygen and put her in the ICU. She was awake and scared, but I was there, and I slept in the ICU room with her. She spent two days in ICU. After she got out of ICU, we contacted our lawyer. We were not ready for her to die, but we knew we had to take care of legal matters in case she didn't make it out of the hospital. We did have life insurance when we got married, but besides that, we never had any planning done. We had over two years to plan before she died, but we didn't know that at the time. Our lawyer drew up the paperwork and helped us immediately get a living will and a last will and testament. These are two completely different things. Living wills are a legal document that allows for someone to speak on your behalf in case you are not able to or you are incapacitated. There is generally a medical power of attorney and a financial power of attorney. They can be the same person, and in our case, it was. Savannah and I had talked at the hospital, and she did not want heart and lung transplant. She did not want the surgery and the antirejection medication. However, us talking about it didn't count for much when it came to medical decisions. So we got the living will done, and I became her medical power of attorney. If she had not been able to answer for herself at Mayo and we did not have a living will, then there would have been a parade of doctors telling me and her kids what could be done to save her. Fortunately, I never had to be in that spot to having to tell the medical team no more medical treatment. The last will and testament was about our property and assets after she died. In our case, we needed a last will and testament also due to the business and property we owned. She willed the business and all the property to me, but I would have gladly had it all taken away to have her better. I also had my will made out at the same time, and I made her a promise that I would look after her kids as my own, and she made me the same promise, but we both knew the chances were I'd end up having to keep my promise. Many other decisions we still had to make, and over time, we did. However, it was important to address those issues and not avoid them before we left the hospital.

When she was transferred to a regular hospital room on their pulmonary floor, we were relieved. However, we realized this was not a sign of immediate discharge. Each day before 5:00 a.m., the Mayo blood collectors would draw blood and get them to the lab. Savannah used to call them the vampires, and they apologized each time they took blood. She used humor to help herself cope with the sounds of machines around her and "vampires" drawing blood each morning. Then there were x-rays, cardiograms, and about every three to five days more draining fluid off her lungs. Then usually the main doctor would come and explain the results of the tests and introduced idea of a medication to help reduce the pressure on the heart and slow the rate of fluid building up around the lungs. It would not be a cure, but it would buy her time. And about once a day, we had visits from the transplant team. They explained how a heart and lung transplant would be the most logical aggressive treatment that could be pursued. She laughed after they visited and called them Dr. Frankenstein and Igor. They explained the risks and urged her to get on the transplant list. She almost immediately decided against it. She talked it over with me. She was scared about having a heart and lung transplant. She also did not think she could handle the amount of antirejection medications. However, her biggest reason was she did not want to deprive someone else younger than her and healthier than her that might have a better shot at survival. Secretly, I hoped she would have at least put her name on the list, but I told her from the beginning it was her decision, and I would support whatever she wanted.

While in the hospital, we thought the medical professionals we encountered were incredibly dedicated people. They all wanted her to get well. At times it did seem they tried to sell treatment options.

Dr. Frantz was her primary doctor at Mayo. He did an excellent job not overpromising and explained things were going to change for her life and all options would be just buying time. She liked him the most. Savannah was not impressed with the idea of transplants. It would mean probably extending her life five to ten years, but she could die during the transplant operation. She would need to take antirejection medication the rest of her life. And there was still a possibility it could be rejected by her own body. One of the transplant doctors talked about how few combined heart and lung transplants were performed each year but arrogantly assured her he would pull it off. Savannah was not impressed and talked about praying about it. The doctor challenged her about her faith and again urged the transplant. That pissed Savannah off and helped cement her decision to not pursue a transplant. But the most important thing that weighed in her decision was the idea of the limited spots on the waiting list. Savannah considered her middle age (forty-eight years old at the time of diagnosis), and her love of others compelled her to pass on the transplant. She talked about how younger people with more life ahead of them should be given opportunity to get transplant before her. They did insert tubing into her chest that was hooked up to a medication pump that she carried with her. The pump provided small doses of medication to her heart directly and ran twenty-four hours a day. This medication needed to be mixed every night, and pump cartridges were switched. Additionally, she took medications to help blood flow to the lungs and diuretics to help drain fluid from the body. We had discussed if she was ever not able to eat if she wanted a feeding tube, permanent drains from the lungs, and other medical interventions that might be used to keep her alive longer. She didn't want any of them. Although they might all extend her life, the pain and suffering with those interventions were not worth it to her.

We spent a month at the Mayo hospital. She celebrated her forty-ninth birthday at the hospital on May 1, 2018. I had gotten a cake from a local restaurant, and several of the nurses and aides sang a happy birthday to her. I know when she blew out the candles that she wished for everything to return to normal. Yet the following weeks at the hospital and the routine of blood draws and tests done almost daily made it increasingly obvious that she would never return to full health, like she had wished for. We tried not to talk about what we were facing mainly because we just didn't want to believe it. We watched a lot of TV. We did crossword puzzles and played games to pass the time. We had family and friends come and visit. We talked about what she wanted to accomplish when she got home. Mainly she talked about getting out of the hospital and getting back to our home. Yet about every four to five days, they would tell her that they needed to drain the fluid off her lungs again. She got anxious, and I could see the fear in her eyes as they got her ready for another procedure to drain the fluid from her lungs. At times, we were not sure she was going to be able to go home. I personally worried she would die at the hospital. Yet one day her lab work came back with better readings, and the latest x-ray indicated fluids around the lungs were not building back up right away. She cried with happiness when they told us we could leave the hospital and return home. We quickly bolted out of there before they could change their minds.

Chapter 2

Return Home and Adjusting to the New Normal

After we were discharged from the Mayo hospital, we went home knowing she was terminal and that she would die. Yet we tried to return to somewhat of a normal life. We contacted home health, and they helped get us medical supplies and nurse needs she had. The machines we got from home health had oxygen tanks and could be refilled. This allowed her to be more mobile. Besides new medication routines and medical equipment she needed, several other adjustments must be made. Those included dietary changes, the setup and layout of our house, limitations to activities, how to avoid depression, etc. It was overwhelming, but we figured it out. The trick was to focus on one or two at a time until they all became part of our new normal. It was a big adjustment when we look back on it, but while we were going through it, we just adjusted to each change. We knew that if we had questions or needed support, there was a twenty-four-hour support available from our medical team. We called Mayo Clinic a few times in the first few weeks back, but after a while, we felt confident enough in what we were doing, and we did not need to call.

Having prescriptions added, and knowing how to take them was important. It was more than swallowing pills. Some medications required taking the medication on an empty stomach, and others suggested eating something beforehand. Then we had to keep in mind that most of the medications caused side effects. Savannah had diuretics, which caused her mouth to be dry a lot, but she couldn't just drink more fluids because she had a fluid restriction. So we learned how to counter some of the side effects. In Savannah's case, she sucked on ice chips or chewed gum or sucked candy. The medications sometimes caused problems with her diet. Sometimes the pills were twenty to thirty pills per day for her. These caused upset stomach and decreased her ability to eat a lot. She got hungry, but some of the pills were large, and her stomach was only so big. Despite the side effects, she had no option but to take them. We never just stopped taking a medication on our own. If she was having severe complications like nausea or vomiting, we would call and consult with her medical team to see if there were other options. Most medications are now made with alternatives that can do the job just as well.

Nutrition guidelines and/or restrictions also need to be followed. This was difficult at first especially when she was used to eating and drinking what she wanted. Luckily, most food ingredients can be substituted such as sugar-free additives, salt alternatives, etc. However, we still had to pay attention to the details and ingredients with our foods. Just because we used a salt alternative did not mean our food was low in sodium. Those labels we had largely never paid attention to now become very important. Keep in mind that processed food, boxed food, instant food, and fast food or takeout food would quickly use up or exceed any dietary limits she had. Home cooking was where we had more control of the additives, and it really made a huge difference. One of her favorite dishes was bone in chicken. When we got that from the local chicken restaurant, it almost immediately hit her sodium limit with one meal. Making at home with our own salt-free alternatives was well within limits she had. Once we started tracking all these nutrients and knew what we should and should not eat, we got accustomed to our new diet. In our case, we found new likes such as swordfish that we might not have ever tried. Next to medications, food and nutrition guidelines were one of the most important adjustments we made.

There were other things we had to consider besides medications and diets. Some of the equipment took up space and had wires and tubing sprawled across your floors. We had carpet and wood floors and throw rugs to add warm and decor. The throw rugs had to be gotten rid of as her oxygen tubing got caught on them when she moved about the house. We had to move furniture around to make room for her walker when she needed that to make sure she had room to get through with the walker. Later we had to move a coffee table out so we could get the hospital bed she needed into our living room. Our bedroom was originally upstairs when we first got home from the hospital, but the flight of stairs was nearly impossible to get up without taking one or two breaks getting up them. We needed to change the layout of our house. We moved the dining room furniture out to the garage, and then we had to move the bedroom downstairs. Luckily, we had an older home with pocket doors that shut from the dining room and living room, and the doorway to the kitchen was a single doorway we covered with a curtain for privacy. We still had one remaining problem, and that was we only had one bathroom, and that was upstairs. Initially, she would try to make the trek upstairs with assistance several times a day because she had to urinate a lot from the diuretics. In the middle of the night, we had her use a bedside commode, and I would empty it in the morning. We had a fundraiser at our bar a few weeks after returning from the hospital, and we received a grant from my employer that helped us convert our laundry room and back porch into a downstairs bathroom. Stairs continued to be a nemesis the rest of the time she was sick. She would go outside and enjoy the flowers we had planted or when she wanted to go to the store, but she had to take her time and needed assistance carrying her purse, her portable oxygen cart, etc. And if we shopped stores, the one thing that stopped us from going in was if they had stairs. Rethinking our house layout took some adjustments, but we got accustomed to it. Besides, like any house, it was only a home with love, and we had plenty of that throughout.

Perhaps the biggest adjustment needed was in our own minds. My wife had a hard time getting used to not being able to do very much. She was an active woman all her life, and we had both worked at least full-time and part-time jobs besides. It bothered her as she became less and less able to be active. We had to have her apply for disability because she was no longer able to work. She tried keeping busy with activities. There were periods of time she engaged in different hobbies and projects to stay busy. She got into gardening, painting, cooking, crocheting, sewing, etc., anything to keep herself busy. Each time she had a new idea, I'd go buy her supplies and materials for her latest ideas only to see she lost interest in a few weeks. I spent too much money at times knowing the result would be the same, but I wanted to make her happy. Best advice for those going through this and wanting to keep busy with projects is to start small and moderate how much you spend on these projects. As the disease progressed, she was less able to do things, and this really made her angry. Her mind was active and wanted to do so much more, but her body would not let her. I can't imagine how that felt, being a prisoner in your own body. The point is, those activities made her feel worthwhile. They made her feel like she was doing something, and it helped in preventing depression. Don't overlook the importance of such activities.

I myself started to have to adjust my activities. I was someone that worked a full-time job during the day, and if the weather was nice, I'd want to take her golfing after work. I worked part-time jobs on weekends and was doing that at our bar until we had to close it. I was never a painter or a crafter, but I did enjoy playing video games and golfing and listening to music. Video games I could play on my phone as she slept or did her craft ideas. However, the hobbies we enjoyed the most were ones we could do together. We cooked together as she told me what ingredient was needed next. We watched shared favorite Netflix series. We played a mini-golf video game and Scrabble almost nightly. As a caregiver, I needed hobbies and activities to keep myself busy as well. There were many times she slept and I was not tired or times she was working on a project that I was not interested in. I couldn't just go to the bar or go with friends to do something fun. I had to stay home and be of assistance if needed. There were lots of dead time. We kept busy with individual and shared hobbies and activities. Even if it was weeding the flower bed, cooking, or as simple as watching TV together, it all helped. Some might think we were killing time, but we used to laugh and say, "At least time isn't killing us." It kept us from becoming depressed.

We were able to discuss difficult subjects (including sexual intimacy, her death, my life after she was gone, etc.) as we busied ourselves. We knew we had limited time left, and doing things together helped us grow closer.

We quickly became aware that we had to be inside most of the time because of her terminal illness. In the winter, it was too cold for her, and in the summer, it was often too hot for her. Even weather she normally like was not as enjoyable as it used to be. Savannah loved going outside in the spring and summer and even the fall. However, with medications having impact on her body and poor circulation often associated with declining health, she found herself inside much more than she had hoped. This affected her mentality and emotions. We were aware of seasonal depression and tried to counter this by opening curtains more, trying to sit near windows, and going outside if she was able to once a day even for a few minutes. We repainted the living room to a lighter color. We had antidepression medications available, but she never used them. I think there were times when she could have used it. Heck, I could have used them and probably should have gotten a prescription from a doctor and used antidepressants myself. It is important to know she did use THC tablets, which did alter her mood and provide some relief to any depression she had. It was important to utilize medical and psychological interventions when dealing with the mental aspects of her terminal disease.

I became more aware of how depression was part of the terminal disease process. Working in hospice for several years, I have not heard many patients or family admit they were depressed. Even Savannah would not say she was depressed. She would say she was having a bad day or a rough day or she was cranky today. To be honest, I knew I was, but I never admitted it. To me admitting it was like admitting I had a weakness. We utilized a variety of strategies to deal with depression. There is an old saying: "Laughter is the best medicine." Early on, we used laughter. Of course, we cried. We cried often when we talked about things she would miss out on. But after a few minutes, she would turn to me and tease me by saying, "Are you crying like a little bitch?" That was our cue to switch the topic and try to focus on something else. She loved reading jokes on Facebook, and friends would tell her funny stories when we talked to them when they visited in person or by phone. During the day, while I was at work, she would watch comedy sitcoms often. She had a wonderful sense of humor that helped us both deal with what we were going through. I previously had lots of training as a social worker in cognitive restructuring strategies. Quite simply, this was taking how we thought about our situation and changing our thoughts about it. For example, if she thought about what she couldn't do, then she would stop this thinking and try to focus on the positive aspects of her life and what she still had or still could do. I am aware of a lot of research that supports cognitive restructuring. Perhaps the more common terminology that most people would recognize for such strategies would be the power of positive thinking. This perhaps was the most important method we utilized. Dying of a terminal illness was depressing, but we weren't afraid to find humor and use positive thinking to counter it.

Her medical team often asked her about depression and suggested counseling and/or medication if needed. Savannah did not ever take them up on the offer for antidepression medication. However, she did utilize THC (legal in our state for medical use at the time). She took THC pills for pain, but she admitted it helped her mood as well. As a social worker in hospice, I know firsthand the benefits of antidepression medications. Often these were utilized by patients, but several times I had discussions with spouses and other family members that struggled with depression before and after the patient had died. These medications have made a difference in millions of lives and should be considered if depression is problematic. Of course, all medications should be discussed with medical professionals and your doctor and utilized as prescribed. It is also important to note that sometimes it took several days or several weeks before she felt the therapeutic levels. Again, we never discontinued antidepression medications on our own without consulting with our doctor. Many times, I have counseled people to talk with their doctor before discontinuing. This is a common issue as a person starts feeling less depressed and then decides on their own that they no longer need the medication. This of course then leads to return of depression symptoms and inconsistent treatment. Of course, both antidepressants and counseling can be a very effective strategy regarding depression. I strongly encourage patients and families to consider antidepressants and counseling if depression becomes problematic during the terminal illness or after the patient has passed away and loved ones are struggling with depression during the bereavement process.

We did most things together through our two-year journey. We watched the same TV shows. We played video games we both enjoyed. We went to the store together. We visited family and friends together either by going out initially or having them visit us as she got weaker. I was still working the last year of her life. Gavin and Heaven had moved back in to help when I was at work. But we had the bonus of having Heaven's children move back in too. The grandchildren were very emotionally uplifting for her. They would wake up before their mom, and Savannah would hear their pitter-pattering feet sneaking food in the kitchen. She would get up sometimes just because she had the grandchildren getting into things and playing before the other adults were up. It was a relief for me, knowing someone was at the house while I was at work. After work, it was back to taking care of her and making sure she had her needs met. So keep in mind as the terminal advances, they will need more people to help. We were blessed that they had gone though some breakups and were in their early twenties and could move back. We charged rent because we didn't believe in allowing our kids to take advantage of us. It wasn't much, but not having to hire private help to stay with her saved us money too.

Depression for her as a patient and me as a caregiver was a reality and not weakness. We utilized positive thinking and humor to counter depression. Savannah had legal THC pills that helped with pain and her appetite and elevated her mood some. Depression medication and counseling can be effective strategies in dealing with depression. We learned to enjoy activities together as we spent increasingly more time together inside. We got additional help from our family, friends, and neighbors and hired a private helper for a while. Savannah needed increasingly more help physically and socially as she declined. When she went on hospice, the COVID-

19 pandemic was in full swing, and there were several days I had to work from home. When it was obvious she was not going to live much longer (the last two weeks), I took a vacation and stayed with her all the time. As a caregiver, it was imperative that I took care of myself as well. The terminal process was challenging to both of us physically, mentally, and emotionally. The most challenging and yet rewarding experience was knowing I was there for her throughout. I would gladly go through it again at any age to just spend more time with her.

We had many adjustments dealing with a terminal illness. Medications needed to be taken and understood. We did not hesitate to call early on if we had questions. Changes to diet we accommodated to by developing new tastes, and substitutes were used. Equipment that was required took room, and we had to be careful that it didn't get caught or unplugged. It happened at times, and we learned. Changing around our house and layout took time and money. The biggest adjustment was within our own minds. It was incredibly and mentally tough to slowly lose her mobility and her independence. We learned to develop joint and individual activities and hobbies that helped us stave off depression. We had to cross boundaries that included helping her in the toilet and bath and eventually help her accept help from others including other caregivers, like our children or hired caregivers. We were not afraid to talk about all aspects of our relationship, including sexual intimacy. Having such conversations, we found out it allowed for more of a mental and emotional connection than just the physical contact of sex. We went through all this, and we grew stronger as a couple. We depended on each other on a realm that was hard to describe but other than what wedding vows described as "for better or for worse." Funny thing is, I never saw our relationship as worse, just changing as the disease progressed. I was next to her in her hospital bed as she slowly slipped away, knowing she was loved, and we were there for each other. To me, I feel content we faced it together.

Chapter 3

Her Journal 2018—Adjusting and Still Hopeful

Savannah started journaling after returning from the Mayo hospital. She had asked me to read the journal after she had passed and apologized ahead of time if she said anything in her journal that was harsh or hurt anyone's feelings. She had needed to vent her feelings in her journal and explained it was the best way to get them off her mind. I completely understood and encouraged her to journal. She started journaling immediately, but we started the actual book writing about a year after she was diagnosed. I finished the book after a few months after she had passed away. We hope the shock of the title got you to look at the book and helped you as we described what we went through and explained it in our everyday experiences. Although the love of my life dies at the end of this book, I hope you feel her warmth, her sense of humor, and her determination and realize this is a book of hope and inspiration. Her journal entries follow. They are indented for ease of reading and know what she wrote in her journal. I occasionally add in some context or backstory to explain what was going on in our lives during the journaling.

At the beginning of her journal, she puts a warning in to explain to myself and the children that she wanted to be understanding of her feelings and in no way wanted to hurt anybody. Also, at this time, we talked about writing a book, so I think she figured that she better put a disclaimer in there.

Savannah's opening statement for this journal book:

This is my life now. The things you read here are my thoughts and feelings. These books are a place for me to vent and for you to one day help you understand what I'm going through. Please don't be offended. These are emotional days for me and I need to vent. I mean in no way to harm anyone. I'm human, I get angry, depressed, happy, sad. These books are so I can vent healthy instead of speaking out and saying things I don't really mean.

May 16, 2018
Rough day today. Reality sucks! God gave me such a wonderful husband and kids though. I'm so blessed. Truly I am blessed with friends, family, and all the prayers and love being sent my way. We grilled out today and it was awesome. I loved the air, the birds, the bunnies in the yards, and even the bugs! LOL! Never thought I'd say that. I talked to Cindy and Terri (friends of ours) via video chat. I miss them so much. I've been crying a lot today. Just being mushy. Looking back on a lot of things and people. God has truly blessed me. The taste of hamburger was awesome from the grill and I didn't get sick. Corn on the cob was Amazing! The most amazing part of today though was the strength my husband and my son had as I sobbed off and on. My husband has always been amazing to me and I've thanked God for him. My son made me so proud and happy because I never thought I'd get the close-ness I felt today with him. It was amazing and the man he is growing into makes me so proud. Wonderful, but rough day. Thank you, God.

Savannah herself had moments in which it dawned on her she was dying. As you can tell, it was not only physical torture as she got sicker but also mental torture. She briefly mentions it here, but the first time was when we returned from the hospital, and she tried going up the stairs and had to stop and sit on the steps because she got so winded. She broke down crying and sobbed, "This really is happening. I'm dying." Other times she would try to do something like cook or do something physical, and she couldn't. Often, she got angry and kept telling herself under her breath, "You can do this," but finally she would ask for help. This was our first day back from the hospital after almost a month at Mayo. I had taken FMLA to be at the hospital, but I was not set to return until the following week. We needed to get settled in and see how much support she was going to need when I returned to work.

May 17, 2018
Had to go have blood drawn today. Potassium low as usual. Been a little stressed today, but we're doing a lot of cleaning. Nurse came to teach us to do dressing changes. Tim was awesome as usual. (I have the best husband EVER!) We're a little on each other's nerves today, but mostly because I'm so used to being independent, but with this crap I need to relax a little. It's hard, so sometimes we butt heads. Had Keegan today and saw MJ. Love them so much. Proud of how hard that girl works, and Keegan is just amazing. Mom, Evelyn, Brittany and baby Megan stopped by. Evelyn cried, I told her it was OK. Get it all out. I love her so much. Brittany told her no crying, but I told her to "Let her cry. I'm dying, so let her cry." We all cried then and talked. It was a good visit. Made supper after another head butting, but relaxing watching tube now. They upped my meds today, so I'm a little slow now. Did I mention how much I love and

appreciate this amazing husband of mine? He fucken ROCKS! I'm lucky and blessed to have him. Anyway, going to try make up for meltdowns and get some cuddles with my man.

Sometimes we would watch Keegan (our grandson) after school when his mom and dad were working later. MJ is Michaela, our oldest daughter. Her mom, Evelyn (Savannah's sister), and Brittany (Savannah's niece) visited this day. She thought it was okay to cry and encouraged us to do so whenever needed to, but after about five minutes, she would encourage us to stop.

May 18, 2018
Today was rough. I don't know how to explain it. I was angry and feeling sorry for myself. I was so embarrassed to ride in the electric cart at Walmart. I've never been so needy. I argued with Tim. The one constant in my life. The rock who holds me high. I was STUPID! Then I cried on top of it and felt even worse. Then the day became better. In the morning I sat out on the step enjoying the beauty of what God has given us and then the meltdown. Then we grilled out! We ate outside too. It was so beautiful. Judy [Savannah's sister], Adela [Savannah's niece], and Janae [Adela's baby] stopped by too. That was good. We've been working so hard to get the house right and I'm going through things I ask myself, "If you're going to die, how much crap do you need to leave behind for people to get rid of?" That's probably why I was pissy, but it's reality and I'm going remember that. They texted me that I got an appointment in Mayo at 8:45 AM! WTF! X-ray first, then blood. Hopefully that's all. I want to be home and not wasting time in Dr. office. Anyway, so Saturday hopefully I

won't be such a grump and whah whah. OH, My HUSBAND IS FUCKING AMAZING!!!! Total negative Bitch! Whah! Whah! Poor Tim.

First off, I never thought she was a bitch. Anyone that knew us knows we loved and adored each other. We never called each other names in our entire marriage. These thoughts were hers, like many women. Society trains women to not complain or cry because they are deemed a bitch or a crybaby. As a social worker and having several female children, I always hated this negative socialization women are indoctrinated with. Even at our home, I don't remember intentionally doing this to our children. However, it is so prevalent in our society maybe I did unintentionally at times. And a quick look on the TV or movies we have watched, I know the message is nonstop toward women. Savannah had been abused as a child and later as an adult in different relationships she had had. She often gave me way too much credit. I was not perfect. I was stubborn at times. I drank too much at times. However, I do know, compared to many of her previous relationships, I treated her more as an equal than any of her previous relationships. But I'd note she had treated me better than my previous relationships before too. We were meant for each other.

May 19, 2018
No entry.

May 20, 2018
Rough day. Went to church. Awesome, Gavin came with. Scott, Evelyn, & Bill (my brother and his wife and my other brother) came to visit. Great to see you them! They're so good to me. His family have pitched in staying with me when he had to work, now they've given money to help us. I owe them a lot. Damon, Tiffany [Savannah's nephew and his girlfriend] and baby came to visit. She's so beautiful and happy like Damon was. I loved seeing his new family. So

proud of him and he's an awesome Dad like his Dad. Then there's the aching I've had all day. Thinking I'm having a reaction or getting sick. So tired and cold, just yucky feeling.

We started going back to church when she felt like it. As you can tell when we returned from Mayo, we had lots of visitors. She loved company, and I often worried she would overdo it with visitors, but it seemed to energize her often. Savannah would visit and ignore her symptoms, but later she felt it in the evening. Besides the side effects, Savannah faced daily challenges with illnesses. Often, she had a cold besides having COPD. Her immune system was very weak, and if there was a bug going around, there was a good chance she would get it. This upset her often because she often thought she was recovering some, and then she would feel sick again for several days. She told me the hardest part of the terminal illness was never getting a break from illness very long. She had the cold several times with congestion. She had the flu several times with diarrhea and fevers at times. It wasn't just illnesses but also exposure to weather that caused complications. If it was cold outside and we returned inside, it would take several hours sometimes before she felt warm again.

May 21, 2018
Had to go to Mayo for appointment today. Sick on my way home. Sick all day, Slept most of it. Threw up on my way home and felt like shit rest of the day. Tired, went to bed early. Felt better somewhat by bedtime.

May 22, 2018
Feel like shit today.

May 23, 2018
Still feel shitty but got to get house done so Marinia and Lincoln will have somewhere to sleep. I'm a bit cranky and sick. Going to have

a nap. Napped forever! Feel better now though. Grilled out, ate too much. Way too much.

May 24, 2018

Marinia's home! Glad she is here, so excited to get to see Lincoln on Friday! Keegan was here today. I told them to get water guns out so they (Marinia & Keegan) could cool off because it was hot today. Grilled out again, but this time I got to go outside to!! They up my meds so that's going to suck cause just started feeling better and now I get to suffer again. Yay! Pain for a holiday weekend! Tim was back to work at far Friday, so life will get back to a little normal for him at least.

May 25, 2018

Still suffering from side effects. Spent most of the day miserable. After supper felt little better got up and did dishes. Lincoln came today! It was great to see him and watch him and Keegan play. God forgive me, I hate Marinia's ex-husband so much for keeping him from us. Oh well at least we get to see him now. Tim had to work bar tonight, so I had to make meds on my own today. Scary but I did it. Heaven is coming home tomorrow! Can't wait to see her. Well, here's to a better day tomorrow.

May 26, 2018

Beautiful day today. Starting to feel better. Painted a bank with Lincoln, Suncatcher with Keegan (well Marinia). Love watching the boys play & craft. Marinia took boys swimming for a bit. Michaela came by for a bit. Heaven stopped in. Made me heart happy. Tim had to work bar tonight and Danno, our friend, sang a song to me on video, some of our regulars were there and said hi on video. I bawled like a baby for about an hour because I miss them all so much. I'm so damn emotional. Watched TV for a bit, then did dishes. Trying to keep busy and trying to stay cool. Yep, thinking today was one of my most favorite days. I love my family so much.

She made crafts like banks, wind chimes, birdhouses, etc., with the grandkids. The grandkids were like a magical elixir to her. She would ignore her illness and try to do something special with the grandkids. When I had to work the bar we owned, I would sometimes Facebook-chat with Savannah to try to include her. Many of our friends wanted to say hi to her, and the regulars were regular customers and friends of ours at the bar.

May 27, 2018
Yay! Going outside today! I'm going to clean out my flower beds, while Tim mows. Can't wait! All done! Yard's mowed, flower beds weeded (mostly). It was HOT!! I did great though. I feel good that I could get out and do something useful. My flowers out back are AWESOME! Proud of the way it looks. I was worried that my flowers wouldn't come up at all but, most of them did. I feel GOOD!! Thank you GOD for giving me a very productive day!

May 28, 2018
Suzy (Tim's sister) came yesterday, took us to breakfast at Perkins today. She's awesome, I love when she visits. Had a cookout today with a lot of my family. Suzy helped get it all ready. Suzy and my family (My mom, my brother Donnie and his wife and their boys, my sister Judy and her boyfriend) all ate outside and visited. Heaven

and the boys came, MJ, Steven and Keegan came. Gavin was here as well. It was beautiful. Everyone had fun, no drama and we all overate! Boys and Heaven stayed late, and we watched a movie with them (Black Panther). Boys and I ate oranges and we had a great time. Tim was exhausted and so was I, so we went to bed early. BEAUTIFUL DAY!!

May 29, 2018

Home alone today. Tim's at work. Gavin's here, but he will be going to work out later. Did laundry, dishes, cooked supper. Tim kept calling me to check on me. He stopped by this morning before he left town. I love him so much. He takes awesome care of me. I hope I show him just how much I appreciate all he does. I try. I try not to get pissy. Went to Walmart to get groceries. It's pouring outside! Going to cuddle up to my man and watch a movie. Thank you, GOD, for another day with my family!

May 30, 2018

Great day again. Got a lot of housework done. Tim hired Patti (a lady he knew from work) to come and check in on me and help me if I need it, while he returns to work. She came today and helped. I always feel better when I can do productive things. Made tacos for supper. Beaver Creek 4 are coming over tonight to play for me, so I'm feeding them tacos. Well that was AWESOME. Great friends that would come over and jam to cheer you up! Very blessed. Emmett loved it too. Thank you, God, for another Great Day.

Patti was the lady I hired to come several days a week for a couple hours each day to help Savannah during the week when I was at work. She had been laid off, but she was an older lady, and I knew she would be consistent in helping us. Just having her over a few days a week for a couple of hours a day brought me some peace of mind as I returned to work. Beaver Creek 4 was a local band of four guys that played classic rock. We had them at the bar before and considered them friends. They came and played in our living room. She loved it.

May 31, 2018

Had to get blood drawn today. Dena and Russ came! Dena and Russ are old friends of mine. I've known Dena for over 20 years. It was good to see her and Russ. Heaven slept most of the day, but boys kept me and Gavin on her toes (LOL). Heaven works so hard to give them all they need. She's a great mom, they're so smart! Tim had to work today but you still managed to have enough energy to watch movies with me Whatever I need, I get. He's the best. Love watching movies with him. Thank you, GOD, for another day.

June 1, 2018

THANK YOU GOD FOR ANOTHER DAY! Well side effects aren't too bad this time. Pretty uneventful day. Cleaned house and Patti came at 2 to help with what I can't do. Kirk & Lori (friends of ours) stopped by. That was cool. It was good to see them. Glad they came because I get stir crazy being here always and alone mostly. Again, Tim had to work at hospice and bar so, home alone. Thank You God.

June 2, 2018

THANK YOU GOD! Thank you for another day and THE WORLD'S BEST HUSBAND EVER!! Not only was I kind of bitch today and he didn't lose his cool, but he took GAVIN & I GOLFING!! I only can putt but still. I Fucking went golfing!! Trying hard to get out of my slump, it's tough. Again, THANK YOU GOD!

I have no idea what she was talking about here. I never thought she was being bitchy. I know there were days she was not feeling good and maybe cranky, but to me, that would be normal for anyone. But again, this is her perception and thoughts, not mine.

June 3, 2018

Went to a bar and help clean there. A lady had to get in early to decorate for grad party. Went to Menards to get flowers for my flower garden & beds. Weeded in flower bed and got solar lights put in. My hubby was awesome of course he dug up all the soil in the flower bed so I could pull the weeds out. Ice cream truck came by and he got us treats! I'm pooped! We made spaghetti and now cuddle time! THANK YOU, GOD, FOR ONE MORE DAY.

She planted flowers in front of the house. She couldn't do this herself but had me plant them for her. She carefully pointed where each plant had to go. Once they were planted, she would weed them and water them.

June 4, 2018

Thank YOU GOD FOR LETTING ME HAVE ANOTHER DAY!! Didn't do much today, but I got my oxygen and cleaned out closet. Made honey mustard chicken, potatoes and strawberry shortcake for supper. Had FaceTime with friends at bar. Bawled my eyes out after. I miss them all so much. So later THE BEST HUBBY IN THE WORLD, took me and Gavin to see the new Han Solo movie! Was great to get out. THANK YOU AGAIN FATHER!

June 5, 2018
Didn't get anything done except dishes. Maybe tomorrow. Wish I could just do things on my own. Thank You God for another day! Heaven and her boyfriend and the boys came today. They cooked for us and then bed.

June 6, 2018
THANK YOU GOD FOR ANOTHER DAY! Very rough day today. Started out with just numb & ok. Tried to get out of my funk. Heaven and her boyfriend, & the boys were here, but still didn't help. I just feel worthless and useless. Planned to go to the store and work in flower beds but nobody available to babysit me. They all were busy. It started pouring rain and hail and I lost it! Tim (my hero) bought an umbrella took me to the store where I cried more then went to Eagle's meeting. That helped. We then watched Supernatural rest of the night. Thank you, Father, again.

We were both members of the local Eagles' Club. I was president for a year. Meetings were not formal, but it was more social for her. She loved visiting with others, which helped her feel better mentally and physically.

June 7, 2018

Increase meds today. THANK YOU, GOD, FOR ANOTHER DAY! Felt much better today. Got laundry done, put some away, did dishes, visited with a friend from the bar. Patti cleaned my bathroom, and did some bar rags & mops, put away more clothes in our room. Went to bar with Tim and saw a bunch of friends. I was so happy to see them all. It was Harold's b-day and I got to hear him sing. Harold is a friend of ours and an avid karaoke singer. I cried a little. Tim of course worried that it was too much for me, but I'm fine. I need to see people! Anyway, thank God for such a great day and good friends. Also, for an awesome HUSBAND!! Thank you, Father!!

June 8, 2018

Thank you Father for another day! Great day. I feel good, going to work in my flower beds. It feels good to be useful. Gavin and I worked in flower beds after Tim and I got more stuff for beds. Went to work with Tim again. I had such a great time seeing all and I even sang one song! Thank you, Father, for letting me have such an awesome day! Thank you.

June 9, 2018

Heaven's coming today I hope it stays clear all day because I want to try to get flower beds done. Heaven came got another flower bed done. It was good to have her hang out with me and do things. Wasn't going to go to the bar, but Tim and came and got me at 10. Glad I went. Got to see Danno and Jason and Kirk (friends of ours).

Sang couple songs too! THANK YOU, GOD, FOR ANOTHER DAY! THANK YOU!

Savannah loved karaoke. In fact, only reason we met was I worked part-time as a bartender at a bar that had karaoke on weekends there. I hated karaoke at first, but she slowly got me to liking it. Then we started doing DJ work with karaoke, which eventually led to us opening our own bar that we did karaoke at seven days a week.

June 10, 2018
Thank you Father for another day! Feel great, a little sore. Going to work in flower beds again today. I first have a big one in the front house that must get done. Worked outside for just a little bit because Gavin was gone, and Tim had to do hospice visit today. Anyway, this flower bed is huge! Going to need some muscle for this one. Rain is coming so going to binge watch Supernatural and hang with my man. I was craving chocolate and Tim went and got me a Bing (a candy bar). I haven't had one in years. Thank you, God, for my husband, family, friends and life in general. Thank you.

I myself tried to stay as busy as possible throughout her terminal disease. I worked during the day. I focused on work at nights and tried to keep her spoiled as I could. As much as I tried avoiding thinking about it, I, too, had moments of realization and panic that the love of my life would die someday soon. Sometimes this was a slow realization such as when I was watering the flowers, and I would start crying and thinking of how the flowers would come back next year, but she wouldn't be here to enjoy them. Other times it was like a bolt of lightning, and I was shaking with grief and sorrow. All these moments were helpful to me to come to grips with the finality of death in this lifetime.

June 11, 2018

Today first I want to thank God for giving me another day. Did housework and took it easy waiting for anybody to stop by to help do flower beds. Well, no flower bed work today. It's okay I'm a little bummed anyway.

June 12, 2018

Thank you Father for another day! I did laundry, dishes (with Patti), worked in flower beds with Judy & Adella. Very productive day. Terri (our friend) and Riley (her granddaughter) stopped by. I've stayed positive today. Riley made a gift for me, the "little" sweetie. Love her bunches. Anyway, I'm so excited the flower beds are getting cleaned up. The front's going to be beautiful! Tim and I had a talk and I'm going to pray harder for him for peace and strength.

June 13, 2018

Heaven boys are coming today! Thank you, God, for another day. Did housework then Gavin I took the boys out to swim. Tim came home and took us all out to play mini-golf and Perkins. I love the boys so much. They're so fun to watch. They do however wear me out, but I will NEVER ADMIT THIS! Thank you, Father! Nikki my friend came to visit. It was good to see her.

June 14, 2018

Thank you Father for another day! Today was a busy day with boys. My friend Allie stopped by with her babies. I'm happy she made it back home and she's doing good. Nicki came over again. She took me for a ride in her Jeep with the top and doors off! It was awesome! Reminded me of my convertible. Meds are up, so I had a few issues, but all in all a great day. Keegan, Tim and I ended today with movies. I bawled a lot, they all hit home. Thank you again Father for another day!

June 15, 2018

Thank you Father for another day! Got my butterfly bushes planted!! Filled pool up, so Keegan can swim today! Really hot day, but my amazing hubby made it all happen. Thank you for such a wonderful hubby. Nicki bought me some wine and I must try it. I can only have one glass a week. Excited to taste them. Tim wants me to go to work with him tonight, so I will. Thank you again God for another day. P.S. Not going to bar, feeling a little pain.

June 16, 2018

Thank you Father for another day! I'm not good this morning. Trying to fight it but I think my lungs need tapped again. Tim's noticing and knows I'm scared but has talked to me about it and we are going to ER. Doctor Day is it working! I'm scared. OMG!!!! THE MOST PAINFUL TAP EVER!! Crap!! It hurts so bad, but it's done. One full jug and a little in another off just one lung. Heaven came up for the night. We all went to SwaggerZ later (Tim and Gavin) had to work. I sang with Heaven, I missed that. She got a little tipsy and said, "Mom, you can't leave me I need you at least another 20 years." What do you say to that?

When she got out of Mayo, the lung taps were not very often. Dr. Day was her favorite local doctor that did them. Dr. Day had good bedside manners and made her feel more at ease. Our children were some of the first and last ones that had these thoughts of realization and panic with the fact she was dying. I remember coming home from Mayo and my wife and I were so busy trying to get everything arranged and set up at home we didn't even think about her being terminally ill. Yet I remember that night of Heaven coming home from going out, and she was intoxicated. She was crying uncontrollably and crying out loudly, "You can't die. I still need you. I still haven't gotten married. Who am I going to talk to when I have problems? This is fucked up." Savannah comforted her and reassured her she would be okay. I remember her asking this question crying when we got home from the bar that night. I cried too inside. I felt for her, and it reminded me how I felt when my mom died when I was only thirty. What I was going through with Savannah would have been something I would have talked to my mom about, but she was already gone.

June 17, 2018

It's Father's Day. Nobody is up yet but me. I feel better today but my lung still hurts from the tapping. Hopefully it will mellow out today. Very angry with me. Feel much better. We went grocery shopping and had lunch at Hy-Vee. I had sesame chicken; Tim had salad. Let's not forget chocolate milk. My lung stopped spasming so I'm happy about that. Anyway, very happy I had another day with everybody. Thank you again Father for each day.

June 18, 2018

Thank you Father for another day!! Did some housework. Started painting again. I LOVE painting! It makes me very happy even if I suck at it. I just love to paint. Spent the whole evening painting and I will start another tomorrow. Thank you, Father, for the opportunity to paint. Will maybe donate to auction? Thank you again Lord for my family and my friends.

She got into painting, something she loved when she was younger. She was a talented artist. Painting was something she planned on doing when she retired. However, now with extra time on her hands, she started painting pictures again. This was short-lived, and it frustrated her because it took concentration, and her hands shook a lot from the medication. Savannah was way too hard on herself. She was a very good artist. She was a sketcher and drawer and could paint and do crafts from several types of mediums. Most of our family and friends complimented her on her artist abilities. Yet she was a perfectionist, and if it didn't look good to her, then she would redo it. She really was a good artist. I wish she fully understood what we saw in her work. She really was talented.

June 19, 2018

Thank you Father for another day to experience all you've given us. I still hurt. Something is weird. Sucking it up though. I know Jesus suffered worse. I painted again today after housework. Tim planted the last of the butterfly bushes. There's a little black bunny that is eating my flowers, little bastard! I'm getting anxious about seeing people this weekend and golf! So excited. Thank you again, Father for another day.

June 20, 2018

Thank you Father for another day! Feeling pretty good, still a little sore. Painted more today. Watch Judy and Anna try to catch their bunny. LOL, that was funny. I laughed too hard. Going to try to find a live trap. Excited for weekend, but I'm scared about doctor visit tomorrow. I don't want anybody here touching my kegs, but Dr. Day. I hurt still and that is scaring me. Anyway, I went to visit Leroy and Dawn (friends of ours). Leroy's having health issues. I pray he's going to be okay. So, it was a good day and I thank you Father for that and all the blessings you've given me.

June 21, 2018

Thank you Father for another day!!!!! Finally got it bath today! I cried; it was so nice. I'm so fricken emotional. Big crybaby over everything. Moody too I guess, but I'm trying not to be. It's hard. You just get frustrated when you can't do things you've been doing for years. I wish I was me again. I wish I were that independent woman I used to be but now I'm stuck being dependent on everybody (mostly Tim) and that isn't fair. I seem to push his buttons some days. I will work on that. Anyway, again, thank you Father for another day with family and friends.

June 22, 2018

Thank you Father for another day. Please let my appointment go well. No tapping, no hospital. I thank you in advance, Amen. Dr. appointment today, Whooh! Hoo! My friend Kim and her husband Mike came today! Well, no tapping, no hospital! Thank you, God! They upped the potassium pills. We talked about spickets. I don't know, what if God says no and he makes my lungs stop filling up? It's nice to have Kim and Mike visit. Getting more excited about this benefit. My Aunt Joyce may come! My cousins are coming, I used to spend every summer with them. My sister Linda canceled, but she's sick.

Thank you again God! P.S. Side effects are minimal, but the restless legs stuff pisses me off.

June 23, 2018

Thank you God, for another day! Woke to cramps in foot, like when I used to dance. They hurt like hell! At least I'm awake!! So excited about Sunday! Tonight's a beach party at bar. Got to get decorations and prices. I'm going and I'm going to make everybody pose with me for surfing pics! Can I my car camping in yard I hope they enjoy their weekend as much as I did. I loved getting everybody to pose with me for surfing pics. My husband is the best. He worries so much about me, but I love when he relaxes, and I get to see him have fun! Thank you, God for another day with family and friends. Thank you for all the blessings you've given me.

June 24, 2018

Thank you God for another day!! Wow! So much family! I am seeing people I haven't seen in ages! I love that my cousins and nieces came. Then all that came to the benefit and donated and bought stuff! The bands, the magician, the customers and Terri for putting this all together and volunteering to serve, sell and donated tips! I'm very blessed woman! In tears of joy because I never thought I'd ever receive such love. It's overwhelming. My old boss came, people I worked with came. It was amazing! Thank you, Father, for all of it. My husband even had a good time.

We had one fundraiser after she got sick. We had low insurance before this through my employer. I was responsible for a large, out-of-pocket co-payment but also eighty-twenty afterward. So our bill from Mayo was like almost $180,000 of which my portion was almost $40,000. We raised about $13,000, which helped a lot, but we still had medical bills coming in, and we needed to add a downstairs bathroom for her. All totaled, we had probably had nearly $100,000 of bills and expenses with this illness. And this was because she opted out of the heart and lung transplant. I'm sure it would have hundreds of thousands more if she had gone for a heart and lung transplant. I always told her it would never be about money. I would work the rest of my life anyway, and if I had not a penny to my name when I died, I would be okay with that. But she didn't want it on her own. She used to say she did not want to take a heart and lung from someone younger than her who had not had a chance to live life yet.

June 25, 2018

Thank you Father for another day! What a beautiful morning! Kim and Mike went home today. It was nice having company. I feel great even after such a busy weekend. I'm a little tired, but happy. I love seeing everyone and I was amazed by the turnout. I did some housework and then rested for a bit. Made supper, but it's hard to do sometimes because of sodium. Tim got me lunch and I had chicken strips (lots of sodium). I figure I will get liquids on track one day like sodium. It's hard to do. Anyway, Thank you God for another day with family & friends.

June 26, 2018

Thank you Father for another day! Got up, got into housework slowly. I think I needed more sleep, that's why I overslept. Feel great. Just watch a little tube after I made cinnamon-French toast! Then I busted ass doing dishes and going to the bathroom. Pissed myself a lot today. At least nobody had to see that or clean it up. Patti had a funeral today, but that's okay, gave me more time to be independent. I'm so emotional again. Cried like a mad woman today and I was honestly a little angry. Glad to be alive. Thank you, Father, again for my family and friends. Thank you for another day!

June 27, 2018

Thank you Father for another day! Had a good day. Heaven the boys came today. Watched them play and Tim mowed then planted my clematises. I love my husband so much. He works hard and then comes home and mows both lots then asks me if we can plant my flowers so he can be my hero. He doesn't know it but he is always my hero, every day. I look at him and I'm amazed that I have such an awesome husband. Thank you, God.

June 28, 2018

Thank you Father for another day! Gavin and I got up with boys and made breakfast. They kill me! They're so fun. Heaven came late, so I didn't get outside until later. Had Keegan today after boys left. I weeded the flower beds out front. When Tim came home, we went out and planted more flowers. Would've been an early night but Tim got called to work so, I will wait up to make sure he makes it home okay. Thank you, Father, for another day and for my hubby (AMAZING HUBBY) and family and friends. Thank you.

June 29, 2018

Thank you Father for another day. Fun day! Got to go to Des Moines to get lights for laser party. Got lights, new mics and did I mention awesome new lights! I'm so excited. So, I didn't want to change my med cassettes at 6 because there was still half a cassette. I waited. I called the specialty pharmacy 24-hour number and they said, "I have to change it!" I will never keep old cassette on longer than I'm supposed to again. Had severe diarrhea all night and I don't like it! Had a great time at bar. Sang some but just had fun. Thank you, Father, for another day with family and friends.

We didn't know it at the time, but medications had to be switched out daily or it could cause side effects. She called the twenty-four-hour emergency number with questions. We changed meds at six every night. This night, she didn't do this at the normal time, and it led to her diarrhea.

June 30, 2018
Thank you Father for another day!! We slept until 11!! Guess maybe we needed to. Still having some issues with side effects. Hopefully it will keep getting better. Heard from Mayo on appointment for consult from transplant team and then from palliative care team. I'm going to say no to transplant. Going to bar with Tim again tonight. Hopefully I can keep my fluids under control. That went well, not. Got to get my fluids under control! Help! Buy shit tons of candy, but not helping. Keep trying. Thank you again Father.

July 1, 2018
Thank you Father for another day! Well, slept well and felt great. Went to hook up lights and get my pans so I can cook at home more easily. I'm so happy I got my stuff back since I can't do anything else. We went and saw my Dad

at Crickets! God, I love that man! He's not doing
so well either. He was so happy to see us. He and
Tim did their usual shots and BS stories. Those
two are like kids! Love them both so much. Glad
our friend Lacy called and told us he was there.
I feel happy. Thank you, Father, for another day!

The guy she referred to as Dad was not really her dad. Savannah's
dad was not ever involved in her life as her parents divorced when
she was very young. But Savannah "adopted" Earl and called him
Dad. Earl was an elderly gentleman and a regular at Crickets (a bar I
used to bartend at). He was a bad influence on me as I found myself
drinking excessively when I hung out with him. Okay, that is not
true. I was as guilty as him because we talked a lot of shit to each
other and dared each other to drink shots. He had a heart disease
and had fluid retention. I'm sure his doctor had warned him not to
drink as much, but Earl was almost eighty and was ready to die. He
just wanted to have a good time until it happened. Besides, he had
told us he was lonely and bored in his apartment. The bars always
had someone he could socialize with. This is true for many elderly
men in bars. They often are lonely and bored and just go to the bar
for socialization.

July 2, 2018
Thank you Father for another day!! Went
to bar today and we made Jell-O shots for rave!
So excited! Anyway, it felt good to be there in bar
doing something. Super tired, so going to bed.
Thank you, Father!

A rave is a party in a club or bar with lights and techno music
and is geared more for younger crowds. We tried to market our bar
to older crowds with karaoke music, but we had hip-hop bands, rock
bands, and even rave parties. We wanted to provide a safe and unique
experience to several different clientele at our bar. We offered karaoke
at one bar seven days a week, but a bar in the ballroom side allowed

for different groups to enjoy a different music and different experience totally.

July 3, 2018

Thank you Father for another day! Going to bar today to decorate and set up for Rave tonight. Heaven, and her boyfriend, and the boys are coming today! Can't wait. Love my babies! Anyway, should be fun night. Will write more later. Oh! Had my first Mt. Dew in 6 mos., don't do that again!! Crackhead! Great night tonight! Both bars were packed! I only screwed up a little by forgetting to order a couple things. Tired but can't sleep. Ugh! Anyway, thank you Father for another day.

July 4, 2018

Thank you Father for another day! I was restless last night couldn't sleep. Stayed up until 5 a.m., then woke back up at 9 a.m. Also, took my mask off again in the night. Woke up with no oxygen on I had hung my mask on hook neatly. Apparently, I think I don't need it. The flushing is getting less tolerable. I get hot. It's been so humid so maybe that's why. Anyway, I thank you Father for another day. Thank you.

Side effects vary depending on the disease and the types of medications. She often described her side effects at night as flushing. I asked for her to explain this better because I was not sure what she meant by this. She then explained it as going through menopause again. She had gone through menopause in her forties and had helped me understand that before. Savannah described her side effects at night as having hot and cold flashes at times. Often, she was covered with a blanket and still visibly shaking. I'd offer her another blanket, but she would tell in a few minutes she would be hot again.

July 5, 2018

Thank you Father for another day! My emotions are getting harder to control. I'm sick of it! One moment I'm fine, then I'm angry, then sobbing uncontrollably. This is worse than menopause. I dislike it very much. I think my magnesium is low, getting those pains again. It just hurts. Keep telling myself to suck it up and stop being a baby. People go through worse. I need to just deal. At least it's not worse. I could be stuck on a machine and bed rest only or and worse pain. Thank you, Father, for being so kind and merciful to me. Thank you for giving me such an awesome support system. Thank you for all the blessings every moment of every day. Thank you for all the experiences I've had, for rescuing me from myself when I needed it, for carrying me through hell! Thank you, Father, for my husband & children, grandchildren. Amen.

July 6, 2018

Thank you Father for another day! So, today I discovered that if I make myself get out of bed, eat then get busy with dishes & laundry, I feel pretty good. I did feel great, then at lunch. I ate, then passed out. I must've needed that sleep. I feel pretty good now, I'm going to try to keep that feeling going. My fluids are under control today for now. Later want to go pull some weeds in flower beds. Flowers are all coming up and I'm excited to see them. Thank you, Father, for another day.

July 7, 2018

Thank you Father for another day! Had a great day with Tim. Went to Sam's Club! Love going on road trips. Went to bar tonight. I had a great time. Took some videos, sang some songs. Good memories were made. I love watching them all have fun. Tried the Moscato tonight, it was awesome. Thank you, Father, for another day. Thank you for my family & friends. Thank you most of all for Tim he's amazing.

July 8, 2018

Thank you Father for another day! Going to work in flower beds today! Kirk and Lori came coming at 3 p.m. Going to get a bath & shave today too. Can't wait!!!! Yea!!!! Got my bath! It felt so good. Thank you, Father, for making that possible. I feel so much better. Still suffering some side effects. Wish the twitches would stop. I hate those. Got my front flower beds done. Thank you, Father, for another day.

July 9, 2018

Thank you Father for another day! I started off full of energy today. Did dishes, did laundry, cooked lunch. By evening I'm tired but had to stay up to deal with body spasms. They're so frustrating. Gavin spent most of the day with me because he didn't feel well. My hubby was very chipper today. That was sweet to see. Also, did I mention, he's so cute he's so sappy and sweet. Well he is.! Thank you again father for another day!

July 10, 2018

Thank you Father for another day!! Good morning! Heaven's coming today! It won't be until later in day but, she's coming so we can have time together. Got to eat breakfast and then get house picked up and candy put away before they get here. Went to Des Moines to return lights we rented. Stopped at Hickory Park to have supper. Heaven got here about 10 p.m. so did we. I love seeing her and the boys. Keegan hardly comes here anymore. Lincoln lives with his dad, so we hardly see them. I miss my children & grandbabies. I'm getting a little tired now. Thank you, Father, for another day.

July 11, 2018

Thank you God for another day! Felt pretty good today had to check scale twice. WTF! Not sure what's going on, but I feel good. Heaven and boys here today. She's filling pool. Gavin's sick, going to urgent care. Gavin's got strep throat! Boys are going to my ex-boyfriend's house. My niece Anna came over and her and I hung in pool. That felt amazing. Got to see my mom yesterday. Never for long but, at least I got to see her. My kids, Tim and his family check on me more than my own. They're amazing. Anyway, thank you Father for another day!

July 12, 2018

Thank you Father for another day! Damn!! Scale is wrong cause today it says I gained three back. B.S.! Got me all excited thinking my lungs were working on their own. Oh well, keep on going. I feel good anyway. Med change night, hopefully it all goes well. Still feel good. Keegan's coming today. Tim took us out to supper. It was nice. I saw friends of ours from the bar Amanda and Kevdog there as we were leaving. Went out to Kennedy Lake and eww!! That was so gross!!

Going home and watch movies. Thank you,
Father, for another day.

Savannah had to weigh herself daily to make sure she was not
retaining fluids and maybe needing to get her lungs tapped again.
Savannah tried to mention it anytime she visited with friends. With
her lack of ability physically, she often felt the only time she could
do anything was when she visited and talked to others when she saw
them. Savannah had incredible memory and often waved and said
hello to people that had come to the bar. Many people liked our bar
because of her.

July 13, 2018
Thank you Father for another day!

July 14, 2018
Thank you Father for another day! Golf
tournament today! Yay! Finally, some fun! Up
early for golf tournament today! Yay! I can only
putt but at least I get to golf! So, I sucked at putting today but it's ok. I love being outside and
also with good friends. We had a great day and
got DEAD ASS LAST again, but it's all good.
Came home, took a nap, had to be bar by 6.
Dead night at bar but we had a great time. I love
when people just have fun and stop boobing on
me. Thank you, Father, for another day. Thank
you for my wonderful friends and family.

Savannah and I loved golfing. We used to golf often, but when
she got sick, she couldn't use her one arm because of the possibility of
loosening the tube in her chest on her left side. Still, she would putt
and even tried golfing one-armed a few times. We were never very
good, but we liked hanging with friends and being outside. Savannah
used the word *boobing*, which meant crying about her condition. She
didn't want people to feel sorry for her. She wanted to be looked at as

normal as possible. Many people often expressed sadness about her condition, which is a normal reaction many have when they find out you have a terminal condition. But she really wanted none of this.

July 15, 2018
We watch movies movie *Midnight Sun*. I cried a lot. BATH NIGHT!!!! Bath was amazing as always, so is my husband. I thank God for each day. Thank you again, Father for another day. Thank you. Thank you. Thank you.

July 16, 2018
Thank you Father for another day! Kind of tired today after the weekend. Up doing dishes, housework, and by lunch time tired and ready to crash. Napped from about 2 to 4:30. Got meds done and packed to go to Mayo. Hate this. Don't see the point in me getting consulted when I'm not going to do transplant. Waste of time for all and gas. Tim and I are a little pissy with each other lately. Not sure how to change that but try not to be so freaken emotional. Anyway, thank you Father for another day.

July 17, 2018
Thank you Father for another day. Did my appointment and came home. Tim and I are pissy again. Don't like it. I don't want this to drive us apart and make us miserable. I've been so emotional lately and get butt hurt easily. He's a great man and I feel blessed to have him, but I feel like he resents me sometimes. I know he loves me but accepting this may be a little too much at this moment. Maybe I'm a little resentful to that I'm sick and people have lived purposely much worse than I ever did and they're healthy. Still I don't

need it to be bitchy and especially not to him. He does so much for me. Thank you, Father, for another day and for my family and Amazing Hubby.

July 18, 2018

Thank you Father for another day! Alone all day. Gavin slept all day. Our hire helper couldn't make it. I was fine though. I went outside. I wasn't going to wait all day. Weeded flower beds and back of house. They took a long time, but it's done. Went to Eagles meeting and then to Hy-Vee for supper. I was going to grocery shop, but I was freezing so bad that I had to go to the car while Tim got groceries. Then we came home and watched a movie. I'm tired and sore and those painful spasms are pissing me off. Thank you, Father, for another day.

July 19, 2018

Thank you Father for another day! Med change day, whooh whooh! Praying for the best. Feel tired today. Did some housework but tired so sat down. Our friend Norma came over and she brought some Larita's cookies!! Did med change. Now feeling yucky and I hurt! I really hurt. Not going to write much more. Thank you, God, for another day!

July 20, 2018

Thank you God for another day! Feel like shit still. Fucking hate this! Oh, well it will pass. So tired and I hurt. Can't stop crying. WTF am I crying for? I feel a little run down. Staying home tonight. I'm such a fucken wreck. Praying tomorrow gets better. Oxygen at 96! I feel like shit though. WTF. Heaven's working in Okoboji tonight and tomorrow. Maybe I will see her on Sunday. She's always busy. Well I thank you Father again for another day.

July 21, 2018

Worked in yard, shopped then went to work with Tim. Not much to write about today. Found out my neighbor who's only eight years older died. Aneurysm. Her twin daughters are so lost. God thank you Father for another day and thank you for a chance to spend time with my family.

July 22, 2018

Thank you Father for another day! Slept in a little. Tim had to work this morning. At 1pm he must go help at Eagle's building to fix sidewalk. Heaven will be stopping by. I watch her and I cry because I know what she's going through. All the things I didn't want her to go through. Oh, well, can't change things for her. I trust God and that I raised her right. I love all my babies so much. Thank you for another day and for all you've given us. Thank you for being my strength, courage, and peace. Thank you for my loving husband and children and grandchildren. Thank you.

July 23, 2018

Thank you Father for another day! Did dishes, did laundry, cleaned fridge, cleaned cupboard, watered plants and made an awesome supper! One month and eight days since last lung tap! Yay!! Thank you, Father!! I feel pretty darn blessed. So much better than the hospital. Spasms in my feet are pissing me off but I can deal with them. I keep praying for them to stop. So thirsty, but I'm being good! Doing a great job today on the liquids. Thank you, Father, for another day and thank you for my loving family and friends.

July 24, 2018

Thank you Father for another day! Up early cause of spasms. They hurt so bad. I need to do better at taking and potassium and magnesium. Did laundry, dishes, Patti and I cleaned fridge and cupboards out. Watered my plants and that's pretty much it. Pretty exciting huh?

July 25, 2018

Thank you Father for another day!! I feel GREAT!! Other than waking up to severe pains in feet again. Fighting it all the way. Did dishes, laundry, Gavin I got a pool ready, fixed vacuum for bar, cleaned house, hung out in the yard with my babies! Wooh! I'm pooped. Going to sleep great tonight, I hope. Heaven and the boys came, and Keegan came down to swim. Grandchildren kill me! They are so fun to watch. I feel so good getting hang out outside. Fresh air, breeze, birds, bunnies, kids… It's like being with God. Thank you, Father, for another day with my family. Thank you for my family.

July 26, 2018

Thank you God for another day. Med change day! Whoo! Whoo!! I feel awesome. Going to hang with grandbabies outside again. Up early cause of pain in feet again. Did dishes, got grocery list ready, helped Gavin get boys fed. Heaven and I took boys outside to pool and

Keegan came down too. Such a beautiful day. Tim came home early said we were having a date night! We went to Market on Central (need to go earlier) then got movies and went home, because it's med change night and anything can happen. I love watching movies with Tim. Thank you, Father, for another day and for my family and friends. Oh! Norma came again today. We sat outside too. She brought me a beautiful Lilly to plant (white & purple). Love Norma.

July 27, 2018

Thank you Father for another day. Up late, did some housework then off to store for bar. Made Jell-O shots (lots of them!!) and that took most of the day. We are going to the bar early because we are hosting a karaoke contest tonight. I'm already pooped. Awesome night! My friends Chris and Kayla prayed for me, along with Chris's children. He got lead singer in Beaver Creek 4! He's such a good singer and person. I just love that family. Thank you for another day with my loved ones and for all the many blessings you've bestowed on me.

July 28, 2018

Thank you Father for another day while, another day. Do a little housework, fix breakfast and go to the bar to prep for tonight's event. I'm so glad I can go this weekend. Poor Tim, I get insecure at times because I feel unattractive and I know he loves me, but I still feel worthless. Then, his friends all try (not all, a few) to get him checking out chicks like they always have. It's hurtful even more now for me. I shouldn't get it let it get to me but it does. It's stupid. Anyway,

I need to work on not being stupid. So, Lord please give me strength knowledge and tolerance to get through without being a bitch. Thank you. Amen.

July 29, 2018

Thank you Father for another day! Stop drinking over limit! It's hard. Great day. Slept late some. Tim needs it bad. Taking a lazy day, we are. I love a day like this sometimes. It's BATH DAY!!!! I love bath day! Funny how the little things like baths and hugs and smiles mean so much more. I've always thanked God for giving man knowledge to invent things like bath and hot water heaters so I can have hot baths. They just mean even more to me now. Anyway, Heaven and the boys will be coming up this week! Will have to get house ready. Thank you, Father, for another day and for all your many blessings.

July 30, 2018

Thank you Father for another day! Busy day! Housework, laundry, dishes, get ready for the most awesome fridge ever! New fridge is coming today. Super excited. Going to get pool ready for boys. I feel energetic and spastic today. Probably because I'm getting coolest fridge EVER today! LOL. Silly I know but it's so nice. Going to learn to slow down and nap sometimes cause I'm worn out and legs are hurting. Too pooped. Thank you, Father, for another day and all the many blessings!

July 31, 2018

Thank you Father for another day. Up early, housework, laundry, cleaned up my room a little, put meds way. Beautiful day. I didn't get outside but I will Wednesday! Heaven and boys are coming today! Got to get it all ready. Took everyone to dinner tonight. Wish the rest of the kids could've come. Sometimes I feel like MJ keeps herself and Keegan away because she doesn't want to hurt. It's okay, but I just wish she knew I love her as much as my own. Both Marinia and Michaela. I wish I could've been there when they were growing up more. Thank you, God, for another day and your many blessings.

August 1, 2018

Thank you Father for another day! Hung out with Heaven and boys all day. Boys love the pool. Had to make my own meds today then went to Eagles meeting then came home and made popcorn and watched a movie with the boys "Tomb Raider". Then prayed with boys Tim also had told them Bible story and then bed because we were pooped. Thank you, God, for another day with family and friends and for all the blessings you've given me.

August 2, 2018

Thank you God for another day! Normal day until med change. Feel like Shit!! Make it stop, Please. Please.

August 3, 2018

Thank you God for another day. Still feel like shit. Did nothing because I can't!! I hurt everywhere! Please stop! Please make it stop! My brother Roy, my mother, sister Evelyn and her daughter Brittany stopped by.

August 4, 2018

Thank you Father for another day. I'm still not my best. Trying so hard to get out of this, but not happening. Started feeling better, then after supper BAM! Shitty again! WTF! Help me Father please. I need you.

August 5, 2018

Thank you Father for another day. I still feel crappy but thank you, thank you, thank you. I need to find a way to deal with this. Going to try to get outside. I need fresh air! Aunt Joyce's birthday today! Love her so much. God, I wish I could travel to see all the wonders of the world with Tim and the kids and grandkids. We'd have such a great time. Oh, well, we will be doing our trip to Adventureland this year, so that will be fun. Thank you, Father, for another day! Thank you!

August 6, 2018

Thank you Father for another day. Feeling a little bit better. Hopefully it stays that way. I have so much I need to get done. I need to feel better so I can. Heaven and boys come tomorrow, so that will be nice. Scratch that, they're just coming to get car but that's fine cause they will be here Wednesday. Going to try and get housework done! Need to get my shit in order! Thank you, Father, for another day!

August 7, 2018

Thank you Father for another day. Rocking the day! Got some of (a lot) my shit done! I feel like Wonder Woman today! Clean house, laundry, clean bedroom (well getting there), did dishes. Heaven and I weeded flowerbeds and planted my plant from Norma! I'm so proud of all our girls. They're each unique and strong. I love them so much. Gavin's on his way to sorting life and making his path. My baby is going to college! So proud! Thank you, Father, for each day! Thank you.

August 8, 2018

Thank you God for another day!! Heaven and the boys are here! Can't wait to get in the pool! Well, no pool. Nobody can get up and clean out and fill it up! Heaven emptied it, but now she's going to work. Oh, well, funny, Heaven's working at bars I worked at. Not funny ha! ha! but weird funny. I wish she didn't have to. I hope so much more for her life. Oh, well, you do what you got to do and live and learn. It sucks, but it's wonderful all at the same time. Each day I wake is beautiful but painful. I thank God anyway. One more day to be with my family, to see my grandchildren play, to hear their laughter, to wake up to my hubby. Yea, no med change! I'll take that!

August 9, 2018

Thank you Father for another day! Thank you. Starting to feel better feel much better today. Back still hurts a little, but I will be okay. I've been trying to get all my stuff done so Tim won't have to. I know one day I won't be able to do shit and I hate the thought of that. I'm so glad the moodiness is from meds are gone, that sucked! Not me at all. My poor family. God, I wish I could do more for myself, I want to work. I feel like a huge burden and like a waste of Tim's life. He deserves to be happy, have fun and not stuck with this weight. Yay! No med changes!

August 10, 2018

Thank you Father for another day! Happy b-day to my niece Adella. I'm so happy no med change this week! Can't handle it! I'm going to try to get out and have fun this weekend! Terri's gone on vacation so trying to help Tim at bar. Feel excited to be getting out! Thank you, Father, for the opportunity to live another day to be able to wake up and do whatever my body allows. Thank you for making the nurse say no med change, we need to back off for a moment. Thank you for all the beauty you surround us all with each day. Thank you.

August 11, 2018

Thank you Father for another day. Last night wore me out some. Slept well. Going to help again today. Man, I wish I could work! Stupid bodies. Stupid me for being sick. Stupid me for smoking all those years. I know, suck it up! I'm dealing with my shit. It's hard though. I want to do is make Tim's life as good as he has made mine. I love him so much. This isn't fair to him. He totally neglects his self, because he wants to spoil me. Thank you, Father, for such a wonderful partner. Thank you for his love and care. Thank you for letting me know what real love is. Thank you.

August 12, 2018

Thank you Father for another day! Happy b-day to my nephew Damon! Golf at noon! How can this day get any better!? Golf today, got angry at myself cause I tried to drive one armed. I could do it before. I was angry and embarrassed, but I putted! I got to stop and realize I almost wasn't here to do anything, so I should be grateful. Came home, did yard work. Well, Tim mowed, I weeded flower beds. They are getting so beautiful. I keep finding plants I thought died are now growing! It's awesome! Going to plant more so next year it will be even more amazing. Thank you, Father, for letting me enjoy your creations.

August 13, 2018
Thank you Father for another day. Happy B-day Gavin. I'm a little moody today. I get angry so easily. Nobody's up or here to help me with things. I got an idea in my head and I plan and pissed cause it's not going right. I got to stop! Heaven and boys are coming, Michaela and her family are coming, Gavin wanted a cookout for his b-day. It turned out fine even with my stress and moodiness. I need to learn to relax. Thank you for Father for all you give each day to me. I appreciate all of it. Please help me to relax and enjoy more instead of stressing so much and please help me kick my moodiness's ass! Thank you.

August 14, 2018
Thank you Father for another day! I'm still moody! Trying so hard to stop. I can't focus. Woke up in pain and tired as hell! Up early then fell back to sleep until 11 a.m.! Guess my body needed. Tim heard me crying this morning and left came back with a foot soaker and Epson salts. He's awesome! I hate my moodiness cause I'm often moody to him. He makes sure I have every-

thing I need and he's so tired. I hate what this is doing to him. Sometimes we cry together about our life and then sometimes we laugh until we cry. Thank you, Father, for the best man I have ever known. Thank you.

August 15, 2018

Thank you Father for another day.! Thank you, thank you! Feeling a little under the weather today. Woke up in pain and kept dozing off all day. Heaven and boys are here but keep dozing off. Can't get much done. Oh, well we will be okay.

August 16, 2018

Thank you Father for another day! I must have needed to sleep, more active today. The grandbabies are crazy as fun!! Bed late up early and run at 100 miles per minute all day! LOL. I wouldn't trade it or them for anything. They all leave today. Grandbabies go to their dad's and Heaven and Gavin are going to 515 music festival. I'm glad they're getting this shit out of their system now cause at least they'll be grown-ups when they get involved again and maybe see there's more to life than just partying. Oh, they worry me. I know they'll be okay. Heaven's a great mom and my Gavin well, he's a great man but I just want them to have good lives.

August 17, 2018

Thank you Father for another day. Well no call from Mayo! Patti sick, so no Patti today. I'm alone until Tim gets here at 1 or 1:30. Feel pretty good today, going to try to get shit done. I need to downsize my shit! The peace and quiet is awesome but I will be happy when Tim arrives. Soaking my feet today too. Mayo called; no meds change until Wednesday! So, I get to enjoy my weekend a little. Yay! Thank you, thank you, thank you.

August 18, 2018

Thank you Father for another day! Marinia, and her husband Justin, and Lincoln are coming today!! Going to golf a couple holes today! Golfed six holes! I golfed one armed every hole but the last! It felt fucking amazing! I love golfing with Tim. I felt normal again. God, I pray I heal if it's your will. Tim needs me and my children and grandchildren need me. I sobbed like a baby, worse, I ugly cried. It was good. Thank you, thank you thank you Father for another day!

August 19, 2018

Thank you Father for another day! Golf again today at noon! Marinia and her family are going. Great day! Thank you thank you for another BEAUTIFUL DAY! Lincoln's gotten sooo big! He came downstairs this morning and said Nay Nay? I missed him so much. I dislike Marinia's ex-husband for keeping him from us. His Birthday we miss. Her ex-husband sucks ass! Forgive me for that, but he does. Marinia looks good. Her and Justin to seem healthy for each other and for Lincoln. He's good with Lincoln. I'm so glad she's happy. Thank you, Father, for another day.

August 20, 2018

Thank you Father for another day! Spent day trying to do stuff like I normally do. Made tie-dye shirts with Lincoln, Marinia and Justin. That was fun. Really glad Marina found somebody so good. Her ex-husband was a total dick! God forgive me for saying that, but he was. Got to get stuff ready for Wednesday. Tuesday is going to be a long day and med change day is Wednesday. Don't know how I will react this time, so I better get shit in order. Anyway, praying for the best. Anyway, thank you Father for another day again. Thank you for my family.

August 21, 2018

Thank you God for another day! Whooh! long day! Today we all went to Adventureland. The kids had a blast. Tim got to ride some rides also. I'm so glad he went on rides, he needed to have a fun day. I didn't ride the rides, but I watched the kids and the grandkids have a blast which made me happy. I love their smiles. I love that I got to spend the day with him all again. Pretty exhausted, so going to go to bed now. Thank you, Father, for another day!

August 22, 2018

Thank you God for another day! Med change day. Very sleepy today, but boys are coming! Made tie dye shirts with boys and Gavin. I love having the kids here. They amaze me, with their little attitudes and smiles. They amaze me.

August 23, 2018

Thank you Father for another day! Well, not going to lie, it's been busy, busy, busy. Marinia and Justin go home to Colorado tomorrow. Sad to see them go, they have a life to get back to you. Wish Lincoln was going home with them, but one day. Back to a normal routine when they go, which is okay. Wish I could do more. Wish Tim wasn't so stressed. He thinks I don't get he stressed about money; he always has been. Oh, well can't do anything about that. Thank you, Father, for another day!

August 24, 2018

Thank you Father for another day! Well, kids are off to Colorado. Silence through the house. I'm going to rest a bit. Caught up sleep some. Caught up housework some. Wooh! What a week. Hope I make it through the weekend. I'm super exhausted. Going to work with Tim today.

August 25, 2018

Thank you Father for another day. Thank you, thank you, thank you! Golf! Yes! Love golf! May not do 18 holes but I LOVE GOLF! Such a beautiful day Thank you Father for letting me see such beauty and be part of it. Thank you cannot express the gratitude I have for being here still. I feel so blessed! Thank you again. Going to go to work with Tim tonight.

August 26, 2018

Thank you Father for another day! Boy am I tired but GOLF!!!! YES!! It's like being with God. You're out in his church of creation and enjoying every bit of it. Thank you. I'm sore and I will probably need a nap later but I love golf. Vegging, eating pizza, and watching movies. Awesome end to an awesome week. Thank you, Father, for all your many blessings.

August 27, 2018

Thank you Father for another day! Tired, sore, but glad to be here. Now to get back to normal as can be. Gavin starts college soon. I'm so proud. Hope he is too. Finally, one of my own babies going to college! Wish we could've helped more but you do what you can. Feel good, just sore. Dr. appointment today with palliative care. Well, that was fun! I like them much. Going to get a scrip for CBD oil or something for pain. Well, back to work at emptying my house. Thank you again father for another day!

August 28, 2018

Thank you Father for another day. Happy anniversary—9 years! Trying to take it easy cause Tim wants to go to the movies and dinner. Heaven and the boys are coming now, I guess. Those boys are such dolls. They asked where we were going and when I told them we are going to the restaurant, they said they wanted to go so of course Papa and I couldn't say no. So, we all went, and I started to have an episode, so Tim took me cruising to get me through. He's so good to me. It's crazy how he is with me. Nobody has ever even been half as good as he is to me. Thank you, Father.

August 29, 2018

Thank you Father for another day. Med change day. Well, handling med change okay, then towards evening I started feeling like crap. I hate the side effects, but my breathing feels great! It's still not as bad as sometimes when I've had med change. Just irritating to have diarrhea then constipation then diarrhea, then more. The back pain isn't as bad as before, but it still hurts a lot. Hopefully the side effects don't last that long. I must be better by Friday because we have our party and the golf tournament on Saturday. Thank you, Father, for another day!

August 30, 2018

Thank you Father for another day! Gloomy day! Still feel yucky. Got up at 8:30 went in took pills, ate toast, woke up at 11:30! WTF! So sleepy. Having a hard time staying awake today. Side effects I'm assuming. Got to feel better by Friday, our anniversary party. I slept off and on most of the day, so not much to write. I really hope I'm better tomorrow. Tired. Thank you, Father!

August 31, 2018

Thank you Father for another day! Yay! Our party's tonight. I love the band that's playing. 7 Minutes Til Midnight. She has an awesome voice. Amazing. Tim will get trashed of course but I plan on enjoying myself anyway. Yay, Tim's trashed. Puking his guts out! I'm so pissed. Oh, well I had a blast anyway. I actually got out and danced twice. Sort of. The lead singer left early, and rest of band took over and rocked! They want them to come back and play. They were awesome. Thank you, Father!

September 1, 2018

Thank you Father for another day! Thank you for letting me golf! It's our bar tournament today! Tim hung over of course! Oh well we are off to golf! Great day. didn't get rained out. I golfed 15 holes before Tim made us leave to get stuff ready at bar. Terri was on Danna's team. She was loud! There were times I wanted to drown her, but it was all in fun. She's crazy! Love her to death. Anyway, thank you Father, thank you, thank you, thank you.

September 2, 2018

Thank you Father for another day! Beautiful day, scattered rain. Members tournament at Deer Creek today and we are in that so, wish me luck. Whooh! 9 holes and we're both exhausted. We didn't go do bad. I had a rougher time and had a meltdown but oh, well. Tim pulled me through! Boy do my muscles hurt though from golfing one armed. Now it's movie time. Thank you, Father, for another day! Thank you. Thank you. Thank you!

September 3, 2018

Thank you Father for another day! Happy B-day Marinia. Rainy day! Off and on. Tim has a day off so we're doing yard work in between sprinkles. We keep having little tiffs about shit. Maybe it's just lack of sex and stress. LOL, but probably. We got a lot done today though. Well, I hope Marinia had a wonderful day today. I'm so happy she found Justin, or he found her. I'm glad they are happy. Just wish they had Lincoln. They're so good with him. Well, it's been a good day and I pray tomorrow is too. Thank you, Father, for another day. Thank you, thank you.

September 4, 2018

Thank you Father for another day!! Thank you, Thank you! Great day for being stuck inside. It's raining, has been all freaking day. Oh, well my flowers are loving it. Had to switch my oxygen tubing. I ran out and it's way too short so I will have to get more. Gavin and I had a good day together. We had a long talk about life and school. I think he was having a meltdown. We talked, we cried. We cooked supper together. We cook together awesomely. That felt good. I love that we talked, it made me feel closer to him than I ever have.

September 5, 2018

Thank you Father for another day! Pulmonology appointment today. Dr. said everything sounds good. She is amazed at how well I'm doing. She took a blood test, will call tomorrow. No long tap today but we will see. I feel okay, but a little tired. Med change today. Mayo never called, but I'm doing it anyway. Hopefully all goes well. We just sat and watch TV until bed while Tim worked and played his video game. Thank you, Father, for another day!

September 6, 2018

Thank you Father for another day! Test results were almost normal! Minimal med reactions, I'm having a good day! Yeah, I am having pain and some nausea, but I think I'll be okay. Again, just did my norm housework, cooked supper. Open mic night at bar so we must go down. Long night made Jell-O shots. Starting to feel a depression coming. It's so intense, but I'm fighting. Please, help me Father. Send warring angels to guide me out of this depressed mode. Amen. Thank you, Father, for another day!

September 7, 2018

Thank you Father for another day!! So depressed! Crying a lot! Do not like this! Hate it! Please stop! OMG! I'm so bummed and I'm being ugly as hell. WTF! Where's this coming from. I can't stop this. It's stupid. I feel like a piece of wasted space. Like I should just die because Tim deserves better and so does my kids. I feel useless and like nobody really cares. God, please surround me with your love and protection. I thank you in advance. Amen.

September 8, 2018

Thank you Father for another day!! Still fighting depression. I hate this! Why? Why? Do I have to feel like that when I got good news? Poor Tim really been letting him have it. Some he needs but others WOW! not me. I'm so such a Bitch! Feeling a little better, fighting it through. God help me get through. I need strength and help my husband understanding also, so we don't end up divorced. I need to do better. I will do better.

September 9, 2018

Thank you Father for another day! Happy birthday our friend Don!!!!! My Gladiolus will bloom soon! Can't wait! Spent the whole day doing much of nothing. Slept late and I can't seem to wake up much. Finally, got out to do some running for bar. Had supper at Hy-Vee. Spent rest of the night in silence pretty much. Took my bath, on my own, I love bath night! Watched some boring movie and ate popcorn. Things have changed so much. It sucks, I know it's hard on everyone but it's stupid. I just need to stop being so emotional. Hard on myself a bit. Thank you, Father, for another day!

September 10, 2018

Thank you Father for another day!! Thank you. Thank you. Thank you! Rough morning already! Meds were left in cooler in the car all night. Oh well, I will call and see if we're okay. I will have to be more diligent from now on. Had to throw meds away cause not good. I'm so glad this depression going away! I hate it. I need to find a way to get me through it always. Don't want to feel like that again. Whooh! That was a train wreck. Anyway, forward march. Trying to get my meds straightened out. WTF you think Mayo would've told me shit.

September 11, 2018

Thank you Father for another day!! So thirsty today and tired. Think my lungs were filling and now my body's draining it. We will see how I feel tomorrow. Just going to try to get through the day as best I can. Father guide me through this day and night. I pray your will for me, and I will follow whatever you say. I thank you for doing in advance. Amen.

September 12, 2018

Thank you Father for another day!! Well, full of energies today! Thank you Father! The pricklies are getting so intense. They kept me up most of the night. Pricklies and toileting. My legs didn't want to rest. I feel good today though. My flowers are looking beautiful. More are blooming. I love that there are purple. Watched World of Dance tonight. I love that show so it will be a repeat for me because we know how much I love to dance and that I always wanted to be that kind of a dancer.

Savannah explained to me that the "pricklies" felt like she was getting pricked by thousands of little needles. This occurred on occasion and caused her great discomfort. We believed it was probably the side effects of her medications or maybe a lack of potassium.

September 13, 2018
Thank you Father for another day! Thank you. Thank you. Thank you. Thank you.

September 14, 2018
Thank you Father for another day! Thank you! Thank you! Thank you!

September 15, 2018
Thank you Father for another day! Golf!!! Found out or friend Harold passed away Friday. Loved him so much, but at least now he's with his true love.

September 16, 2018
Thank you Father for another day! Tired.

September 17, 2018
Thank you Father for another beautiful day! Thank you! Tired.

September 18, 2018
Thank you Father for another day! Tired.

September 19, 2018
Thank you Father for another day! I woke up this morning wishing someone would shoot

me. Don't even know how to describe the pain I was in. If somebody had cut my foot off it would have been a relief. Maybe I've had too many years of ease and have become soft. I've been through some pain and this was one of the worst pains I've known. I've been extremely tired lately. Hope I'm not getting sick. Please Father don't let me be getting sick.

September 20, 2018

Thank you Father for another day! Boys are here! Yay! I love seeing my boys. I'm still tired but enjoy watching these guys so much. Also at least a talk to me. I hate sitting here talking to anybody and they are on their phones and then I repeat what I said, and they still don't really talk or respond. These two just want to know everything for now. Worried about Heaven though. She needs to get here soon, I'm alone. Gavin's at school, Tim's working.

September 21, 2018

Thank you Father for another day! Happy birthday to my awesome Hubby! Trying to stay positive today. Feel a little better, energy-wise. I'm so excited about the band tonight. I know Tim will probably get trashed but it's his birthday and he works hard so party on baby! Besides 50 is a big birthday. He still looks younger than me. He's just starting to get more gray, but he's so sexy.

September 22, 2018

Thank you Father for another day! I danced a fast song! Okay, so it was only half a song, but I did it! Tim had to be at bar at 9 a.m. this morning for a wedding people. Poor babe, hungover, hardly any sleep. Wow, Tim didn't get back until 3 pm. He's getting a nap, then we must be back at bar at 4:30 p.m. He's going to be so tired. Hope he's not his usual crabby self when he's tired, I don't want to fight. Can't wait to sing also! Maybe, he will let me sing something new.

September 23, 2018

Thank you. Thank you. Thank you, Father, for another day! I feel okay today. A little tired but ok. Today we must go get a plant for Harold's funeral. We had lunch at Hy-Vee after getting plant and I got to finally go into the New Dollar General!! It's nice. I love they moved it so close. Anyway, got a remembrance for Harold at bar tonight so, going to that.

September 24, 2018

Thank you Father for another day! Feeling kind of crappy and tired. Trying to get up and moving but not doing so well. I just want to feel normal again. Think my lungs are draining again. I always get like this or I did push it too much this last weekend. I'm tired and peeing a lot. No freaken energy. I just want to get up and do things so Tim can relax. He's so stressed. Hate that I'm causing his stress.

September 25, 2018

Thank you Father for another day! Oh my gosh! Please help us. Our relationship is so strained now. I hate this. I don't want my time to be spent with the love of my life fighting. I don't know how to help him deal. I'm having a hard-enough time myself. So, I beg you Father, guide us, assist us through this. I don't want to die, and I don't want to lose what we have either. I need him and he needs me. Amen.

September 26, 2018

Thank you Father for another day! Ugh! This is stupid! Still feel crappy, a little better, but now it's med change day! Oh, well, it could be worse. Guide me Father, hold me in your arms and surround me with your love and guide me with his tolerance, wisdom, and I thank you so much. Thank you.

September 27, 2018

Thank you Father for another day! Brrr! I'm freezing! Guess we're going to have an early winter. I'm handling side effects well. Sometimes I feel like I'm watching a movie. My life. It's weird. I feel the pain, but I don't feel like this is my life. I'm trapped in a shell. I used to work every day but can't now. I try. So, I assume the role of a housewife. I love cooking and cleaning but when I can't do all I want, it bothers me. I just don't feel connected to this body other than pain. Maybe that's good, maybe not but I will figure it out.

She loved cooking and started experimenting with foods she had never tried before. She made swordfish and special low-sodium, high-potassium meals. She stuck with the cooking hobby, and we found some good dishes at times.

September 28, 2018

Thank you Father for another day! Got to make Jell-O shots today! Tim is going to bring actual bed down so we can sleep on instead of air mattress. Going to work with him. Still hurt but got to do something it's freaking cold!!

September 29, 2018

I thank you Father for another day! It's still freaking cold!! Going to work with Tim again. Wish I could work. I tried but it's hard. Kind of like me trying to dance. It's sad, I get so winded. Maybe, someday! LOL

September 30, 2018

Thank you Father for another day! Happy birthday to my brother Roy! I love Sundays! I get a bath!! Worn out a bit need to soak for a while. We've been going through our clothes and I've decided I have way too many. Who was the clothing hoarder!? Maybe it's because I always got me hand-me-downs and never had enough. Who knows but WOW! Going to get rid of a lot!

October 1, 2018

Thank you Father for another day! Still tired, not sleeping really well. Poor Tim, I keep him up with all my tossing and turning and potty runs. I hope and pray that he never looks back at me and says wow what a pain, keeping me up always. It's got to suck. Called my brother Roy yesterday to tell him happy B-day. Talked for a while. He has heart trouble too.

October 2, 2018

Thank Father for another day! Thank you, Father, for bacon! I love bacon! LOL, I'm silly over bacon. Feeling a little better, still tired though. Hopefully I will sleep better tonight. Painting a lot still. It's so relaxing. Re-covered kids table today. Heaven's coming, she has to work tonight so I will see the boys tomorrow. Haven't seen Keegan or Michaela, Marinia was going to Skype with me but didn't. Gavin's busy with school and work too.

October 3, 2018

Thank you Father for another day! Feeling pretty good today. Just haven't been sleeping so good lately. I'm tired but something wakes me up. Love the memory foam mattress and the new pillows Patti gave me. Been painting a lot, still in painting mode. Going to try to get outside today in sun if it comes out like they say. Yes, got some sun! Med change not going so well already. Not happy! Got a lot I wanted to do tonight. Oh, well, maybe tomorrow.

October 4, 2018

Thank you Father for another day! I pretty much slept the whole day away. I am so tired and weak. I wanted to try to paint more, but med change put me down. Finally, by late afternoon I did get dishes done and supper made but then I was down again. Oh, well, they say sleep is my friend. Hopefully I can do more me tomorrow. I don't want to waste my time sleeping all day and night. That's med change though, it's a crapshoot! Well, good night.

October 5, 2018

Thank you Father for another day! Went to work with Tim. I still feel shitty but need to get out! I'm so yucky and grumpy. I need socialization! It's been rainy and cold, and I felt like crap. It'll do me good to get dressed and get out of house. I've been in my PJs for days. I'm going! Making myself do it.

October 6, 2018

Thank you Father for another day! Happy Birthday Evelyn. Glad I went to last night. I really need it out. It helped. I still feel a little yucky, but I think it's getting better. I just got to keep moving and get this worked out. I really need to feel better. Poor Tim, having to deal with my grumpiness and my weakness. I feel like a shitty wife. I'm trying hard to keep myself under control. He works so hard to keep me happy and pampered. It's wearing on him and I can tell. I don't need to be pampered. I need his touch, his arms and his time. He does all that and more.

October 7, 2018

Thank you Father for another day! Tim's brother and sister-in-law Scott & Evelyn's came for a visit and to dropped off hospital bed. Feel better today. Went to bar and decorated some for Halloween. Still got to do more but got company coming. Making homemade chili tonight! OMG! My chili was awesome!! Hit the spot. Great visit with Scott and Evelyn. It was good to see them. Michaela & Keegan stopped by. Keegan got glasses. He looks so smart and very handsome. All in all, it was a busy day and I'm tired so I hope I sleep good tonight. Good night.

October 8, 2018

Thank you Father for another day! I feel ok. Didn't sleep well. Got up early, did dishes then ate lunch and crashed hard! Something I can't have anymore is Salisbury steak because it made me so tired and I think dehydrated. Heaven and the boys came and stayed for a while. Tim got to have some time with the boys. I got some photos, but it reminded me of when the boys used to spend every weekend with us. Makes me cry knowing I won't get to watch them become men.

October 9, 2018

Thank you Father for another day! I'm doing okay. Just trying to keep busy so I don't get depressed. Heaven and the boys are going to come visit. Excited about having somebody to talk to. I mean somebody new. Plus, having is going to help me get through stuff so I can declutter my life and Tim's. I'm up for it and I am happy about it. Wish me luck.

October 10, 2018

Thank you Father for another day! Feel all right. Got movie night at bar and am excited about that. Med change today so hopefully it goes okay.

October 11, 2018

Thank you Father for another day! Feeling crappy today. Sleeping a lot today.

October 12, 2018

Thank you Father for another day! Feeling better. Making myself do stuff. Kind of have a pissy attitude today though. I don't like this. I'm so negative today. Got to fight the urge to blow up. WTF! I need help! Going to the bar tonight, not sure if that's a good idea, but I'm going. We will see. It may be just what I need, some social activity!

October 13, 2018

Thank you Father for another day! People are so stupid! I got really frustrated at bar and angry. There's no controlling my anger when I'm in that way. Got to pray harder for a better reaction. I'm tired, but also frustrated cause my mind wants to do things but my body doesn't. Also, I must wait on others to take me to do things & that sucks. I don't want to be a pain, so I don't say anything and get nothing done. Oh, well it is all good.

October 14, 2018

Thank you Father for another day! Still pissy. Not sure what the hell!

October 15, 2018

Thank you Father for another day! Started off the day okay but by afternoon, I was a sobbing baby and tired! I feel very crappy! Tim's so awesome he came and helped me finish cooking supper, then we cuddled and watched movies. I think I fell asleep for a bit also and it helped. Hopefully tomorrow will go better. I'm just tired of being sick. I don't want to be sick. I never been a sick person. I FUCKING HATE THIS! I really feel worthless on days I can't do shit! Just how I feel sometimes.

October 16, 2018

Thank you Father for another day! Beautiful day! Got up early, did dishes, cleaned stove, did laundry, clean more in bedroom. I feel very productive today. Listened to my Susan Tedeschi CD and Stevie Ray! Made me feel so good! Made lunch and more laundry and passed out. Funny

I always need a nap now. Haven't needed a nap since I was little and even then, I just lay there and hum a tune in my head or pretend I was on some exciting journey. I was always dreaming big.

October 17, 2018
Thank you Father for another day! It was a good day. Didn't sleep much at night. I made myself get up and do stuff. Fix my hair and went to work with Tim at bar. I bartended (sort of) tonight. I love little kids! They're not afraid to ask questions. They asked me, "What happened to your nose?", "Why do you need that?", "When you are you taking it out?" They love to learn, and they like when you tell them the truth. They make me happy!

October 18, 2018
Thank you Father for another day! Not much energy today. Freaking med change. Couldn't get past nausea this morning. Started on dishes & laundry but had to lay down. Patti made me lunch because I was still down. I hate being so weak! Stomach hurts, back hurts, I'm nauseous and my feet feel like somebody's pulling them apart, down the middle up to my knees. Oh well could be worse! I could be dead. Be thankful for living another day. Which I am but I need to be more grateful and not give in.

October 19, 2018
Thank you Father for another day! Thank you. Thank you. Thank you. Thank you. Thank you! Feel like shit today! WTF I hate this but I still it's better than being dead. Going to sleep now.

October 20, 2018

Thank you Father for another day! Still feel like shit! Stayed home all freaken weekend!

October 21, 2018

Thank you Father for another day! Got out to Perkins with Tim's sister Suzie. I love her. Started feeling better then shit again. Getting antibiotics since I'm coming down with something!

October 22, 2018

Thank you Father for another day. Still shitty! Tim's stressing.

October 23, 2018

Thank you Father for another day! Felt better today, but not sure how long that'll last. Still yucky, moving a little slow. Got dressed, did dishes, slowing down now. Made supper and cleaned a little. Yep, felt pretty good and woke up at 2 a.m. with shit's and can't sleep. Fuck! I hate being sick!

October 24, 2018

Thank you Father for another day. Yucky!

October 25, 2018

Thank you Father for another day! Yucky!

October 26, 2018

Thank you Father for another day! Feel shitty, but I need out of here! I need conversation with anybody who talks! Okay make yourself go; bitch don't be weak! I went, still crappy!

October 27, 2018

Thank you Father for another day. Still feel a little crappy, trying to fight it, but I think it's worse.

October 28, 2018

Thank you Father for another day! So, sleepy. Slept most of the day. Got worse as night went on. Sick and tired of being sick. Give me a fucken break, please!

October 29, 2018

Thank you Father for another day! Still sick! Sleepy almost done with this antibiotic. Never taking it again!! Levofloxacin never, ever, ever again! Puking!

October 30, 2018

Thank we thank you Father for another day! Sick! Sleeping a lot still.

October 31, 2018

Thank you Father for another day! Feel like crap! And now for med change. I was starting to feel better a little but then med change fucked me up. No visitors. Happy B-day Judy. Happy Halloween. I dressed up to hand out treats tonight. At least I did dishes, laundry and some cleaning, after supper shit got bad. Med change today and now not doing good. FUCK I was hoping I be okay, damn!

November 1, 2018

Thank you Father for another day! Feeling very, very shitty today. Tired. Happy B-day Don Juan and Tanya Jean. Still shitty! Tired. Yep still shitty! Sleep at least I can eat now. I'm so hungry and I wasn't eating much cause of the reaction to antibiotic. I'm so hungry.

November 2, 2018
Thank you Father for another day! Yucky! Stayed home again! I need sun and I need social interaction.

November 3, 2018
Thank you Father for another day! I will make myself get up today and go out. I can't take it anymore! I'm going freaken nuts. Went, glad I did but still felt crappy. I pray and hope Sunday goes better. I need to feel good.

November 4, 2018
Thank you Father for another day! Yes! I'm getting there! Finally! We're going to try cleaning living room today and Tim's going to move stuff around. We're also doing family night with Michaela, Steven and Keegan. Gavin joined us. Tim's always trying to make life easier for me so we ordered food, but I wish we could just cook stuff at home cause it's better for me sodium wise. It's hard to stick to a diet when he always wants to just spoil me. Oh, well we'll figure it out.

November 5, 2018
Thank you Father for another day! Feeling way better. More energy, eating more and awake more. Wish we could get outside and get yard prep for winter.

November 6, 2018

Thank you Father for another day! Cleaned my kitchen and am getting ready for bathroom to be built! Yay! Getting shit done! Cleaned all day then made supper. I love cooking! Slept like crap last night so maybe tonight I will sleep good since I did so much today. Hopefully. Tim's working his ass off. Gavin's back to working and the girls all have their lives. I need to be busy or I will go insane! Oh! Marinia's pregnant!

November 7, 2018

Thank you Father for another day! Slept like crap last night! I feel okay though, tired but okay. House is getting cleaner and less cluttered. I'm getting my kitchen cupboards back and I'm happy. I can't wait to get it done and bathroom in! I can't wait for that! It can't happen soon enough. I've been cooking again. I think it's been helping me get better. I'm feeling more and more like me. No visits from anybody. Oh, well I'll be okay. Just need to get busy and stay busy.

November 8, 2018

Thank you Father for another day! Feeling like crap again! Damn it! I'm sick of being sick!! I hate this!

November 9, 2018

Thank you Father for another day! Sick still can't go anywhere! Tim's working late so even if I did feel okay can't go to the bar. No socialization this week either. Heaven's busy, Gavin's busy, my family never visits (Roy does), no friends come over. I'm alone as usual. Oh, well be a big girl. You've been alone most of your life you're fine.

November 10, 2018

Thank you Father for another day! Tim's working today in Okoboji Spirit Lake. I still feel shitty. Patti is coming today. Still no family, no calls, nothing. I miss my grandsons. I used to care for them all and now I can't babysit. I hardly see any of them. All my boys. God, I miss them all. I wish the kids could visit more. Even MJ is too busy. Tim's my saving grace. He's been amazing. Thank you, Father. I'd be dead without him & so alone.

November 11, 2018

Thank you Father for another day! Sleep, sleep, sleep! I'm just going to sleep. Tim has to work again, and my body is tired. I just want to feel good. On my way, I know it! Sleep.

November 12, 2018

Thank you Father for another day! Yay! Feeling a lot better! I have a dr. appointment today to talk about getting a nurse to come check on me twice a week. They say it's cause am not getting out. They're also trying to talk me into having an aide come in but I can do stuff still. Sometimes I feel like they want me to just give up. I ain't dead yet and if I can do for myself, let me! Man, I hope winter goes fast!

November 13, 2018

Thank you Father for one more day! Feeling better today. Last night Tim took me to the new steakhouse after dr. appointment. The food was good. The portions were huge, and we hit it early before it got packed. I had a pork chop, baked potato and broccoli. I tried sour cream on my potato (never had that before) and of course I had to get a to-go box. I'm busying myself today cause he's working late again. Love cleaning my home and cooking.

November 14, 2018

Thank you Father for another day! Well, I feel great and it sucks cause now it's med change day. Keeping my hopes up though for a good day. Keep praying. The house is starting to look better cause I'm getting all stuff gone through and getting rid of stuff too! I wish my mom would come stay with me a little. It makes me cry. I guess I shouldn't fret, we've never been that way. I love her so much, wish she knew. Oh well, I'll just be that way with my kids all 4 of them, because I love them all. They will always know that.

November 15, 2018

Thank you Father for another day! Still doing good. Getting through depression. I'm crying a lot, but that's good. Letting out a lot of pent-up anger, sadness and pain. Patti not here today, so I can do a lot to the house today (LOL). My nurse came today she was fun. I liked her. She talks a lot and doesn't mind that I'm gabbing off her ears either! Tim and I were both in a sarcastic fun mood tonight and I laughed so hard I cried and couldn't stop! My ribs hurt so bad from laughing so much. Thank you, I needed that!

November 16, 2018

Thank you Father for another day!

November 17, 2018

Thank you Father for another day!

November 18, 2018

Thank you Father for another day! So sorry for not writing for a while. Haven't really been in mood. I will vow to do better.

November 19, 2018

Thank you Father for another day! Sleeping a lot in the day cause hard time sleeping at night. I'll be okay. Got to get house ready for boys, Heaven says they'll be coming and spending the night with us. I'm so happy cause I haven't seen them for so long! I need my grandbabies.

November 20, 2018

Thank you Father for another day! Getting house ready and food for Turkey day! Heaven and boys will be here! Can't wait! I'm cooking some awesome food lately! Tim and Gavin keep saying I'm making them fat! Whatever!

November 21, 2018

Thank you Father for another day! Yay! Family get together day! I love family gatherings. Wish we'd have more. There're all so funny. Getting closer to date for guy to come put my bathroom in. Can't wait for that! Rest. I need rest. Going to sleep. Okay, I'm delusional. Turkey Day is tomorrow! Boys are fun as always and I love that Heaven is spending time with me.

November 22, 2018

Thank you Father for another day! Happy Turkey Day! Yay! I love Turkey! Fun day! Heaven and boys are hanging with me today. Watched movies all day with them. I love spending time with them all. Going to sleep good tonight.

November 23, 2018

Thank you Father for another day! Recovering from yesterday. Staying home tonight. Sleep, sleep, sleep.

November 24, 2018

Thank you Father for another day. Working vendor show today. Please, let me make it the whole day and thank you in advance. Well, made it! Work until end. Visited some, then tummy started hurting. Sleep.

November 25, 2018

Thank you Father for another day! Relaxing and resting today with hubby. Back day! Not! Too tired. Watched movies again with my man. I love him so much. I need to do something special for him. He does so much for me. Think I'll buy him some real nice shoes for work and some for play.

November 26, 2018

Thank you Father for another day! Wish they were working on my bathroom. I really can't stand the commode! It smells, it's gross and I hate that Tim must empty it after working all day. I'm getting bored and depressed. I need to do something. Wish I could do go to work. I've always work. If I didn't work, I had children to take care of. I'm going crazy!

November 27, 2018

Thank you Father for another day! At least my cooking experience is getting better! I love cooking. Sometimes I think I should've went to school for that and then I'd be I cook meals for weddings and stuff in the ballroom and every day but let's be real with this crap going on with my health, where was I going?

November 28, 2018

Thank you Father for another day! It's our monthiversary and he sent me roses. He's the best man, husband, friend & lover a woman could ask for. I wish I could do more for him. I wish I had money, so he never had to work his ass off again, but then he'd probably change. Neither of us would be the same person if we'd been born with money or had money. Oh well, happy with our life just wish I wasn't sick.

We started celebrating our "monthiversary" right after we got married. A monthiversary is like an anniversary in which we celebrate our marriage with each other, but instead of yearly, we celebrated the twenty-eighth day of every month. Sometimes we would go to the movies. Other times we would eat out or go to see live entertainment. And many times, we stayed at home and watched movies together and ordered in. Sometimes I'd get her roses or a card, and she would make me a special meal or get me a card or a small token of love in return. We kept our romance alive throughout our marriage. And as she got weaker, most of the time we just stayed home and tried to spend quality time on our monthiversary with each other.

November 29, 2018

Thank you Father for another day! Felt bad that it was my ex-husband's b-day and Debbie (my other mom or my ex-mother-in-law) had to suffer. It's so sad. She's such a good person. I wish she'd find her prince. She taught me so much and loved me as her own. My brother's widow's children (including my brother's children) posted how sad they were that he had died and how they loved him. Wish they'd known my brother,

Frank. Sad they never knew him. He and his son Damon were close, but I don't think Damon remembers him, he was very young. Sad.

November 30, 2018

Thank you Father for another day! Happy B-day to my friend Dena! I miss her bunches. Hope your day is awesome. Too bad we don't live closer, it'd be great. One day I hope to go to Wisconsin and visit her and her husband Russ and find Daddy Joe's grave. One day.

Daddy Joe was one of her stepdads growing up. Savannah told me how they used to get beat by one of their stepdads when they were kids. Savannah reported that they got beat so bad that the school called child welfare services, and they got involved. She loved Joe because he didn't beat them, and he treated them as humans. He'd listen to them and tell stories to them. Savannah did report she knew he was an alcoholic, which led to her mother divorcing him eventually, but she always thought highly of him. Even though he was an alcoholic, according to Savannah, he was always good to them as kids. After her mom divorced him, she lost track of him, but she spoke of him often and saw him as a major positive influence on her life. He had died years before, but she was not sure where he was buried. He was a Native American and was buried on a reservation in Wisconsin somewhere, but she was not sure where. We had always talked about going up there and asking around and maybe finding his grave. Another interesting story she told me about Joe was that he told her when she was young that his tribe believed you could come back after you die as a spirit creature. Joe used to tell her if he died that he'd come back as a black crow. Occasionally, if we were outside and she'd see a black crow, she'd say, "There is Daddy Joe checking on me." Savannah told me if she came back as a spirit creature, she'd want to come back as a butterfly. So now when I see a butterfly, I think of her and smile and feel her watching over me. I feel her love as the butterfly slowly flies away.

December 1, 2018

Thank you Father for another day! Happy B-day Daddy Joe! I miss you so much. I always could talk to you. Wish my children and grand-children had known you. I wish my husband had known you. You were awesome to us kids. They will never know how much you loved us and the things you taught us. I know you were an alcoholic, but you were never cruel to us and you treated us as people not punching bags. I'm grateful to have had you in my life.

December 2, 2018

Thank you Father for another day!

December 3, 2018

Thank you Father for another day!

December 4, 2018

Thank you Father for another day!

December 5, 2018

Thank you Father for another day! Happy birthday Emmett! So excited! Can't wait to see all the boys! We're taking Keegan with us and that asshat Jon is going to let us have Lincoln for the party too! I miss them all so much! However, we never see Lincoln until Marinia gets him. I bet he's grown up so much. I see the photos Marinia posts on Facebook and it melts my heart it to see he's doing good with kids in school I used to worry about that. He's going to have so much fun playing with all the boys.

December 6, 2018

Thank you Father for letting me wake up today, for another day with my family. Thank you. A little worn out today from Emmett's party. What a blast. Funny, how stuff wears me out. Hell, getting dressed is a marathon for me. Hell, everything's a marathon for me. Sad too cause I used to be very productive person. I just get bummed thinking about it.

December 7, 2018

Thank you Father for another day! May get to go out! Excited do something and see people. I'm getting depressed and I don't want to. I want to be happy it's on one of my favorite time of the year. I've always loved it because you see more family and people act nicer and are more loving. Too bad they weren't like that all year round. I love Christmas movies and the songs. I love decorating the tree and house. The world is a much prettier place at Christmas time.

December 8, 2018

Thank you Father for another day! Yay! Heller Family Christmas day! Had a great time at the Heller Christmas. Great day. Tim got to relax a little and hung out with his brothers. I got to visit with Michaela. Tim's niece Tanya came and talked to me. We have talked before; but then she was depressed and unhappy about her marriage. This time she was happy and on her own, getting a divorce. I'm glad she talked to me and I'm glad she changed her life. I started feeling crappy when we got home, don't know why but I did. Maybe I'm just worn out. Need to sleep.

December 9, 2018

Thank you Father for another day. Feel better today. Doing med change today because nurse didn't call until Friday. Got to pick out a bathtub today! I'm so happy, they start on bathroom tomorrow! We went to grocery shopping too! We're going to try to swordfish! I'm so excited! Swordfish was awesome. It was very good. I think our friend Don would like it! Starting to feel med change. Watching movies with my man then going to get some sleep hopefully. I must get shit done before guys come to start bathroom. Wish me luck!

December 10, 2018

Thank you Father for another day. They start on my Bathroom today!! Crying with joy! Hope it goes quickly because I need a bathroom. Full of energy today! For a little bit anyway! I must keep busy or I get depressed. Cooking & cleaning house are about as crazy as I can get. I started painting again. Oh, how I love to paint. It's getting sunny out. I love it when it's sunny. I wish I could go outside for a bit, but oh well, I'll have to settle for soaking up the sun as it comes through the window. I got to do something to keep from going crazy.

Her journals often refer to how she loved the sun on her face, and it made her warm and revitalized her. If you are a caregiver and they want to go outside, then allow them. If you need help getting outside, then help them. If you can't do it safely, then wait until you have help like home health or hospice or family or friends to help you. I considered how she felt staying inside all the time and how depressing it was for her.

December 11, 2018

Thank you Father for another day! Getting house picked up because kids are coming tonight for family night. It'll be MJ and family and Gavin and us. I'm going to make tacos. I'm glad somebody is still interested in family night. It sucks at Heaven and Bean don't live near. I miss all of them being near. I love my babies. I miss my grandbabies. Painting a self-portrait for Tim, want to surprise him. Bathroom is progressing slowly, but it is progressing! I will feel better when I have freedom to use toilet and tub whenever I want!

December 12, 2018

Thank you Father for another day with my family! Another day of painting because I'm bored as hell. Don't want to stop because I'm thinking too much about how much of a waste I am. I will not succumb to this. God please, give me strength to fight these dark feelings. I know I'm not a waste. I hope and pray I get through this and rise like a phoenix. If I survive this, I'm going to live! I mean really live, try things I've always been afraid to, do things I've been always been afraid to, love like the way God intended instead of being the scared girl.

December 13, 2018

Thank you Father for another day! Thank you, thank you, thank you! I am damn grumpy! Fighting urge but I'm losing battle! God, please don't let me get mean, please. I don't want to be cruel and crazy. I like that I'm a kind, caring person who cares about not hurting people's feelings. I just want to get through this as me as much as I can. Don't let me lose me. Father, please. I painted and Iris for Evelyn, Tim's sister-in-law today. OMG! I got it done in one day! It's amazing! Very grateful and proud of this painting. I can't wait until I can give it to her.

December 14, 2018

Thank you Father for another day! I woke up in pain this morning at six something, so I got up the dishes and went to living room to take meds. I took my meds and then must've passed out and woke up at about noon! There went my damn day! Tim came home early and then he took me to bar to make Jell-O shots. Went home for a bit then came back to bar for about an hour just to see everybody and get out a bit. Also put me in a better mood! I missed everyone so much!

December 15, 2018

Thank you Father for another day! Spent the whole day watching war movie with Tim, ugh! I hate war movies, they're long and boring and yes it was history, but I already learned that shit and I was not needing to be reminded. Guys like that shit though. Made meds are now waiting to go award prize money for Fill the Ballroom contest. He doesn't want to go. He forgets that I'm trapped here 24 hrs. 7 days a week and I need out! We argue about getting rid of bar, but I don't want to because then I'm dead. I will never get out, never have anything to hope for (work wise). That's just my thoughts. He works hard I know and is tired.

December 16, 2018

Thank you Father for another day! Last night was some fun. Loved seeing everyone. A little tired today, but I'm okay. Tim got called away for hospice. Our friends Kayla & Chris stopped by. I love them so. Weird but I feel like they are my children. They exude happiness to me. For some reason they are special. Anyway, bath day! Had a date with my hubby, at Perkins, then grocery shopping. Yay! Fresh air! Doing med change even though nurse from Mayo didn't call again, WTF. Oh well, hope my reactions are small or none. Wish me luck.

December 17, 2018

Thank you Father for another day! Well, made it through the weekend. Med change was yesterday. Mayo never called, but I know what to do so I did, and I felt like shit! Tired, nauseous, poops, life is fun! Headache bad held on all day, slept off and on and then the meltdown started. I cry so much for no reason, well it hurts, so many times a day. I just remember what he suffered for all of us and know my pain pales compared to his. I'm grateful that I'm here and I'm grateful for all I have been given. Lindsay Joey shared deer meet sticks with us, so good.

December 18, 2018

Thank you Father for another day!

December 19, 2018

Thank you Father for another day! Had a great day today. Got up early, did dishes, passed out on couch about 10 woke up at noon. Got ready for Keegan's Christmas program. It was really nice, but I'm really worn out. Fell asleep again woke up at 5. Made swordfish for supper and rice. It's so freaken good. Later went shopping for present for my nurse Mallory. Tonight, now watching movies and visiting with Marinia. She picks Lincoln up tomorrow. I can't wait to see him. So glad she made it home.

December 20, 2018

Thank you father for another day! Thank you, thank you, thank you. I feel pretty good today although I woke up in pain. My damn feet! I think my body's trying to work properly. I feel changes. It's so weird and I don't know quite how to explain it, but something happening. Watching movies with my man. I think he's getting sick or just stressing and not talking about it, he's short with me sometimes or maybe it's me. Whoever, whatever, it needs to stop!

December 21, 2018

Thank you Father for another day. We're going to have all grandbabies tonight! Yay, like old times. Only somebody else will have to do the baths for Emmett & Kalem. It's going to be fun but very exhausting. Very happy they're all here! Think my man is sick! Ugh! He can't get sick. I can't take care of him. Going to pray hard he is okay. Found out my friend Pam passed away. Sad, she was sweet.

December 22, 2018

Thank you Father for another day. Busy day! Got to get stuff done for the karaoke contest. I really hope I can get this stuff done. I feel so stupid and worthless some days. I want to do stuff, but I need to remember I can't do the things I used to, not all of them anyway. Good that Marinia and Lincoln are leaving early in the morning. I've loved having them here. I'm going to miss them. Found out her ex-husband broke up with his girlfriend broke up, I hope he gives Lincoln to Marinia. She's such a good Mom and Justin is such a great Dad.

December 23, 2018

Thank you Father for another day! My family Christmas today. Feel like crap! Cooked the bird, made the cranberry stuff and had a good time at family Christmas. I still feel like shit and it's beginning to show. Hope I can get much needed sleep tonight to prep for Christmas with my babies. Don't want them to see me like this. I wish I felt better. Oh well, I just keep praying.

December 24, 2018

Thank you Father for another day! Busy day! Trying to get house cleaned up for kids tonight. Still tired from Saturday and Sunday but got get stuff done. Maybe I can get a nap later. Done with shit until 3 so getting a nap! Yes! Thank you, Father, for letting me get my nap and food was good. Thank you. Kids were full and happy and then they left. Glad they all had a good time. Love having them all here but tomorrow I see lots of naps for me.

December 25, 2018

Thank you Father for another day! I realized today what whiners and crybabies people are today. So sad people are so emotional broken fucked up. We've gotten lazy and selfish.

Not what God put us here for. Grow up. Myself included. The things we are hurt by are so childish and the major stuff is even worse. No wonder we have children who think they're owed it all and they don't need to work for it. We've destroyed humanity.

December 26, 2018
Thank you Father for another day! Thank you.

December 27, 2018
Thank you Father for another day!

December 28, 2018
Thank you Father for another day! Thank you, Father, for taking my pain this morning. I'm sorry I was weak, and I know you suffered much worse for me. Thank you, it was proof that you were will take unbearable pain for us, so I will continue trying to be strong too. It's bitter freaken cold today and I cannot get warm! WTF! I just need to be warm and healthy again. Got to get these fluids under control! I'm so thirsty though. I wish I was normal, and I could drink whatever I want to, how often I want to.

December 29, 2018
Thank you Father for another day. Feel yucky!

December 30, 2018
Thank you Father for another day! I got a call last night from my brother Roy saying my niece's husband (piece of shit!) hurt their 1-year-old. What kind of piece of crap hurts a baby! They

had him arrested but still, WTF?? This hurts so bad because it brings back all those things when I was a kid. God, help my niece, give her strength to raise her children without their father. Help her and her children break from all he has done to them.

December 31, 2018

Thank you Father for another day! Yes! New Year's Eve! Hopefully this year will be much better! Not just because of me but for all the families who lost loved ones or had some tragedy happen. Here's to all the memories and moments created this year and I pray many more good memories and moments happen next year. I'm going to our bar tonight to see all the people. I love and get some more memories for my past and start some new ones for my future. I'm going to wear my New Year's red dress and try to wear heels! I just got to make it there. I just want to feel normal a little. I need to feel normal. Anyway, I'm going even if I feel shitty because Savannah doesn't miss New Year's Eve! Ever! I'm shooting off confetti cannons tonight! It's going to be fun as shit! See you next year!

Chapter 4

Her Journal 2019—Continuing Decline and Realization

January 1, 2019

Thank you Father for another day. I got sick today. Gagged on phlegm and puked my guts up! Ugh! Wish the nausea and phlegm would stop. I'm going to bar to help clean up from party last night. That'll be fun, it was a real mess! Well, we went at 1 and made it home by 6! Wow, that was a lot! Tim, Don Willy, Keegan and I cleaned up entire bar and ballroom and stairs and main lobby. Anyway, that was a real workout! I'm tired as hell. Going to eat and veg out.

January 2, 2019

Thank you Father for another day! Feeling pretty good today. Up at 7:30 and doing dishes, laundry, and feeling fresh and new. It's weird. I think my lungs drained or whatever from when I threw up yesterday. I swear it was 2 pounds of phlegm! Probably not but it looked that way. Med change today, so far so good. Not feeling too bad tonight, but we we'll see how long that lasts. My nurse came today said my lungs sound great!

Bathroom is progressing, can't wait!! Picked out paint and stain. Wall heater getting put in and they are working on floor tomorrow.

January 3, 2019

Thank you Father for another day! Puked again this morning. I swear lost another pound. So much phlegm! Better out than in! LOL. I feel great after though. I spoke too soon, feel like crap. Slept a lot today. Tim's working late as usual, on call. Had supper alone because Gavin was out too! Took all day but starting to feel better. I ate 2 pork chops! They were so good! Well just going to watch TV as usual until somebody come home and have someone to talk to. Oh, Mom stopped to drop off a body pillow for me. It's nice, but two minutes and she was gone. Wish she'd stay once.

January 4, 2019

Thank you Father for another day! I had a lazy day. After I got up and did dishes, I sat down and watched movies and slept. *Lifetime* is addictive! Tim work late as usual. They work him like a horse or a dog whichever is worse. When he gets home, he still must work on computer until way late. He's trying to focus so he doesn't talk much, and I don't want to bug him. Sometimes I do and we must just butt heads. Miscommunication on both sides. I love him so and he loves me, so we get through it, but sometimes it's tough. At the end of day, we pray together, cuddle, kiss each other and thank God for each other as always.

January 5, 2019

Thank you Father for another day! Slept a lot today. Leaving for Rochester tonight. Got to pack up our stuff. I'm going to go in the swimming pool! Well, up to my waist. Hopefully, Tim will use hot tub for a bit. OMG! I've never been so pissed off! When you pay money for a clean room, why can't it be clean? Ok, they did the rest. Just not the garbage, sink and counter, or tub. Gross, and Tim doesn't care! Ugh! Then I open soap and it was already used. Gross! Fucking Gross! He doesn't care!! Aggh! But I do!

She was a neat freak. LOL. She had a part-time job for several years cleaning hotel rooms as a housekeeper on weekends. She knew what to expect and look for to see it if it had been cleaned. Me? I was a guy. If I knew were my bed was at the end of the day, that was good enough for me. They say opposites attract. In this case, that is true. I was the slob, and she was the neat freak. I do find it humorous how different we were in some ways but got along so well too.

January 6, 2019

Thank you Father for another day!

January 7, 2019

Thank you Father for another day! Well it's appointment day! So scared, but also can't wait to show Dr. Frantz how well I'm doing! First appointment at 7:40 a.m. Here we go! Well that wasn't as bad as I thought. My Dr. was shocked how well I'm doing. All my test turned out good! My gosh, that was a day! Not just for me, but poor Tim. That was a lot of walking around for him. Glad, it's over and that I am doing better! Not just fooling myself. Thank you, Father, for it all! Thank you for giving the Dr's knowledge to use those meds. Thank you for your love. Thank you for all the people praying for me.

January 8, 2019

Thank you Father for every day! Yay! So happy to be home again. They're working on my bathroom! Felt good sleeping in our bed last night. I feel good, like energetic and all, but mostly happy and relieved. Anyway, I'm doing great! A little tired but will be alright. I got to make my lungs drain somehow and I will feel even better. Other than that, I'm doing great. Med change tomorrow. Hope it goes okay. It'd be nice if I had a good easy med change once. Oh well, not holding my breath.

January 9, 2019

Thank you Father for another day! I'm so excited, they're getting farther on bathroom. Can't wait! Med change seems to be doing okay today without much of a twitch! Yay! Maybe I will get to go out this weekend! I hope so. I miss everybody so much. Wish my mom would come and visit, but it is it's okay. Heaven is coming. She's going to wash my hair and cut it. Can't wait to see her and the boys! I love my hair. It feels so much better now! I have a bad rash and it itches around my neck and scalp often, so I had my hair cut short. Goodbye long hair, but it looks ok. Just got to get adjusted to it. Heaven always does a good job.

January 10, 2019

Thank you, thank you, thank you, thank you Father for another day! Well, still feel tired, but good. Now if I could sleep. Tim's working a lot as usual. Wish he'd get a break. Him and I are good. We love each other, but we've been cranky with each other. Can't talk business at all because all just not agreeing on things. It's probably a phase but hate it! Oh well, we will get through it. Thank you, Father, for guiding us and getting us through. Thank you.

This was a time we were debating on keeping the bar. She was no longer able to work, and we hired people to work the bar for her. However, they sometimes would call in, or there were problems at the bar with a customer, and I'd have to go down there during the week and take care of it. And the business was starting to die down too. People that used to come to see her stopped coming, we had inconsistency in our bartenders, and it hurt our service and reputation. Whatever money I got in a weekly check at this time was being put right back into the bar to buy supplies and advertisement. So we weren't really making money at it, and yet she wanted to keep it, and at times and other times, she didn't want it. And I had back-and-forth feelings about it as well.

January 11, 2019
Thank you Father for another day! I'm so excited! I want to go out and I feel like I can! Bathroom is at a halt until Tuesday, but it's so close to being done. Bummed that Tim will be working away all weekend, but what can I do. Well, not going out! Side effects happening now! Damn it!! Why? I just want one weekend occasionally with no reaction and I want to feel great. Tim got called in and I feel like shit! Sleep.

January 12, 2019
Thank you Father for another day! Still feel crappy. So tired of feeling like this way. I feel like I'm a prisoner here inside my body. I just wish

I could have a little fun some way or another. I just want to scream. I see him and how tired he is, but he can have a fucken beer! He can go out of the out if he wants.! His life doesn't depend on momentarily feeling good and then oops, you feel like shit! So no, you must stay in again. Oh well, he needed rest anyway.

January 13, 2019

Thank you Father for another day! Pissing my guts out! Feel a little better today. Maybe I can get out. Yay! Got out a little, but now back to feeling shitty! Oh well. I'll get over it. I'm so thirsty! Got to get a grip on myself! I just want to drink continuous. Being this thirsty is crap! Limited to 8 cups of fluid per day. What the fuck! No alcohol! Just a splash of wine a week! Bullshit, bullshit. No hot tub. No getting chest wet. Fuck this! But you're supposed to be happy thankful and pleasant because at least you're alive! I've never been free. My whole life somebody has controlled me. Now I have this disease that controls me. I'm sorry. I'm weak.

January 14, 2019

Thank you Father for another day! Whoop Whoop! Thank you, Father, thank you! I'm still not happy still not a happy person, but I am thankful for all I have. Tim and I are stressed, but we will be okay. We always get through. I just think he forgets, I'm the one dying. Any decision I make, I have one opportunity to choose the right option, because I may never get a chance again. Oh well, maybe he'll get in one day. Now he wants to keep bar! He may want something to do when I'm gone! Keep it. You can't have a partner though, because you trust nobody. But whatever. I'm done dreaming. Done caring. Just done.

January 15, 2019

Thank you Father for another day! There is something about cashing in life insurance policy. Betting the check is sweet, but when you get it cleared, reality smacks you in the face. You're going to die! Now suck it up and do what you need to. Live out some dreams. I'm going to take our family on a trip to the ocean! Not today though, because I'm sick now!

At a certain point, it dawned on her, "OMG, I'm going to die." Despite denial and all the talk of medications and treatments and new procedures, there were moments in which the reality came cutting through, and we were overwhelmed with grief and panic. My wife had these moments, I had these moments, and our kids and family had these moments. This was one of those moments it dawned on her. This was normal. Working in hospice for many years, I have noted the desire to live by many patients who claimed they were ready to die. Sometimes it is verbalized as acceptance and readiness, but as death closes in, many times I have seen a struggle to let go. This is sometimes difficult to discuss. I know a few times I hid my fear and thoughts of her dying, thinking it would somehow speed up the process. I know there were times she avoided talking about it because she didn't want to upset me or the kids. However, I think it is important to not overlook or dismiss it. It is part of the realization and part of the loss of death. As she got closer near the end, these conversations with the kids and I were some of the most heartfelt and helpful in the grief we were all feeling. She and I shared our Christian faith each night when we prayed, and we had an absolute faith in the afterlife and resurrection in a heavenly home. We believed that heaven was a place without pain, and we were surrounded by loved ones and the glory of God. Despite these strong beliefs, there were moments she just marveled about the beauty in her life and cried because she was going to miss her life and her loved ones. We accepted these moments and supported each other. Sometimes these moments came at unexpected times, and yet later, we realized the timing was perfect for us.

January 16, 2019

Thank you Father for another day! Feeling great, but it's med change day so we will see. Going to do what I can and pray I have no reactions. Yep, here we go. No sleep tonight! Fuck!! Feel like shit!

January 17, 2019

Thank you Father for another day! Please let me feel better today. Going to sleep a lot today. Still feeling yucky.

January 18, 2019

Thank you Father for another day! Finally, feel a little better today! They're finishing details of bathroom today! I LOVE MY BATHROOM! It's the nicest I've ever had. Today we are going to pay off car! We cashed in my life insurance. We are paying off the Buick and the house, so Tim doesn't have to worry about those two. Also paid loan on my Malibu. The house will be paid off next week! This feels great though. Tim won't let me pay some of the medical bills. Instead we we're planning a family trip to the ocean! Grandbabies and babies and we are paying for all. That's what I want to do. Show my grandchildren the ocean and gather shells with them.

We had talked about taking the kids and grandkids on a trip, but she was never well enough to go. She had oxygen on twenty-four hours a day and, most days, could go out for a couple of hours without feeling sick afterward. There was no way she could have made a long-distance trip even if we flew because she would have been wiped out just getting there. And she would not have the energy to go to the beach and collect shells with the grandkids. But our denial of the seriousness of the disease at least gave us hope that could happen someday. Hope is very powerful and served us well often. After she passed, I told the kids I was not doing Thanksgiving or Christmas or buying presents for them anymore as they were adults now. Besides, memories are more important than gifts anyway. I did tell them that I plan on booking a trip every year on her birthday. I will rent a big vacation home and kind of fulfill her wishes to do this with the family. Our first trip was scheduled in Colorado on May of 2021. I hope to keep doing this annually with them as a tribute to her and kind of force our kids and grandkids to stay connected with me. They frustrate me sometimes, but like her, I love them all very much. She would be happy about this. Besides, she'll be there with us.

January 19, 2019
Thank you Father for another day! Puking!
Having a hard time staying awake and breathing.
My sinuses are so plugged. My throat hurts from
breathing through my mouth. So thirsty!

Diuretics made her mouth dry and thirsty all the time. She countered this by sucking on candy or chewing gum often. If she wanted suckers or gum or candy, I would go to the store and buy her several bags of what she requested.

January 20, 2019
Thank you Almighty Father for all you've
given me and for all you've taught me. I humbly
thank you for each day! Amen. Tim and I both
have been sick. Miserable and grumpy we are.
No visitors. Oops! Spoke to soon. Heaven came
by! That always makes me feel good.

January 21, 2019
Thank Father for another day!

January 22, 2019
Thank you Father for another day!

January 23, 2019
Thank you Father for letting me wake up today and feel better than I have in days!

January 24, 2019
Thank you Father for another day, thank you! OMG! I discovered that I actually like steak!

January 25, 2019
Thank you Father for another day! Thank you, thank you, thank you.

January 26, 2019
Thank you Father for another day! Even if I feel like shit! Thank you for every day you've given me and any future ones you bestow on me. Going to sleep.

January 27, 2019
Thank you Father for another day! Thank you so much!

January 28, 2019
Thank you Father for allowing me another day, even though my mood has been discouraged and disappointing. Thank you, Father, for every breath you've given me. Amen.

January 29, 2019

Thank you Father for another day! Thank you for all you've given me. Every breath I've breathed, my home, the people in my life, my car, everything, all of it. Thank you. Amen.

January 30, 2019

Thank you Father for another day!

January 31, 2019

Thank you Father for another day! Thank you so much for all you have given me.

February 1, 2019

Thank you Father for all you have given me. Every day, every sun and every evening, every minute of every hour. Help me to be always grateful for all I have and help me to honor you always with my gratitude. Amen.

February 2, 2019

Thank you Father for another day! Help me to enjoy every moment of it! Amen.

February 3, 2019

Thank you Father for another day and all that you've given me. Especially my amazing, loving husband. Amen.

February 4, 2019

Thank you Father for another day! Thank you for all of you giving and all you will give us each day. Bless me to be strong, tolerable and patient today. Thank you, Father. Amen. Puking again. I hate puking! Yuck!

February 5, 2019

Thank you Father for another day! Thank you for all you've given me and my family. Happy birthday Mom.

February 6, 2019

Thank you Father for another day! Happy birthday a Keegan! Puking again.

February 7, 2019

Thank you Father for another day! Happy birthday to Heaven's dad! Got my approval for CBD oil! Yay! Maybe I can finally get some dang relief! Now the weather just needs to cooperate so I can make it to Des Moines to get it.

February 8, 2019

Thank you Father for another day. I Feel little better, but I got a rash that's bothering me. At least today I can get up and do something. Must have drained, because my oxygen is at 97! Things are looking up! Now it just needs to fast-forward through the winter. I been a little depressed. I think feeling sorry for myself because nobody comes to see me. People say they care and that I inspire them but, I need to have socialization to be inspired sometimes. Nobody calls. I feel like I'm pestering them. Thank God I have Tim and my children. At least they spend time with me.

February 9, 2019

Thank you Father for another day! Yay! My meds came. Now just got to figure out all new stuff. This rash is driving me crazy! Hard to sleep at night when all you do is choke on phlegm and itch everywhere! I hope it goes away soon.

I'm still sleepy. So, think I need to rest. Well, fell asleep and still tired, but rash is going away. It's not as bad or as itchy. Tim is coming home early. We're going to cook supper together and do dishes. Hanging with my honey playing Scrabble then Tiger Woods on PlayStation. Then probably to bed early, as he gets worn out by Saturday night and needs to crash.

February 10, 2019
Thank you Father for another day! Thank you for the relief in pain and part of this dang rash being gone. Thank you for all you've given me. Bath day!

February 11, 2019
Thank you Father for another day!

February 12, 2019
Thank you Father for another day!

February 13, 2019
Thank you Father for allowing me to wake up today, to see my husband today, to enjoy the sun and air and the warmth of my home, the food I eat today, the fluid I drink. Thank you, Father, for it all. Amen. Happy birthday Lincoln.

February 14, 2019
Thank you Father for another day. Happy Valentine's Day!

February 15, 2019
Thank you Father for another day. I suck at writing in here. Sometimes I get a little sad (a lot lately) and start drowning in my pity party. I've

had a good cry though and I think I'm clawing my way out. I just feel alone sometimes, but then I remember I'm the people who truly love me are here. It's just I've always been a person who likes a lot of company and nobody (well a few) come to visit. In their defense I don't call them because I don't want to bug anybody. It also hurts that hardly any of my so-called friends have stopped to see me. Hell, neither has my sisters, brothers, or my mother. I'm good though! My husband and kids are the best.

Our children, families, and friends were made aware of her diagnosis and prognosis of her condition. Initially, we got lots of visitors and offers of support. Then we fell into a routine, and days turned into weeks, and weeks turned into months; and after about a year after she started getting sick, the steady stream of family and friends trickled to an occasional visitor and, in winter months, not many visitors at all. After a year went by, we all kind of didn't think about the terminal part of her disease.

February 16, 2019
Thank you Father for another day! I'm going to get my card for CBD oil today! Then I can make an appointment and go get the stuff! Picked up Lincoln. We went to Des Moines and got my CBD stuff. I got pills and oil. It does help. I wasn't sure about if it was going to help, but it does! Yes, finally some relief. I've had a busy day. So tired going to have to go to bed early.

February 17, 2019
Thank you Father for all you've given me. Thank you for each day.

February 18, 2019

Thank you Father for another day and all you've given us!

February 19, 2019

Thank you Father for another day! Puked again. Heaven and boys are coming. Susie and the girls are coming with little Mia! So many visitors. Yay! Got to get house ready.

February 20, 2019

Thank you Father for another day! Thank you for all you've done for me and all you will do. Thank you. It snowed like crazy and it's still snowing! Winter finally brought snow. Everyone is bitching about it, but it's winter. WE GET SNOW IN THE WINTER IN IOWA PEOPLE! I'm still have that rash. It still itches like crazy! Even in my ears.

February 21, 2019

Thank you Father for another day and all that you've done for us every day. Happy birthday Debbie. I have an awful rash. It's even on my ears and it itches so stinking bad!

February 22, 2019

Thank you Father for another day on Earth with my family. Taking new pill for reaction and itch. It needs to kick in soon because this old girl has torn her body up itching!

February 23, 2019

Thank you Father for another day! Thank you. I'm puking and rash is going away, but not very quickly.

February 24, 2019

Thank you Father for all you've given me, all you will give me, and all you give my family. Thank you for taking my pain. Thank you for saving me.

February 25, 2019

Thank you Father for all you've given me and all I can give in the future. Amen.

February 26, 2019

Thank you Father for all you've given me and all I will receive it in the days to come. Thank you, Almighty Father, for life itself. Amen. Heaven called. She's so scared. Health issues and it doesn't sound good, but we will see. Praying all is fixable for her.

February 27, 2019

Thank you Father for another day! Thank you, Father, for all you've given and all you'll give in days to come. Amen. Heaven called, she may have an infection, Crohn's disease, or colon cancer! I pray it's an infection she can get rid of.

February 28, 2019

Thank you Father for every day you given and give and will give me. Help me to live each day as I should following your will. Thank you, Father. Amen. Well, Heaven's cancer scare is over! She has an infection that is treatable. Thank God! My hubby is an awesome hubby! He surprised me with strawberry shortcake for dessert tonight. It was amazing. It's our 9 years 6 monthiversary. We argue and stuff, but mostly we love and enjoy each other.

After almost two years of opening the bar, it had come to an end. Our last day of running our dream business was February 28, 2019. We sold our initial, everything except the karaoke equipment because it was ours before we ever opened the bar, and I always thought I might get back into deejaying after she had passed as I loved music, and I knew I would need to stay busy after she had passed away. We got about a quarter of our initial investment back by selling the liquor and tables and chairs and coolers and other items. We just needed to get out of it altogether. However, we needed to not have to worry about the business so much and focus more on making sure she would be taken care of. We never argued or even talked about it after that day.

> *March 1, 2019*
> Thank you Father for another day! Thank you for all you given me and all you will give. Thank you. Tell my brother Frank happy birthday and I love him, and I miss him so much! Amen. Tired today. No Patti, Gavin went to Des Moines, Tim's working, mom and Judy busy, Heaven doesn't answer, alone again like usual. Sad. Rash is starting again. It's pissing me off. I can't stop digging. Tim and I are arguing again. Oh, well, it keeps my blood flowing! LOL. Trying to be as good of a patient as I can. God, help me to be better for my husband. He's the best and I love him so. Amen.

> *March 2, 2019*
> Thank you Father for another day! Thank you for all you've given and all you will give. Guide me today keep me on your path, thank you. Amen. Going to go to the store today to get sheets and then to Golf on Central to visit with friends. Made it to store and got some flannel sheets! Got a new comforter to point. Went to

Golf on Central then ate at Olde Boston's. I forgot to turn pump on when I changed meds! Didn't discover this until way later (SCARY!). Went to Sneakers after we ate, I started feeling weird. I should have checked pump. I made it home and discovered my pump wasn't on. Hopefully it will be well.

March 3, 2019

Thank you Father for another day! Thank you for all you've given us and all you will give! Amen. I feel a little rough today, but I'm going to indoor golf today! I went. I had an awesome time. I saw Danno! I was a little embarrassed because I saw him and instantly cried. Many of our friends were their including: Jason, Lacey, Olivia and Briar were there. We played with Barry, Don Willey, and Cindy. I had to golf one-armed, but I had I drive that out drove everyone! I can't wait to golf. I feel like my lungs are filling up today. Please Father don't let that be it.

March 4, 2019

Thank you Father for another day! Thank you for all you've given me and all you will give in the days to come. Still have rash. Dug chest raw again. I woke up digging at it! No Patti again. I feel better today somewhat. I feel worthless! I slept most of the day. Think my lungs must be draining again. I'm breaking out with rash and spots where I have scabs from the last break out. I can't resist itching! It's bad. Almost like chicken pox or measles or Poison Ivy. The very tips of my fingers itch! It's driving me NUTS! I keep dreaming this rash is because I am healed and don't need the medicine anymore.

March 5, 2019

Thank you Father for another day! Thank you for all you've given and all you give in the present and in the future. Thank you for blessing me each day Father. Amen. I think my lungs are training because I feel better today, and my oxygen level is higher. I'm peeing like crazy. Hopefully I will continue to feel even better by end of the day. Now if my hot water pipe would thaw in my bathroom, I can get an awesome bath tonight! We'll see. Yes!! My pipes thawed!! I get a bath! Thank you, Father! Thank you, Tim! It felt so good! I will sleep great tonight! Rash is still here. I look like I had chicken pox, scabs everywhere from scratching.

March 6, 2019

Thank you Father for all the blessings and for the blessing of each day! Thank you. Puking, but I feel good. That bath was wonderful.

March 7, 2019

Thank you Father for all you've given me and all I will receive. Thank you, Father. Amen.

March 8, 2019

Thank you Father for another day! Thank you for all you've done and all you will do in my life. Thank you. Amen. Happy birthday to my sister-in-law Becky!

March 9, 2019

Thank you Father for everyday you've given me and all the days that will pass. Thank you for every breath I breathe, every tear I cry, every ache and pain, and even the nausea. Thank you for keeping me humble my whole life. Bless me to be patient, kind, humble and loving to all until I pass. Thank you, Father. Amen.

March 10, 2019

Thank you Father for another day! Thanks for all you've given me and everyone else. Thank you for the love of my husband and children and grandchildren. Amen.

March 11, 2019

Thank you Father for another day! Thank you for all you've given me and all you will give. Thank you, Father. Amen.

March 12, 2019

Thank you Father for another day.

March 13, 2019

Thank you Father for another day. Thank you for all you've given me. Guide me to focus on living rather than dying. To honor you in every way. Thank you for all you will do in our lives. Amen.

March 14, 2019

Thank you Father for all you've given me. Thank you for every day I wake up. Thank you for all you will give in the days to come. Guide me today and every day to your will. Amen.

March 15, 2019

Thank you Father for letting me wake up today and every day prior and every day in the future you give me. Thank you for all your blessings. Amen. Puking!!! A lot!! Everything I drink!

I'm way too emotional! Oh well, I don't care anymore. I mean that little to you and all I've given has been unnoticed. That's okay. No matter what you're my children and I will always love you and I always have.

March 16, 2019
Thank you Father for all you've given me, every day every hour, every minute. Thank you. Guide me to honor your name and your will. Amen.

March 17, 2019
Thank you Father for another day! Thank you for all you have given and all you will give in the days to come. Guide me to follow your will for me and comfort me and pain and sadness through all this. Thank you, Father, in advance and I accept it. Amen.

March 18, 2019
Thank you Father for another day and all you've given me and all you will give. Thank you. Amen. Happy birthday Mary! Got to talk to my sister, who I haven't seen or talked to in years! God, bless her. I love her so much she's such a good soul.

March 19, 2019
Thank you Father for another day! Please guide me to do your will. Amen Puking.

March 20, 2019
Thank you Father for another day. Thank you for all you've given me and all I receive in the

days to come. Guide me Father, through this day to do your will. Amen.

March 21, 2019

Thank you Father for giving me another day. Thank you for the many blessings I receive daily. Thank you for all the blessings I will receive in the days to come. Guide me to follow you will today. Amen. Sick and sleeping a lot.

March 22, 2019

Thank you Father for another all you've given me and all I receive in the days to come. Thank you for another day. Guide me to your will. Thank you. Amen. Been feeling so crappy lately. I just need exercise, sun, fresh air, and some social interaction. It would help so much. Excited that maybe I will get out this weekend. Promised Norma I'd come to wedding.

March 23, 2019

Thank you Father for all you given me. Thank you for carrying me through each day. Guide me to your will. Amen. Got out of the house! Went dresser shopping, then to Norma wedding (Elvan's too). But we all know weddings are really for the brides (LOL). Thank you for giving me the strength to get out, Lord. I ate a piece of ham and wedding. Probably shouldn't have. We will see. It was an awesome day and I thank you for the son, Father. Amen.

March 24, 2019

Thank you Father for another day. Thank you for the many blessings I receive from you. Thank you for all the gifts I will receive in the days to come. Guide me to your will. Amen. Scott and Evelyn are coming today. I'm cooking ribs. I'm so grateful for my husband's family. I love visiting with them. Starting to get sick. I think I may have pushed myself too far because of my cabin fever! Hopefully it will get better.

March 25, 2019

Thank you Father for all you've given me and all you give me in the days to come. Guide me your will today and every day, Amen. Dry heaves all day. Father, I thank you for being with me and carrying me through my illness and my pain. Thank you for placing this amazing man in my life and thank you for giving me the brains to accept him. Thank you for each of my children and grandchildren and all my family and friends (Tim's family included). Thank you for all you've given me and carrying me through all of it from birth to my end. Amen.

About this time, she started reporting having upset stomach often. Supplements like vitamins or potassium tablets often made her stomach feel acidic and nauseated. Sometimes she would vomit. Lack of some nutrients caused muscle aches and muscle spasms.

March 26, 2019

Thank you Father for all you've given me today. The days before and in the days to come. Guide me to your will. Thank you. Amen. I feel better today (somewhat). After lunch maybe my tummy will stop torturing me. I got dishes done and I washed my hair! Heaven and the boys came to see us today. They stayed for supper. Papa had a great time with boys too. I love watching him relax and be a kid. I mean he put his phone down and work and paid attention to what they were doing and joined in. Made my heart very happy.

March 27, 2019

Thank you Father for every day you've given me. Thank you for the strength you give me to fight addiction with alcohol and drugs and bad people in my life. Thank you for always being there for me. Today I pray that my brother's wife gets help and get happy. Amen. Thank you. Amen. Feeling even better today. Didn't puke, no dry heave and more energy! Not going to push it, but a little. Made some awesome freaken chicken tonight. It was yummy! Still have the stupid rash. Still itches so bad I can't stop itching!! Maybe it'll get better tomorrow.

March 28, 2019

Thank you Father for another all you've given me and for getting me through each day. Thank you for giving me your love and surrounding me in it. Guide me, as always to your will. Amen.

March 29, 2019

Thank you Father for giving me another day. Thank you for all the gifts you've given and the ones you will give it in the days to come. Guide me to your will. Thank you. Amen.

March 30, 2019

Thank you Father for another day. Thank you for your many blessings you given me and all you'll give in the days to come. Guide me to your will for me. Thank you and Amen.

March 31, 2019

Thank you Father for another day! Tim's sister Susie is visiting. Puking today.

April 1, 2019

Thank you for another day. Guide me to your will. Thank you and Amen. Puking and sleeping today.

April 2, 2019

Thank you Father for all you've given me. Every day, every hour, guide me to your will. Puking.

April 3, 2019

Thank you Father for another day. Thank you for the many blessings you given me and all you will give me in the days to come. Guide me to your will. Amen.

April 4, 2019

Thank you Father for another day. Thank you for all you've given me each day and in all the days to come. Guide me to your will. Amen.

April 5, 2019

Thank you Father for all you've given me and all you give in the days to come. Guide me to your will.

April 6, 2019

Thank you Father for all you given me each day and all you will give in days to come. Guide me to your will. Amen. Rough day.

April 7, 2019

Thank you Father for another day. Thank you for all you've given everyone and all you will give in the days to come. Guide me to your will for me. Thank you. Amen. Little better.

April 8, 2019

Thank you Father for all you've given me and all you will give in the days to come. Guide me to your will. Thank you. Amen. Rough day, puking.

April 9, 2019

Thank you Father for all you give me. Each day. Thank you for letting me wake up to my husband each day! Thank you for all you will give in advance. Guide me to your will. Amen. Sick today, not doing well.

April 10, 2019

Thank you Father for another day. For all you have given me and all you will give in the days to come. Guide me to your will. Amen. No Patti today. Ill again, sleep, sleep. That's all I get done. That and pissing and shitting, then puking, and ITCHING!! Getting real sick of this crap! Felt good long enough to make supper, then yuck again. WTF!

April 11, 2019

Thank you Father for allowing me another day. Thank you for all the blessings you've given me and the ones you'll give in the days to come. Thank you. Guide me to your will for me. Thank you. Amen. Feeling better. Spoke too soon! Felt like shit for most of the day. Keegan came and hung out. He's so funny. My grandbabies make my heart smile. Talked to Dena my friend for a while. I miss her so. Having a hard time sleeping again. Going to be a long night. Mayo still hasn't called. Got to find other number for Diana the Mayo nurse.

April 12, 2019

Thank you Father for another day. Thank you for all the blessings and miracles you give us all. Thank for all you'll give in the days to come. Guide me to your will. Amen. Woke up early for going to bed at 3 AM. Feel shitty and yucky. Hopefully it's passes quickly so I can get shit done today. Hopefully it will brighten up and warm up outside too. Double-dosed on my "pot pills". I guess I got a little high. Ordered a sectional (purple), curtains, and area rug from Wayfair on Wayday!! Tim's going to have a fit. Men always do, but he's wasted way more money on booze and gambling.

LOL. I remember this well, and I also admit she was right. I was upset because we had originally talked about buying a couch, a purple couch. I didn't mind the purple couch, but she added expensive curtains and a pricey throw rug. I remember we were arguing back and forth, and as we were going to bed, she told me to roll over and go to sleep or she was going to fucking knock me out and put me to sleep. I started laughing loudly because I knew she was right, and she'd reached her boiling point. So I shut up, and I went to bed. We were arguing back and forth, and it was stupid that I was upset about the cost. It just shows you Savannah was willing to stand up for herself, which I was glad of. So often I worked in hospice with elderly people, and they rarely wanted to argue or want to cause a bother for anyone. Savannah had the right attitude. If she felt strongly enough about something, she would let you know. LOL. The couch was given to Michaela, our daughter, after she passed. It was expensive, but it didn't matter. I'm glad she got her purple couch and her new curtains and her throw rug. It was worth it to see her happy, and I was an idiot for arguing about it. We both told visitors about our argument, and we laughed about it later.

April 13, 2019

Thank you Father for many blessings you give me. Thank you for all you'll give in the days to come. Thank you for blessing me 26 years ago with Heaven. Guide us to your will. Amen. Puking!! Happy B-day Heaven! Indoor golf tournament today! I was awesome for a few holes! Thanks. Seeing them all was so fun. I miss all of them so much. Went to supper with Heaven and then I had to rest. Thank you, Father, for wonderful day.

April 14, 2019

Thank you Father for blessings you've given and thank you in advance for all you will give in the future. Guide me to your will. Thank you and Amen. Feeling pukey today! Everybody is sleeping in, except Gavin. He left for Texas today. Heaven recovering from a night of birthday drunkenness. My Wayfair order are coming early!! Heaven says she'll help me paint and stuff. I'm so excited! I spent a lot of money, but I will never do that again.

April 15, 2019

Thank you Father for another day! Guide me to your will for me. Thank you for all the blessings you've given, and you'll give. Amen. Puking. No Patti today. After I got stomach too settle, I did laundry, dishes, and cleaned my bathroom thoroughly! I hope and pray that since we went down on infusion rate, I just keep getting better and am able to have a somewhat normal life. I can't keep going the way I was. Rash is starting to go away. Can't wait until it's gone!!

April 16, 2019

Thank you Father for all you've given us. Thank you for each lesson, each time. Thank you for all you will give in days to come. Guide us to your will. Amen. Yay! I didn't puke, not that I didn't have dry heaves, but it's getting better! Heaven came. No Patti, so I spent most of the day alone. Heaven helped me get through some much-needed purging of stuff! Yay! On my way to getting rid of stuff I've needed gone for a long time. I'm so excited. Can't wait to do more. She's also going to help with living room and kitchen fix up.

April 17, 2019

Thank you Father for all you've given and all you will give in the days to come. Guide me to your will. Thank you, Amen.

April 18, 2019

Thank you Father for all you've given us and all you'll give in days to come. Guide us to your will. Amen.

April 19, 2019

Thank you Father for another day and all you've given and all you will give. Guide me to your will. Amen. No puking!! 3rd day! I got to go outside today!! Cleaned out my flower beds out front. Got to get new fences around front flower beds. Lincoln's coming for entire weekend!

April 20, 2019

Thank you for another day father and for all you've given me and all you will give. Guide me to your will. Amen.

April 21, 2019

Thank you Father for another day and all you've given us and all you will give. Thank you. Amen.

April 22, 2019

Thank you Father for another day! Thank you for all you've given me and all you'll give in days to come. Guide me to your will. Amen.

April 23, 2019

Thank you Father thank you for all you give given me. Thank you for all you will give in days to come. Amen. Om gosh! I puked so much this morning! Fucking diarrhea all day long day too! So thirsty, so hungry. Painted the dang living room in between the shits! Heaven and the boys came, and I had Keegan! Heaven helped me paint. We took boys outside and I had to come back in, but Heaven played with boys. Tim needs a break from work, he's worn out.

April 24, 2019

Thank you Father for letting me wake to see another day! Thank you for all you do for us and all you've done and all you will do in our lives. Guide us to your will for us. Amen.

April 25, 2019

Thank you Father for just everything. The comfort you've given me and the relief are amazing. Thank you isn't enough I know. Guide me to your will and I thank you again. Amen.

April 26, 2019

Thank you Father for all you've given us and all you'll give. Thank you for a husband who will put up with his wife buying a PURPLE COUCH! Amen.

April 27, 2019

Thank you Father for all you give, will give and have given to me each day. Guide me to your will for me. Thank you. Amen.

April 28, 2019

Thank you Father for another day and all you given me. Blessed me with patience and comfort through today. Thank you for all you all give in days to come. Thank you again and Amen.

August 29, 2019

Thank you Father for all you've given me and all you will give me in the days to come. Thank you. Amen.

April 30, 2019

Thank you Father for all you've given me and all you will give me in the days to come. Thank you for the comfort and relief from the rash. Guide me to your will. Amen.

May 1, 2019

Thank you Father for another day. Thank you for all you've given me and all you will give in the days to come. Thank you for the comfort and carrying me. Guide me to your will for me. Amen. Yay! I'm 50! Today!! Thanks for letting me be here today to see it!

May 2, 2019

Thank you Father again for another day. Thank you for all you've given me and all you will give in days to come. Thank you. Amen.

May 3, 2019

Thank you Father for giving me another day with family and friends. Thank you for carrying me through all this and every day to come. Amen.

May 4, 2019

Thank you Father for letting me see another day! Thank you for all you've given me and all you'll give in the days to come. Best birthday party ever! Tim got the band Road Hard to celebrate at Sneakers. I had such a blast, I was sick, but I had a blast! I've been sick all day, but I'm going to stay medicated so I can go. I'm are all night, but will pay for that, but I don't care. I saw lots of people today for my party. Michaela and Steven and Keegan came! Tim's sister Suzy and his niece Monica came! I saw lots of friends there today as well including: Danno, Barry, Sheryl and Wally, Betty and Charlie, Don, Terri, Belinda, Dawn and Leroy, and Susan, I started puking after I got home. However, not from alcohol because I only had one shot of wine, but more from side effects or medications.

May 5, 2019

Thank you Father for another day. Happy birthday Michaela. Puking. Had to go slow all day! I feel it wasn't worth it to see everybody and I have some fun! Getting worse, try not to. It's MJ's birthday and we have to make it to her day. She decided movies and dinner and at our house. Yay! I can stay in and rest more.

May 6, 2019

Thank you Father for another day of life!! Thank you for carrying me through. I could never repay the many blessings you bestowed on me. Amen.

May 7, 2019

Thank you Father for all you've given and all you'll give in the days to come and all you give daily. Thank you for carrying me through each day. Guide me to your will and keep me strong and positive through all the pain and restrictions. Amen.

May 8, 2019

Thank you Father for everything you given and all you will give us in the days to come. Guide me to your will for me. Thank you for carrying me every day. Amen!

May 9, 2019

Thank you Father, for all you given, giving, and all you'll give in days to come. Thank you for carrying me through this each day. Give me strength and courage to withstand all guide me to your will for me. Amen.

May 10, 2019

Thank you Father for carrying me through another night. Thank you for all you've given will give. Guide me to your will for me. Amen. Rough night last night! Puked in the afternoon. No more red freezer pops or popsicles because I think they made me sick. I made beef stir-fry for dinner and was sick again. It felt like somebody or something was making every vein in my body swell so I much that they were splitting. Oh my gosh it hurt! Couldn't move at all because it would hurt to move anything.

May 11, 2019

Thank you Father for another day and every day after this in advance. Thank you for the many blessings you've given us. Thank you, Father. Amen. Puking.

May 12, 2019

Thank you Father for all you've given me and all you'll give in days to come. Your love and blessings have been the greatest gift. Guide me to your will. Thank you again. Amen. Happy birthday to my Arlayne (my former sister-in-law and I consider a good friend yet). I was puking today again. Feel like shit! Dammit why today! Michaela brought me the most beautiful card and orchids. Heaven came today, but nobody stayed because I was fucking miserable.

May 13, 2019

Thank you Father for another day! Thank you for all you've given me past, present, and future. Thank you for carrying me through every moment. Guide me to your will and grant me strength and courage to follow. Amen. Starting to feel a little better. I need to get a get better so I can go on trips still. Tim's worried I shouldn't go, but I'm going damn it! I will fight this shit tooth and nail, I'm going!

May 14, 2019

Thank you Father for carrying me through another night. Thank you for all you've given, all you give, and will give. Guide me to your will for me. Amen. Puking as well dry heaves. I'm not in the best shape but I'm packing for a trip tomorrow. My nurse Mallory came today. She said my left lung, she could hear air and usually she can't! That's awesome. Gives me hope. I keep dreaming I'm healing. They must take me off meds because the meds are hurting me. A girl can hope!

May 15, 2019

Thank you Lord for all you've given me. Thank you for allowing me to wake this beautiful day! Thank you for many blessings you have given and guide me to your will. Bless me with patience, kindness, strength, and courage. Thank you for carrying through all of this. Amen. Puking more today. Got to Estherville. Going to rest up for rest of the day for visitors tomorrow. I hope I'm able to get out, but if not, I hope people stop by to visit.

May 16, 2019

Thank you Father for all you've given me, in the past, present and future. Thank you for caring me through it all. Guide me to your will for me. Thank you. Amen. Feeling better today. OMG! I'm getting visitors like crazy. Family and friends, I saw today included: Debbie and Jeff, Dallas, Samantha, Roy, Lace and Brandon and two babies, Evelyn and Brittany and baby. I cried happy tears a lot! This town hasn't changed much. Some, but not much. Wish I could have seen Grace my sister, but she doesn't talk to us a family anymore and that's the way she wants it.

May 17, 2019

Thank you Father for all you've given, give and we'll give in days past and days to come. Thank you for caring me through. Guide me to your will and strengthen me. Grant me courage also to face all I have coming. Thank you and Amen. Jeff (my ex-husband's son) stopped by again. Love that kid. I hope Brad is very proud of him, he's a good man. Going to karaoke tonight! I'm not going to quit trying. I pray I can sing. I SANG! It felt great and didn't even hurt this time.

May 18, 2019

Thank you Father for another day. Thank you for coming through all the pain and misery. Grant me strength, courage, and tolerance to walk with you through it as you guide me to your will. Thank you. Amen. My friend Debbie came to visit again today. I'm so glad I got to see her. I'm so happy she finally met somebody that she's happy with. She's a good woman and has suffered so much, she deserves a good man and life. Had supper with my sister Evelyn and her husband Dexter. I'm so glad she has a good man too. She also deserves it.

May 19, 2019

Thank you Father for another day! Thank you carry me through this all. Grant me strength and courage to get through. Thank you. Amen. Puking. Going home today. I'm so glad I went on this trip. I saw so many people I've been wanting to see you for a very long time. I didn't get to do much, but the trip did a lot for me. Also really enjoyed the time Tim and I spent together. He needed this as much as I did. Thank you, Father. Today I'm sick, but I'm stopping by to see my sister Linda and her husband Alan.

We didn't know it at the time, but this was her last trip to see her family up north. The trip took a lot out of her physically, but it helped her mentally and emotionally to see her old friends and her family where she grew up. She loved them all and wished she could go on more trips, but she realized after this trip she could not travel overnights very often anymore. Any talk about taking our kids and grandkids on a family trip to a beach somewhere ended after this trip. She was reserved to the idea that she would not be able to this before she died. She never really talked about with me after this trip, but I know it saddened her.

May 20, 2019

Thank you Father for every day. Thank you for all your many gifts you've bestowed on us. Bless us all with peace, harmony, and love. Guide us all to your will. Amen. I've had the dry heaves today. Taking it slow because I'm still feeling a little beat from the trip, but I'm glad to be home and I need to clean it! If the damn rain would stop, I could go out and plant my flowers before they all die! Oh, and the temp need to be warmer!

May 21, 2019

Thank you Father for the many blessings you give us all each day. I know I'm small and your clock is busy, but I know you are with me daily. Thank you for always being with me. Thank you. Amen. Gavin is babysitting Heaven's boys and Keegan will be here after school. I'm so happy to see them all. Gavin taking them all to a movie. I'm glad because Keegan wants to be included and I like watching them bond. I love getting time with our grandchildren too. It's always fun. I wish I could do all I used to with them. I love them. I love them so much.

May 22, 2019

Thank you Father for another day! Thank you for the many blessings you give every day. Thank you for carrying me through this turmoil. Bless me with courage, patience, and peace. I thank you in advance. Amen. My boys (Emmet and Kalem) are here. They always make my day! I love when all grandchildren are here. Heaven had time to hang out with me today for a bit. That was nice. I' always get sad to see them go. My rash started again! I'm so pissed! It itches so bad, but I'm trying to fight it. Oh, well could be worse.

May 23, 2019

Thank you Father for another day! Thank you for carrying me through this turmoil. Guide me to your will. Amen. Dry heaves again today.

Keegan came after school today. Spent most of my day resting off and on. Got dishes done and laundry started. Patti wasn't here today. She had stuff to do. Judy came this morning and we talked. That was nice. She helped me through the morning. Gavin came back to get more clothes. He is now working until Sunday. He leaves in morning to back to Des Moines.

May 24, 2019
Thank you Father for many blessings you given me. Thank you is not enough for all you've done. I only hope to honor you each day with my faith, love, and gratefulness. Thank you again. Amen. Puking.

May 25, 2019
Thank you Father for all you've given me. Thank you for caring me through this turmoil. Guide me to your will. Thank you. Amen.

May 26, 2019
Thank you Father for another morning. Thank you for the many gifts you given me. For carrying me through all of this. Guide me to your will. Amen.

May 27, 2019
Thank you for all you've given me. Thank you for caring me through another night. Guide me to your will. Puking again today. Tim's brother and sister (Scott and Pam) came to visit. It was great seeing them. Heaven's boys and her spent day here too. I love when we have company, because there are days, I feel I'm alone. Nobody talks because they are always on their

phones. When you say something, and they act like they're listening, but you can tell they aren't. I get so frustrated.

May 28, 2019

Thank you Father for many blessings you've bestowed on me daily. Thank you for caring me during my time of trial. Thank you for giving all you had so we all may be saved. Guide me to your will. Amen. I had dry heaves and puked a little later. Happy monthiversary!

May 29, 2019

Thank you Lord for all you've given me. Every day, every breath, every moment, my family, my life. I am very grateful for it all and all the beauty of each day that you've given. Thank you for giving us a path to Salvation. Guide me to your will. Thank you again and Amen.

May 30, 2019

Thank you Father for all the many blessings you've bestowed upon me each day. Thank you for guiding me, Amen. No puking or dry heaves today!!!!!

May 31, 2019

Thank you Father for the many blessings you give each day. Thank you for always loving me and caring me through this journey of mine. Guide me as you always have, to your will! Thank you, Father. Amen.

June 1, 2019

Thank you Father for another day. Thank you for all you do for each of us. Thank you for the many blessings you give us all and carrying me through this turmoil. Amen.

June 2, 2019

Thank you Father for all you've given me. Thank you for carrying me through this hard journey. I ask for extra strength and guidance for some bad things are coming at me. I'm fighting against them, but I am weak. Thank you in advance. Amen. Dry heaves again today.

June 3, 2019

Thank you Father for the many blessings you given and give every day. Thank you for carrying me through this trial and my journey. For making me a better person. Thank you, Father. Amen. God grant me patience and tolerance to withstand the loneliness and anger I feel. Please make me stronger Lord.

June 4, 2019

Thank you Father for yet another day! Thank you for carrying me each day. Strengthen me to tolerate all I must and keep my mind of good faith. Thank you, Father. Amen. Heaven and boys have been here since Tuesday. Love when the boys come. Love my kids but my mood is off. Trying hard not to be pissy with Tim and kids, but sometimes we don't care if they're rude to me. I wish I could just scream at them (not the babies). I'd say, "Hey! When somebody's talking to you it's all rude to be on your phone and then act like that person did wrong."

June 5, 2019

Thank you Father for giving me and teaching me. Thank you for the many blessings you given me and carrying me when I'm weak. Thank you for your mercy and the stripes I must bear. Amen. I hate the way I look, I'm angry about everything. Mostly I'm pissed mostly at myself for wasting the life God gave me. All my life I've tried to be good, but it's so hard. I take all this shit like a fucking sponge and I'm so sick of it. I'm not fucking selfish. I respect others and I just want to receive the same thing.

June 6, 2019

Thank you Father for a carry me through another night. Thank you for the many blessings we all received from you daily. Please guide my mind and soul to your will. Grant my husband some peace and comfort through all this also, I thank you in advance. Amen. I'm still not feeling the best, but it could be worse. My feelings are... My entire hopes, dreams, all shot! This crap has me so fucked up. Even the way I look. It could be worse, but I have a hard time remembering that.

June 7, 2019

Thank you Father for carrying me through the night so I may wake to another beautiful day. Thank you for loving me and guide me through my journey. Amen.

June 8, 2019

Thank you Father for carrying me through another night. Thank you for your many blessings you've bestowed on us. Thank you isn't enough to ever repay you. Please guide me to your will and teach me what you must. Thank you. Amen.

June 9, 2019
Thank you Father for another day! Thank you for the energy and strength to go to service this day. Thank you for all you've given and all you do. Amen.

June 10, 2019
Thank you Father for letting me live another day. Thank you for carrying me through this. Thank you for the many blessings we have all received from you each day. Guide me to you your will. Amen. A little rough, but I'm good. I love when I don't have to spend my morning puking or dry heaving. Thank you, Father!

June 11, 2019
Thank you Lord for another day! Thank you for all you do for me and the many blessings I receive from you. You've amazing, I thank you. Amen. Heaven and boys are coming, and I will have Keegan! I love when the kids all come.

June 12, 2019
Thank you Father for another day. Thank you for all you've given and give daily. Guide me to your will, replenish me with hope, love and peace so I may do as I am supposed to. Thank you. Amen. Dry heaving again today.

June 13, 2019
Thank you Father for another day. For blessing me daily with your love. Thank you, Father, for carrying me through all this. Amen.

Diarrhea and not much energy today. Just resting. My cooking skills are becoming damn amazing! Love that I have time to cook now! Got to keep fighting this shit. Doing more talking with Tim. We've been having some real deep conversations lately.

We had many deep conversations during her illness. We talked about how I would keep an eye on the kids and grandkids after she passed away. I promised I would always be a resource for them and give them advice if they asked for it. I promised her they would be treated equally in my will, and any assets I would have would be split between them and any future wife if I ever remarried. We talked about that too. She suggested that someday I might marry again. I assured her I would not. I understood that even if she died while I was still in my early fifties that I might live another forty years. However, having such a deep and committed relationship that we had I knew was rare, and it would not be easily replaced. She did want me to have another relationship again eventually. We had that conversation, and although it was difficult to even consider such a concept, I knew that just made our relationship that much more unique and special. In every relationship I've ever been in, I never had the conversation of dating someone other than whom I was seeing or living with at the time. For us to have this conversation was not out of jealousy but for her love for me. She had enough love for me that she hoped that I would find love again and wouldn't be lonely. This kind of love and conversations like this only made me love her that much more.

June 14, 2019
Thank you Father for another day and how many blessings you bestow on me and my family. Thank you for always loving me and saving me. Amen. Worked in my flower beds today! Sun was finally out. I love being out here, it's my meditation, my church. My hollyhocks have so many bugs on them, I can't wait! I'm going to plan to

make a fountain. I need that sound. The yard is looking so nice and Tim is starting to see how the work is worth it. Maybe he'll love it as much as me.

June 15, 2019

Thank you Father for another day. For all your blessings you've bestowed on us. Thank you for your love and protection you surround me with. For the strength to go another day. I pray for continued guidance to your will. Amen. A little rough feeling today. Got to go to Des Moines and pick up Gavin by noon. Went to lunch with Gavin and then took us to Botanical Gardens. I've never been there. That was awesome. At least Gavin celebrated Father's Day with us. Spent rest of the day cleaning, and shopping, and then recovering from the day.

June 16, 2019

Thank you Father for another day! Thank you for each blessing we've received from you. Thank you, Father. Thank you for your continued guidance each day, amen. Happy Father's Day! Feel yucky today, but not going to show it. Got to do something for Tim. I can't believe I'm married to such a good man. Thank you, Father. Problem with oxygenator. So, no golf today. Going to take him out to supper though. I got him the deck shoes I wanted to get him and a robe. He needed because his robe was worn out. Heaven stopped by. We had a good talk.

June 17, 2019

Thank you Father forgive me another day to know love and the beauty which you created. Thank you for the many blessings each day brings. Guide me to your will. Amen. Threw up. Went for a walk today. A very short walk. To the end of the block and back. Guys are putting in stone patio and garden. Yay! Heaven and boys are coming! She's going to help me get shit done!

June 18, 2019

Thank you Father for another day. For all the blessings I received and the ones you give daily! Got my bath last night and dressing changed. Having the boys spent the night. It's raining again so may not get outside.

June 19, 2019

Thank you Father for another day. Thank you for the many blessings I received from you daily. Thank you for surrounding me in your love and carrying me on this journey. Guide me each day to your will for me. Thank you, Father. Amen.

June 20, 2019

Thank you Father for another day getting me through last night. Thank you for caring me each day on my journey. Thank you for the many blessings we all received from you daily. Guide me to your will for me and strength to deal with all that I must. Thank you, Amen. Started puking at 1:30 a.m. along with diarrhea.

June 21, 2019

Thank you Father for carrying me through another night. Thank you for holding me close and guiding me on my journey. Strengthen me please too face what I must. According to your will for me. Amen. Happy first day of summer!!

June 22, 2019

Thank you Father for carrying me through another night. Thank you for loving me and walking with me on my journey. Bless me as you will and strengthen me to face all. In your name I pray. Amen. Happy Birthday our son-in-law Steven!

June 23, 2019

Thank you Father for holding me close each day and carrying me through each night. Thank you for the daily blessings. Thank you for your continued guidance. I pray for more strength each day. I know you've granted it to me. Thank you again Father, Amen.

June 24, 2019

Thank you Father for every day, every hour, every second, for every blessing you've given us all. Thank you for your continuous love and comfort. Strengthen me to become what you will is for me. Thank you. In Jesus's name, Amen. Dry heaving today again.

June 25, 2019

Thank you Father for carry me through another night. Thank you for the many blessings you've given us all. Thank you for the sacrifice you made for us all. Bless me Father to be on the path and to do your will. I thank you in advance, in Jesus's name. Amen.

June 26, 2019

Thank you Father for your sacrifice and the many blessings you give us each day. Thank you for caring me through this journey. Thank you for your love. Amen.

June 27, 2019

Thank you Father for carrying me through each day and night. Thank you for the many blessings I've received all my life. For strengthening me for my journey. I pray for more patience and strength to deal with what's ahead. I thank you in advance. Amen.

June 28, 2019

Thank you Father for all you've given me each day of my life. I could never repay the things you've done for me. Thank you. You are an awesome Father; I don't need to tell you. Thank you again, Amen. Happy monthiversary Babe! 9 years 11 months!

June 29, 2019

Thank you Father for another day. Thanks for each day and the many blessings you give. Guide me on my journey and strengthen me to be as your will. Thank you. In Jesus's name, Amen. Went to my nephew Jake's graduation party today. It was so hot! It was okay but didn't really get to talk to many. A friend of mine wouldn't come say hi. That bums me out, but I get it. He says he can't see me like this. How does he think I feel looking in the mirror every day? The old me isn't gone. I'm still here, just weaker and a little worn. Oh well.

June 30, 2019

Thank you Father for carrying me through another day and night. Thank you for the strength, courage, and love you surround me with. Strengthen me not to be depressed or stuck in my misery. I thank you in advance. In Jesus's name, Amen. Feeling yucky! Wow! I am not moving from couch today! No Heaven today. Gavin will be home soon. Tim is yucky too today. Must be the ham we ate. The 4th of July is coming and I'm hoping to get a cookout with family, but who knows.

July 1, 2019

Thank you Father for letting me wake again. Today I thank you for all you've given me. I pray for strength, patience, and tolerance, not only for me but for my husband to. Thank you again Father, in Jesus's name I pray. Amen. Feeling kind of crappy. Better than Sunday. I think I ate some bad ham. Hopefully we'll get better soon. My hollyhocks look amazing! Almost all the blooms have blossomed. My flower gardens are awesome! They finally finished my patio and garden in the empty lot! Yes, wish I had my health so I could really go to town. Got my hair did today.

July 2, 2019

Thank you Father for letting me see today. For the many blessings you've bestowed on my family and I. Thank you for the sacrifice you made for all of us. I pray for you continued guidance each day. Please give me strength, patience, courage, and love, in Jesus's name. Amen. No Heaven and the boys today again. Well, Heaven came by, but didn't get time with her she was busy with friends, but I got to see her. Got pool up today! Wish I could have got in it. I love my husband. I just wish he didn't think I need all I dream. I'm simple.

July 3, 2019

Thank you Father for another day. Thank you for all you've given me and continue to give us daily. Father I pray for healing patience, and courage to get through my journey. Thank you in advance. I also thank you for my soulmate. He is amazing. Amen. Puking. Last day of this week for Patti. Tim is taking next four days off! Hopefully we get shit done too. Hopefully I have a good four days so we can golf too! It's been so rainy and humid that I can't be out. I can't take it. Painted part of the porch today, it turned out nice.

July 4, 2019

Thank you Father for another day. Thank you for the many, many blessings you've bestowed on us. Guide us Father to your will for us. Grant us strength, patience, and courage to do what we must. We thank you in advance, in Jesus's name. Amen. Boys are coming today. We have boys and Keegan. I'm in heaven with my babies here even when they're naughty. We're hanging out at the pool in the yard. I love watching them play and hearing them laugh. Papa mowed and then came and splashed with the kids. It was so funny. Kids loved it. I love seeing him be a kid.

July 5, 2019

Thank you Lord for another day. Thank you for allowing me to have another day with my husband and babies. To enjoy another sunrise and the many other blessings you give us all. Please guide me to your will, thank you, again. Amen. Last day with boys. We didn't let them watch TV or play video games. They made bird houses and feeder. They played with Keegan all day and we told them stories and taught them to mow. They passed out on the way home. They had some sunburn from being in pool all day Thursday. Poor things.

July 6, 2019

Thank you for all you've given me each day. I thank you for every hour, my family, my friends, life, all of it. Guide me to your path you will for me. Thank you for your sacrifice and love and mold me to your will. Thank you. Amen. Stayed inside all day because I was feeling pretty crappy, but I got through it. Maybe I'll get out tomorrow. Gavin put in my raised garden bed finally, but I'll have to do planting. At least it's done!

July 7, 2019

Thank you Father for another day and the many blessings you give us daily. Thank you for my new grandbaby! Thank you for your continuous love and protection. Please guide me to your path you've chosen. Thank you. Amen. Worked outside in my garden today. Well only the afternoon because I was yucky until about 3. I love working in the yard and it helps my anger a lot. I pray mostly the whole time I'm out there after I curse at the weeds. It's my church. My garden for God. No Heaven Again.

July 8, 2019

Thank you Father for another day. Thank you for your sacrifice and the many blessings we all receive daily. Please watch over me and guide me to be more like you. Bless my family today as they go about their day. Thank you, in Jesus's name. Amen. Puked a little. I think it was pineapple.

July 9, 2019

Thank you Father for another day. Thank You for all you've given me. For your guidance, your love, your strength, and shelter. Thank you for all the miracles you give me daily. Thank you in Jesus name, Amen. Puking!

July 10, 2019

Thank you Father for another day. Thank you for those everyday miracles and the blessings you given. For the sacrifices you've made. I pray for guidance. Continue to put me on a path you've chosen for me. I pray for patience and strength to carry on. Thank you. In Jesus's name, Amen. I just want to feel better and I get my stuff done. I hate just sitting here waiting to die. Helping watch boys today! Gavin leaves on Thursday. I so love my grandchildren. Sometimes I feel like they are the only ones who want to spend time with me. Not true, but just how I feel sometimes.

July 11, 2019

Thank you Father for another day. Thank you for the many blessings you give us and for the miracle we receive each day. Strengthen me on my journey. Thank you, in Jesus's name. Amen. Starting to feel a little better, not much, but better. Sleeping a lot. Boys are gone. Gavin is gone. Got to visit with Heaven some. I was very happy about that. That girl, I worry so much for her and boys. I feel like she's living my whole life. I pray for them a lot. Gavin just needs to get out on his own. Once he does, the change will help him become who he will need to become.

July 12, 2019

Thank you Father for what you have given me. Thank you for your love and support. Thank you for carrying me through each day. Thank you for the daily miracles we receive all around us. For guidance and shelter. Thank you again, Amen. Not the best day, but okay. Tim had day off. We rested mostly. Think we needed that. I guess we don't realize how little sleep we've been getting. Just glad I'm not puking every day. I need to get outside! So many things I want to do. Tired of being locked up and nobody else to talk to. I need visitors!

July 13, 2019

Thank you Father for all the many blessings and miracles you given me daily. Thank you for your strength, support, guidance, and love my entire life. Thank you isn't enough, but I have only that and my faith and I love to give you in return. In Jesus's name, Amen. Didn't feel great, but I need to get out of here! Went to karaoke at Crickets! Didn't get to sing, but Tim did, and I had a blast talking to everyone. I love watching him have fun. He needs to relax more. He's so stressed and always wants to control. God has control.

She was right about me. I was trying to stay busy and tried thinking if I worked hard enough and planned well that maybe we could avoid her death altogether. I was stressed all the time because I believed I had some control. However, as the disease wore on and she got closer, I realized how I had no control, and it was up to her and God when she would pass away. It was very humbling for me. Thank God that our Father in heaven taught me these lessons through this experience. We really don't control as much as we think.

July 14, 2019

Thank you Father for another day with family and friends. Thank you for all you've given us all and for the miracles we receive daily. Thank you for life and all your guidance and support, your love, and your shelter! In Jesus's name, Amen. Feel okay today. Went to church, then golfed with some friends (Don, Barry, Cindy and Belinda). Then came home and got garden watered and some done on carousel fountain. Maybe tomorrow I can get pool clean and filled and get in it! I would love that. Before summer ends and I'm stuck inside again!

July 15, 2019

Thank you Father for taking me in your arms and bring me to this day. I'm amazed at how much you love an imperfect soul like me. Guide me and use me to your will and to share your blessings with others. Thank you, Father. Amen. Covered in blotchy red spots this morning. Feeling okay, but a little yucky. Think I'm going to drain. I can feel a meltdown coming. Yep, it's happening. Funny Tim calls when I have one (I don't tell him always). At least it wasn't bad. Had more meltdowns and flushing. I hate this, but it could be worse. I could be dead already. I'm just going to try to be positive.

July 16, 2019

Thank you Father for leading me to another day. Thank you for the many blessings I receive each day. Father I ask that you lay hands on me and heal me if it is your will. If not that you strengthen me for my journey. Thank you, in Jesus's name. Amen. Puked a little phlegm today. Didn't puke again all day but I have the dark red spots all over me and the rash is starting again. Ugh! Damn this rash it itches so bad! Woke up in the middle of night with pain in my foot so bad, then both feet. Tim my knight came to my rescue with the CBD oil. Thank you, God.

July 17, 2019

Thank you Father for all you've given. Thank you for caring me on my journey. I pray for your continued guidance, use me to teach, to love. Thank you, Father, Amen. No Heaven, no boys. No call or stop by. She's busy. She's got to find a home soon. Gavin called, video chat. Him and Awkward (his friend) are doing okay. Awkward met a girl! I'm flushing, but it had an okay day. Got bathroom cleaned and dishes done. Can't go outside because of the humidity. Oh, well soon hopefully.

July 18, 2019

Thank you Father for allowing me another day to be with my family. Thank you for all you've given me and your love and support. Thank you, Father. Amen. Feeling okay. Did dishes, cleaned my bathroom, and did a little dusting. Gavin called (well video chatted) while Rascal Flatts was playing. That was awesome. I'm starting to flush and I had a couple meltdowns today. Really bad one late, but my amazing hubby got me through. I love him so much. Thank you again for my husband Father. I'm so blessed.

July 19, 2019

Thank you Father for all you give me and everybody else in this world. Thank you for always getting me through the rough stuff. I am nothing without you. Amen. Dishes today! Ugh! Did dishes, but that's about it. Gavin video chatted during Aerosmith so I can see! That was awesome! He's so sweet sometimes. Started flushing. So, Tim thought I should get out a bit. So, we went to grocery shopping at MIDNIGHT! LOL, that way hardly anybody was there. Got to stop over drinking fluids, but I was thirsty, and I had diarrhea. Still needs to stop.

July 20, 2019

Thank you Father for another day. For all you've given so I may be saved. For the many blessings. For carrying me through this. Thank you for your love and guidance. Amen.

July 21, 2019

Thank you Father for another day!! I have faith in you alone to heal me and guide me to your will. I trust in you the Almighty Father alone. Thank you for your blessings. Amen.

July 22, 2019

Thank you Father for another day. Thank you for surrounding me in your love and your arms and carrying me through the night. I am truly blessed by your love and grace. I trust only in you, have faith in you alone, you're my Father, my healer, my savior. In Jesus's name, Amen.

July 23, 2019
No entry.

July 24, 2019
Thank you Father for all you give me and everyone. For the miracles we all receive each day and I thank you for letting me witness it all. Please guide me today and give me strength to get through what I must. Thank you, Father. Amen. Well heaven and boys are moving in until they find a home. I love waking up to their little voices. I just adore my grandbabies even when they're naughty (all of them). Maybe heaven and I will talk more for now. Tim and I had a date! We went to Perkins. I had a really good meal. Went for a cruise through Dolliver Park. I love nights like this when we take time to just love each other. Thank you, Father.

July 25, 2019
Thank you Father for another day of family, emotions, life, and daily miracles. For keeping me calm when stuff and people make me angry as hell! Thank you for the peace inside me. Father I trust in only you. Amen. My patience is thinning lately. I'm fighting implosion so bad. People really know how to push your buttons! Gavin leaves today. Heaven is her busy self. My boys are at my ex's and MJ rarely visits. What has happened in families is sad. Too many ungrateful, selfish people. Just sad! They all don't know what

they're missing in each other. Heaven and the boys are going to be moving in for a bit. I'm running out of room, but I'm throwing out a bunch.

July 26, 2019

Good morning Father! Thank you for letting me witness another day of your love and miracles! Guide me in body, mind, and soul today as every day. Thank you, Father. Amen. Getting nervous about going to Mayo because I just can't seem to get better. Oh well, I'm an old broad, I'll be okay. Just got to relax. I feel better so I'm just going to clean. Yes! I'm proud of myself. My home is getting better. Cleaned a lot. Just going to relax and pack for our trip to Mayo on Saturday.

July 27, 2019

Thank you Father again for letting me witness another day of your miracles. Thank you for carrying me through the night and give me strength to keep going. You're an awesome Father and amazing! Thank you again, Amen. Trip to Mayo today and I'm sick with diarrhea. Ugh! I feel crappy! What the hell, is this is there a rule that says I must be miserable always? I swear just because I was happy! Be tough, pray. Can't sleep. Maybe tomorrow I'll feel better. This bed is comfortable, just can't sleep. Tim is sleeping good though. I'm glad he needs it. Hopefully this red marks all over me go away.

July 28, 2019

Thank you Father for another day for me. Thank you for the miracles I've been allowed to witness. You are an awesome Father. I trust and have faith in only you. Amen. Well, felt crappy when I woke and fell back asleep. Felt better after I got up and we went and ate. Then hit Walmart for snacks. WTF No Pepsi in hotel or microwave and no popcorn! Anyway back now. Ate supper and feel much better.

A couple of times a year, we went to Mayo Clinic for testing. This was one of her last trips to Mayo, and she had been sick weeks beforehand and had no energy. As we got checked into the hotel and she was thinking about the testing the next morning, she sobbed and cried loudly, "I'm going to die. I'm going to die." I offered her a shoulder to cry on and tried to reassure her, but I was speechless. However, the next day, she did her testing and had good results that time.

July 29, 2019

Thank you Father for allowing me to witness another day of your love and miracles. Guide me today as every day on my journey and mold me to your will. Thank you, Father, for it all. Every minute, every hour, every day and week, and on and on. Amen. Mayo today. Whooh! Whooh! 1½ years bitches! Hopefully it goes well. Praying. Didn't sleep well at all. Well, I'm not better, but I'm not worse. I'm not at a standstill. They're going to adjust my meds so I'm not so miserable! Must have blood tests every week though to make sure I'm okay. Going home now. Heaven is still in mood, but oh well. Got to see Gavin!

July 30, 2019

Thank you Father for another for all you've given me. For all you've carried me through and letting me witness another day. I'm truly grateful for all you've given me. Amen. Tim had day off. So, we spent day outside. He mowed, and worked in my garden, and we got my pool filled up! Gavin and Heaven and boys are all gone for day, so it's just me and him. Always feel good when I get outside. Electrician came and got the garage with power again and we have an outlet outside now!! Yay! Gavin's growing up and I'm so happy. Heaven, she'll be better when she gets her life back. For her I hope it's soon!

July 31, 2019

Thank you Father for all you've given for me and to m. Thank you for always having me cared for. I'm truly grateful for all you have given me. Each day, life, family, everything. Please guide me Father in thoughts and actions every day. Thank you. Amen. Been outside most of the day. Diarrhea again! Shouldn't have had popcorn! Planned to go outside and in pool but looks like rain and golf canceled because Tim had to work late.

August 1, 2019

Thank you Father for carrying me through another night. Thanks for allowing me to witness your miracles daily. I'm very grateful. Please grant me patience, strength, peace and compassion for others as I journey today. Thank you, Father. Amen. Got outside. Weeded flower beds, walked, and then cooked supper. When Tim came home, we went golfing. I almost did 9 holes. Got to do 18 on Saturday so I hope I can do it. I will just make sure I take my pot pill and oil with me, maybe that's that'll help. I need to not get so frustrated with myself because I can't hit far enough one-armed. I lost a lot of muscle over this 1½ years. It sucks!!

August 2, 2019

Thank you Father for all you've given me, for your sacrifice so that I may be saved. Thank you for each day is truly a miracle. Father guide me through my day with patience, strength, compassion, and love so I may walk closer to you. Amen. Happy B-day to my friend Lora! Trying to relax a little today so I can do well tomorrow. I hope it works. Marinia's family will be here next week. Can't wait to see them!

August 3, 2019

Thank you Father for all you've given and give every day. Bless me with strength, health, and positivity today. Again, thank you Father. Amen.

August 4, 2019

Thank you Father for letting me wake me awake to another day with my family. Thank you for all the many miracles we all receive daily and the sacrifices you made for us. I pray each day for your guidance, strength, and patience for others and for myself. Thank you, Father. Amen.

August 5, 2019

Thank you Father for all you've given all of us. Thank you for letting us witness the daily miracles you've allowed us to witness. Guide us all to your will Father. Today as every day, I pray for strength, courage, peace to get through whatever I must. I thank you in advance. Amen. Marinia,

Justin, and Lincoln and Ilana (our newest grand-child and first granddaughter).

August 6, 2019

Thank you Father for allowing me another day. I'm forever in your debt. Thank you for all the strength and comfort you've given me. Thank you, Father. Amen.

August 7, 2019

Thank you Father for all you've given me. Thank you for the daily miracles. That you allow me to witness. Please give me extra strength Lord in dealing with my adult children. Help them to see why I'm disappointed in their behavior of late. I don't know why they've become this way. Well I do… because they've been given too much, and it has destroyed the things I taught them. I'm so saddened by this. I mean I know they must grow, but my poor grandbabies. My children always came first before any habit, any pleasure, anything but God. I just don't under-stand this era.

One of our favorite venting subjects was how younger gener-ations seem to be directionless and controlled by their phones and social media. However, we did sound like our parents complaining about my generation…LOL. The reality of dying for her was she wanted our kids to be happy and successful. As I've gotten to know all our kids differently now that she has passed, I think we overlooked how good the kids we really do have. They all work, none of them are in prison, and they have great kids (our grandkids). I visited with our children whenever they came over, but the more in-depth con-versations such as how they are truly doing in life, Savannah was the one for those conversations. However, now sometimes they tell me how they are TRULY doing. Although we were venting about their generation, if she were alive today, we'd agree that the next generation is better than our generation when it includes independent thinkers getting their own needs met and not sacrificing their own and more accepting of others of different race, culture, sexual orientation; and they are more likely to argue their point. Savannah, more than I was, was timid most of her life partly because of the abuse she experienced as a child and societal expectations on women to be passive and take what life dished out to them. We were both thankful that our three girls are very opinionated and can stand up for themselves.

August 8, 2019

Thank you Father for all you've given me and the many miracles you allow me to witness each day. I pray for more strength each day to deal with what I must. Thank you, Father. Amen.

August 9, 2019

Thank you Father for all you've given me. Thank you for allowing me one more day to witness all your miracles. As always, I'm praying for your will over me. I pray for patience and strength to deal and wait for whatever I must go through. Amen.

August 10, 2019

Thank you Father for all you've given each of us. All the miracles. All the sacrifice and your love. Let us not be greedy and impatient, but tolerant and peaceful. Help us to be patient and full of your light. So, we may show what we've been given and endure what we must. Amen. Happy birthday to my niece Adela! Thank you, God, for allowing me to wake this day.

August 11, 2019

Thank you Father for allowing me another day on Earth. Thank you for all your miracles, your sacrifice, your love. I pray for your strength, patience, and faith daily so I may endure what I must. Bless all our children with strength, patience, faith, and knowledge as they journey their way. Thank you, Father. Amen.

August 12, 2019

Thank you Father for all you've given to and for me and my family. Thank you for always loving me and never failing me. Bless me Father with knowledge and strength to continue my journey today. Thank you, Amen.

August 13, 2019

Thank you for another day Father. Thank you for all you've given me and the daily miracles you allowed me to witness. I pray Father that you'll bless my family to be peaceful and tolerant of each other. Thank you, Father, amen. Happy birthday Gavin! Amen. Had a fight with Heaven again. This hurts so bad. I'm losing everything. I was a real crappy Mom apparently. Funny because I forced her to stay in my home until 18. She has a totally different memory. Oh well, I'm crazy. I deserve all this. NOT!! Guess I just pray and fuck it! They will never get it. I love them all so much. I hate this and all of this, but they just use me, and I have always taken it. I feel so frustrated with all of them—Tim, Heaven, Gavin, and myself. The only sanity that I have is my grandchildren. But I'm sure they can all replace me. Fuck this shit! So tired of this. My whole life has been this way and I just take it.

WHY? Why can't they just see? Why am I stupid to believe everything would change? They're all like… I NEED, I NEED, I WANT, I WANT, GIVE TO ME, and Screw YOU. When you don't do what they want or see it the way they see it, they know how to hurt you. I hate that I am emotional. I hate that I failed! I apologize to everyone for being a failure. I apologize that I am weak. It'll all be over soon. None of them will ever have to worry about me doing a shitty job anymore. Then I'll probably burn in hell because I didn't live up to God's expectations either. LOL. Me and Heaven are so funny! I'm so glad we are done arguing. She and I have always disagreed on some of her memories. So, we will leave it at that. We're good and that's better, now I wish Gavin would do what he needs to do.

I think it is important to note that the disease process slowly changes you sometimes. Savannah started really stressing at times toward us living in the house. I noticed at about this time in her disease process that her tendency to let things go changed to her becoming more easily pissed off and more willing to argue it out. She was still the beautiful soul type, but she started becoming more agitated toward others in the home over little things such as making sure we put the strainer back in the sink after dishes, putting toilet lid seat back down, making sure the lint trap was cleaned out before using the dryer, etc. They were stuff in the past that she wouldn't have even thought about or cared about too much. However, looking back on this change for her was the fact that physically she was weaker, and she couldn't do very much. Previously when she was healthy, the dishes were done mainly by her, the toilet seat might have been left up, and she would have just put it back down, and the laundry lint trap would be cleaned by her. So I think that was why it started to bother her more because she didn't have the energy to even take care of simple chores.

August 14, 2019

Thank you Father for getting me through yesterday. Thank you for discussion with Heaven. You saved me again and again and I've grown in many ways. Thank you, Father. I can never repay you. I only try to honor you. Thank you, Amen.

August 15, 2019

Thank you Father for all you've given us all. Thank you for allowing me another day of miracles. I'm praying for peace in my family. I'm at odds with myself and my family. Bless us all with understanding. Thank you, Father. Amen. My stomach feels crappy, but my oxygen is 97! What the hell!!? I'm so tired too. Just some sleep. Haven't been sleeping much at night.

August 16, 2019

Thank you Father for letting me rise from sleep. Thank you for your sacrifice and the daily miracles we can witness daily. Grant me peace, strength, and courage today on my journey. Amen. Felt crappy all day. Hung out here mostly. Tried to go golf, but there was a tournament and we were too late. We just watched movies and played games all night.

August 17, 2019

Thank you Father for allowing me another day. Thank you for the sacrifice you made for us all and the daily miracles we get to witness. Father I pray for strength and understanding for what lies ahead. Thank you, Amen. Still didn't feel well. Laid around all morning. Went golfing with Keegan. Papa was way grouchy! We only golfed 7 holes before he made us leave. I hate when he's a jerk. I think its diabetes or something. It seems to be when he's hungry, tired, or excited. I don't know, but it needs to be fixed. We came home and I worked in my flower beds.

August 18, 2019

Thank you Father for the miracles of life. Thank you for taking care of us and protecting us. You're awesome father. I pray for strength, knowledge, and patience for me and I thank you in advance. Amen. I'm going to church today! Whether I feel good or not. I'm not going and I'm going to golf too! I did it!! We went to church and I felt crappy, but I made Tim take me and we golfed 9 holes! I wouldn't let him tell me I couldn't, I had to go. Our friends (Don, Barry, and Belinda) we're out there so we golfed with them. It was great day. We came home and I worked in my flower bed. Thank you, Father.

August 19, 2019

Thank you Father for allowing me another day. For always being there for me when nobody else is. Thank you for your sacrifice and all you've given. I know I wouldn't be here without you. Today I pray for healing in my family and strength. Thank you in advance. In Jesus's name, Amen. Heaven and Gavin came home yesterday. Haven't really spoke to either of them. I will never get it. They go to these festivals and blow all the money they have and then expect shit not to be behind. I know Heaven will go to work to get money, but Gavin will whine about "how you broke he is" and it's stupid. Tim helped me walk around entire block! I did it!!!

August 20, 2019

Thank you Father for another day. Thank you for all you've given me, every miracle you've let me witness, your sacrifice. Thank you for granting me with patience, empathy, and strength. Bless our family with love and make us stronger. Thank you. In Jesus's name, Amen. Lord I ask for healing in my family. Especially my son. Father, I need help with him, He needs you. Thank you. I will forever love my children, but they really scare me some days. So proud of my daughter protected me today. Never thought I'd see that. My son needs peace in his body and mind.

At this point, we had a full house. Savannah and I had converted the dining room into a bedroom so she didn't have to use the steps to go to the bathroom. Gavin was in one bedroom. Heaven was in another bedroom. Our two grandkids (Ennett and Kalem) had another bedroom upstairs. Heaven and Gavin would argue at times. Savannah and I had arguments occasionally. Both Gavin and Heaven argued with their mom occasionally. On this day, Savannah explained how Gavin was complaining about having to pay rent while he was staying in our home. I mean, we will always help our kids, but we do not believe kids should be dependent on their children. Thus, as adult children living in our household, it was an expectation that you had to pay rent. It wasn't a lot and more for the point that they couldn't live with us forever. Anyway, Gavin was arguing with Savannah, and Heaven stood up for her, and Gavin stopped arguing. For those that question how anyone could argue with a terminal person, it's easy. LOL. Savannah sometimes admitted to me that some of our disagreements were more for the interaction, and us arguing sometimes made her feel more normal.

August 21, 2019

Thank you Father for allowing me to rise above my situation and greet the day. Thank you for all you do and have done for our family. Please grant us patience, empathy, strength, and courage to go on this journey. Thank you. Amen. Puking! Feel real crappy. I just don't understand. My oxygen levels are great, but I'm so yucky day and night. No energy. My body is hurting, and it makes no sense. Well, it does, I'm dying. It's just getting more real. Really praying for strength and courage.

August 22, 2019

Thank you Father for allowing me another day. Thank you for all you've sacrificed and all you give. You're amazing. Father I pray for healing in my family, it's much needed. I pray for strength and courage daily. Thank you, Father. Amen. Feel a little better. Not puking, but stomach is just yucky always!

August 23, 2019

Thank you Father for everything you've given me to me. Thank you for every day. In you only I trust. Bless me Father with strength, courage and patience. Thank you. Amen. Puking! I really need help Lord. I need strength and courage. My emotions are getting me down.

August 24, 2019

Thank you Father for allowing me another day. Thank you for all I have and receive daily from you. Nothing is possible but through you. Amen. Puking! I'm getting weaker! I'm so depressed about the way I feel, and that Tim is sitting here suffering too. We can't go do stuff because I'm always sick. Now I know why people get so depressed and suicidal. I hate this. So, I'm praying for angels to help me.

August 25, 2019

Thank you Father for all you've given every one of us. Thank you for this day and allowing me to be a witness of your love and miracles. Thank you, Amen.

August 26, 2019

Thank you Father for every second, every hour, every day, every minute. The daily miracles you've given me are amazing! Even though I'm miserable I know you are with me. Thank you for loving me. Amen. Feel a little bit better today, but I think my tube has infection.

August 27, 2019

Thank you for all you've given me. For each day and every miracle, I've been allowed to witness. You're awesome and I thank you endlessly. Amen. Feeling a little better. Tube site is still red at top. Things are so crazy here with everybody living here. At least I'm not puking, not moving much because still nauseous.

August 28, 2019

Thank you Father for all you've given me and for the sacrifice you made for us all. Thank you for getting me through each day. Guide me as always. Thank you, Amen. Happy anniversary to my hubby and me! Our 10th Wedding Anniversary!! This is stupid. I feel crappy still. Have no clue what's going on. Can't get outside.

This sucks. We ordered in for supper. I couldn't go anywhere.

August 29, 2019

Thank you Father for all you've given me. Thank you for your sacrifice so my family and I are saved. Thank you for the daily miracles we all receive. Amen. Feel a little better. My nurse came check my site. She sent photo to Dr. Frantz and they made me go to ER. No infection in tube site, but they're checking my blood. They let me home to wait for other tests because that takes two to three days. My sodium was low too. So, I have to put more in my diet.

August 30, 2019

Thank you Father for all you've given. For your sacrifice so we might be saved. Thank you for caring me through each night and comforting me. You're amazing and I'm so very grateful to have been allowed to witness all your miracles. Amen. Went shopping today for a dress because mine still hasn't come. Found one, got shoes, headbands and all done. Can't get too worn out, got to prep for our wedding on Saturday.

August 31, 2019

Thank you Father for another day! Thank you for all I have and will receive from you. For the daily miracles and life. I am nothing without you. Thank you, Amen. Happy wedding day!

We celebrated our wedding anniversary every year. We did two wedding ceremony renewals, one after five years and one at two years. We wanted to share with the world our love we had found. We were married on August 28, but we had to wait for this day on a weekend to have the ceremony because many had to drive and worked during the week. We invited tons of family and friends and hired our friend to deejay. We rented the Moose Lodge, and we had a complete ceremony and food and reception all right there. Several of her family came, and several of my family came. She was very weak, and I could tell she didn't feel well, but she honestly still was as beautiful as the day I married her.

September 1, 2019
    Thank you Father for another day. Thank you is not enough to repay all you've given. Guide me to honor you in every way. I have nothing without you. Thank you. In Jesus's name. Amen. My friends from Wisconsin Dena and Russell came over with their son Lee and his family. We had a good visit.

September 2, 2019
    Thank you Father for another day. Thank you for all you've done for me and my family. Please guide me to be better person today and every day. Thank you, Father. in Jesus's name, Amen.

September 3, 2019
    Thank you Father for a miracle of life. Thank you for allowing me to witness your daily miracles and my family. I know nothing is possible without you. Bless me Father to be your example. In Jesus's name, Amen! Happy B-day Marinia.

September 4, 2019
    Thank you Father for miracle of another day. Thank you for all you give, all your love, and the lessons. Bless me to be strong and guide me.

Open my mind so I see the path you've chosen. Bless my husband to believe in himself and me. Help him see my strength. Thank you, Amen.

September 5, 2019

Bless me father to be more the way you've chosen for me. Thank you, Father, for another miracle and all the ones before. Thank you, Father. Amen.

September 6, 2019

Thank you Father for another day and all the miracles you've allowed me to witness daily. Strengthen me and guide me to your correct path. Thank you, Amen. Stomach feels crappy, but oh well, we're just going to stay home all weekend. Crappy weather is going to bum me out.

September 7, 2019

Thank you Father for another day. Thank you for the many miracles you perform every day. We are nothing without you. Amen. Pretty uneventful day. Spent most of it alone. Tim was sleeping in. I got dishes done. Feel crappy and my stomach just hurts. Ventured out to look for dressers, but we didn't find one. Venture down to Sneakers for karaoke. Sang one song but shouldn't have. I get winded so easily. I love to sing though. I can't believe I've ended up like this. It makes me so sad, but it could be worse, I could be stuck at home and never get out.

September 8, 2019

Thank you Father for another day. Bless me this day to accept what I must, strength to get through it, and to know your presence is with me. Thank you, Father. Amen. Crappy weather. Made it to church today! Wish we could golf, but it's raining, and I feel yucky. 10 years of marriage and I realize how things have changed. Some for good and some worse. Well at least I know who we really are. Same old same old mistakes. Too late to fix now. I love him dearly and I know he loves me, but we don't act like we did when we first got married. Probably because of my sickness. We don't snuggle as much because he is usually working on paperwork at night or I hurt when he tries to snuggle. We have gotten accustomed to each other which is good in a way, but also seems like we have lost our spark.

September 9, 2019

Thank you Father for giving me another day. I'm amazed by you. Bless me with your patience and love to deal with what I must. Amen. Happy Birthday to our friend Don.

September 10, 2019

Thank you Father for love and guidance. Thank you for allowing me another day and to receive the miracle of life. In Jesus's name, Amen. Painting Hall today!

September 11, 2019

Thank you Father for all you've given me. Thank you for allowing me another day and to witness the many daily miracles you give us all. Bless me father to be more like you. Thank you. In Jesus's name, Amen.

September 12, 2019

Thank you Father for all you've given me. Bless me to be more like you. Thank you. Amen.

September 13, 2019

Thank you Father for all you've given me. Thank you for all the miracles I've been allowed to witness. Bless me to be more like you. Amen.

September 14, 2019

Thank you Father for all you've given me. Thank you for allowing me another day to witness the daily miracles and the beauty you've given. Bless me to be more like you. In Jesus's name, Amen.

September 15, 2019

Thank you Father for all you've given me. Thank you for life itself. Bless me to be more like you. Father grant me patience to handle the pressure of life and all the problems that are appearing. Father grant my husband some relief and patience for me, so he's not so growly all the time. Thank you. In Jesus's name, Amen. My mom's going to church with us!!

September 16, 2019

Thank you Father for getting me through another night. Thank you for loving me. Guide me Father to be more like you. Protect my family today and bless us all with the need for harmony and peace. Thank you for life itself and the daily miracles we all receive. In Jesus's name, Amen.

September 17, 2019

Thank you Father for another day. Thank you for carrying me through my rough patches and walking with me daily. I know I have nothing without you. Bless me to be more like you daily. Thank you. In Jesus's name, Amen.

September 18, 2019

Thank you Father for a miracle another day and thank you for caring me through it all. Amen. I think I'm draining again. I'm bawling over everything and on top of it I'm aggressive as fuck! I think I tore my infusion site. I think all the redness is from me tearing it! That'll be my luck. Trying to get more done in my house. I'm pissing off everyone. I'm so tired of trying to keep all of them happy. They don't worry much about my feelings. They do somewhat, just they want it all now. I can't do it as fast as that! Deal with it. Not going to sit on my ass and going to die slowly either.

September 19, 2019

Thank you Father for all you've given me and my family. Help them all appreciate the help we try to give but stop taking advantage of it and complaining about it. We try so hard to help and sometimes I let rudeness destroy me. Help me father to your this and not hurt so deeply from ungratefulness. Guide me to your will and bless me with patience and silence of a saint. Amen.

September 20, 2019

Thank you Father for another day. Thank you for all you've given me. Father I'm asking for repair of my family, if it is your will. Bless us with your patience for each other and peace in our home. Thank you. In Jesus's name. Amen.

September 21, 2019

Thank you Father for all you've given me. Thank you for your life. For carrying me on my journey. All the blessings you given me. I could never repay. I am nothing without you. Bless me today to be more like you. Thank you. In Jesus's name, Amen. Happy Birthday Tim! Going to try to make his day special.

September 22, 2019

Thank you Father for all you've given me. Thank you for caring me through my journey. Thank you for loving me. Bless me to be more like you. In Jesus's name, Amen. Going home today after lunch (brunch) with Tim's family. Then hit the dispensary for pot pills and then home. I suck at gambling. I lost $50 altogether. Tim does good though. Feeling a little crappy. Think trip was a bit much for me or I overdid my sodium or liquids.

September 23, 2019

Thank you Father for all you've given. Thank you for a good weekend with my hubby and his family. Father guide me on my journey and bless me to be more like you. Thank you in advance. In Jesus's name, Amen.

September 24, 2019

Thank you Father for allowing me another day. Thank you for all you've given us all. Bless me to walk closer to you and be more like you. Thank you in advance. In Jesus's name, Amen.

September 25, 2019

Thank you Father for life and all you've given everyone. Thank you, for none of us would be without you. Bless us all to be more like you. Amen.

September 26, 2019

Thank you for all you've given to the whole world. Thank you for loving me and life itself. I am nothing without you. Bless me Father to appreciate all you've given and to be more like you. Thank you. Amen.

September 27, 2019

Thank you Father for all you've given me. For all you sacrificed and all the beauty of your creation. Thank you for life itself. Bless me to be more like you. Thank you, Father. Amen. Went to Moose Lodge after painting kitchen and listened to Beaver Creek and then went to Cricket's. It was an early day though. I had to go home because I didn't feel well, but once I got home. I was up late. It was our friend Jerri's b-day and I'm glad we saw her.

September 28, 2019

Thank you Father for another day. Thank you for all you've given me and the rest of the world. You're awesome and your creations are awesome. I'm sorry man mutated, raped, and defiled it. Bless us all to be more like you. Thank you. Amen. My friends Dena and Russ came to visit! Great visit. I talked their ears off. Then we did what we always do…stayed home and watch TV and played a video game. Happy monthiversary Tim.

September 29, 2019

Thank you Father for all you've given me and the world. None of us have anything without you. Bless us all to be more like you. Thank you. Amen. Didn't make it to church today. Got up early, but it's a blah day. I don't feel like doing anything. My hubby is sleeping. I'm freaking bored!!

It was important to note that after a while, I needed extra rest. It seemed like at times she never slept. I often stayed up late with her, watching TV or playing video games with her, and then having to head out or do phone calls early in the morning. By weekends, I was wiped out. I slept in if I could or tried to take naps when she napped. As a caregiver, I knew it was important to take care of myself, so I started napping when I had a chance.

September 30, 2019

Thank you Father for all you've given us and me personally. Thank you for all the beauty you created and I'm sorry man corrupted it. Bless us to be more like you. Thank you, Father. Amen.

October 1, 2019

Thank you Father for everything. I have no one and have nothing without you. Thank you for your love. Comfort me and guided me my entire life. Thank you and bless me to be more like you. Amen.

October 2, 2019

Thank you Father for all the wonderful creations you given us. Thank you for your love and guidance. We are nothing without you and would have nothing without you. Bless us all

to be more like you. Thank you, Amen. Happy
B-day dad (my biological father Harold)!

October 3, 2019
Thank you Father for all you've given us all.
Thank you for your sacrifice. For all the beauty
you give us daily. We're nothing without you.
Bless us to be more like you. Thank you, Amen.
I am going to go see a Dr. today because of infu-
sion site. I don't trust Dodge! Wish me luck.
God, please help keep them from screwing it up.

Savannah was referring to the Fort Dodge hospital and doctors here. Even though the home health agency associated with the
hospital did an excellent job with her weekly, occasionally we would
need to go to urgent care or emergency room on weekends. On these
occasions, she wasn't as familiar with the doctors, and she was petri-
fied that they would try to flush the infusion tube or try to remove
it. Sometimes the doctor covering the weekend would not know the
information on the infusion site and ask such questions. She won-
dered if they didn't understand. I knew that doctors in such settings
often only glanced at the chart before seeing patients in the emergency room. Often ER doctors dealt with infusion sites but rarely did
they see one like hers. So if they suggested removal or flushing of the
infusion site, she became very nervous. I simple understood that we
needed to educate the doctors at times about her infusion site because
it was not as typical as other types of infusion sites. I knew from my
work at hospice that some infusion sites were easily replaced and
were flushed. So the doctors, when they asked these questions, were
familiar with other types of infusion sites. I often reassured Savannah
to relax as her anxiety would make her reluctant to go to the doctor.
For the record, I felt they provided adequate care when we had to go
to the hospital. I never had a complaint, but it still didn't stop her
about worrying that they would screw it up somehow.

October 4, 2019

Thank you Father for all you've given me. Having you get me through every day is awesome. Thank you for strength to keep moving and not giving up. I am nothing without you. Guide me and bless me to your will. Thank you, Amen.

October 5, 2019

Thank you Father for all you give me and everybody else. Thank you for the sacrifice you made so we can be with you. Guide me to be like you. Amen. Puked today!!

October 6, 2019

Thank you Father for all you've given me. Thank you for your love, support, and guidance. Bless me to be more like you. Amen. Happy to my sister Evelyn! Nauseous today! My boys are coming home today. We are going to go pick them up. Heaven will be home later. Noticed puss pocket on infusion site.

October 7, 2019

Thank you Father for all you given. For returning my grandsons and daughter home safe. I am nothing without you. Bless me to be more like you. Amen. Puking again today!!

October 8, 2019

Thank you God for loving me and all you've done for the world. Thank you for life and beauty. Guide me to be more like you. Amen.

October 9, 2019

Thank you Father for another day. Thank you for all you've given me. I am nothing without you. Amen. Puking today!

October 10, 2019

Thank you Father for holding me close. Thank you for all you have given myself and the world. Blessed me to be more like you. Amen. Puking again today! Last day of antibiotics!

October 11, 2019

Thank you Father for all you've given me and the world. I wish I'd done better for you. Thank you for loving me anyway. Please guide my family and choices today. Help me focus and be more like you. Thank you, Amen.

October 12, 2019

Thank you Lord for another miracle of life today! Thank you for all you've given. We are nothing without you. Bless us all to be more like you. Thank you, Amen.

October 13, 2019

Thank you Father for all the miracles we receive each day. Thank you for life and all the beauty you've given us. Bless us to appreciate and respect all of it and each other. Bless us to be more like you. Amen. Spent day at home. I painted more in the kitchen, but then I had to sit for rest of night. The morning started out rough, but then I got busy in kitchen painting while Tim watched game. It was too cold to do or go anywhere. I'm sad winter is so close.

October 14, 2019

Thank you Father for you all you've given me. Thank you for all the beauty you've created for us to witness each day. Bless us all to be more like you. Amen. Drove to pick up my mom and went to the store to get stuff to make chili. I feel like sometimes people forget I don't get to go places much. I hate being a pain in the ass, but I get tired of always waiting on everybody. Then I feel like I've interrupted their day and I hate asking Tim to go when he worked all day. Anyway, my chile rocked! Next time I can't do cumin or red pepper. Maybe something made me itch bad. Did I mention my chili was AWESOME!

October 15, 2019

Thank you Father for all you've given and the daily miracles you create, and we witness. We're nothing without you. Bless us all to be more like you. Amen and thank you. Thank God I'm not a phone face! So sad that you can't sit and talk to people, but they never move their face from their phone! Sad.

October 16, 2019

Thank you Father for all you've given. For making me who I am. Thank you for giving me compassion, love, hope, kindness, and strength. I'm nothing without you. Bless me to be more like you. Father, I thank you in advance. Amen.

October 17, 2019

Thank you Father for the many blessings we receive each day. Bless with patience for each other and acceptance reach other. Bless us to be more like you. Thank you, Father. Amen.

October 18, 2019

Thank you Father for all you've given me. For every daily miracle I witness. For being my Father, my shelter, my savior. Bless me to be more like you. Bless me with compassion, love, and patience to deal with everyday trials I go through. Thank you.

October 19, 2019

Thank you Father for all you've given. Thank you is all I can say, but it will never be enough. I'm nothing without you. Father, I'm asking that you push me to be more like you and all my family. Thank you, Amen.

October 20, 2019

Thank you Father for all I have & all you've given. We are truly blessed. Thank you. Bless us all to be more like you. Amen. Yay! Church! So happy I'm going. I saw Lori my friend again. I'm so happy she's clean! She chased me down to say "hi". I love her so much. I pray for her a lot.

October 21, 2019

Thank you Father for all you've given, all you created, all I'm allowed to witness. We're nothing without you. Bless us Father to be more like you. Thank you, Amen. Between my illness and this weather, I don't know which is worse! Thank God for my grandbabies light up my world. Their laughs, their smiles, their orneriness! It all makes me happy. They don't care how I speak, just that I'm talking to them. They love attention.

About this time, we had decided we did not need Patti anymore since we had Gavin and Heaven, and her two boys were living with us. We had a few disagreements at times, but having the kids and grandkids there, I believe, helped her depression. She got frustrated with us all at times, but I noticed she reported less depression with the two grandkids in the home. They really made her smile. The rest of us, I think, frustrated her often, but this was not who she usually was. Her emotions went from self-pity and depression to anger to us adults in the home. To me, this was a positive in many regards. The frustration with us was part of her fight-or-flight instinct. If she was fighting with us, then she was still fighting to be alive. She usually felt bad after arguing with one of us, but I always encouraged her to speak her mind.

October 22, 2019

Thank you Father for all you given me. I'm nothing without you. Father bless me to be more like you in my daily routines. Fill me with your grace and love. I thank you, Amen. People don't just get how it is for me. They go when they want. They don't have to have somebody to do things for them. I was a free, independent woman and now I'm a fucking prisoner. I don't see my friends. I don't get to golf much. I can't dance. I can't hardly sing anymore. I'm lost and I've been trying so hard to adjust. I'm trying.

October 23, 2019

Thank you Father for all you've given me. Bless me be stronger and all ways and to be patient and loving. Thank you, Father. Amen. I'm so aggressive and frustrated with everybody and everything. Trying so hard not to let this taking over me, but it's hard. How would you feel if your life was always busy and then bam, you have to wait for everyone to do anything? You lose all independence and humility is stripped. Makes a person want to get ripped something fierce.

October 24, 2019

Thank you Father for allowing me to witness another day. Thank you for the many blessings I've received and will receive. Thank you for freeing me. Bless me to be more like you. Thank you, Amen. Trying to make myself do things and be active, but it's tough. Feeling like I'm getting sick or something going on with me. Getting worried about not trying to focus on this crap. I want to do stuff, but no energy and breathing is getting worse.

October 25, 2019

Thank you Father for loving me. For allowing me to wake every day. I am nothing without you. Thank you, Father, for your sacrifice and patience. Bless me to be more like you. Thank you, Amen. Feeling like my lungs are all getting full. Been sleeping a lot during the days. So maybe I'm draining. Had diarrhea a lot. So, thinking I'm draining. Just getting scared it won't be able to hold out until they drain.

October 26, 2019

Thank you Father for letting me rise again today. Thank you for daily blessings you've given us all. Bless me to be more like you and strengthen me. Thank you, Amen. I'm not doing so good today. Really scared I may have to get lungs tapped. Oh well, it's been long time since that's been done. More worried about who will do it. Hope Dr. Day is around if I need her. I trust her. Didn't like this hospital so much. I may drain and be okay, but we'll see.

October 27, 2019

Thank you Father for allowing me to rise this morning. Thank you for sacrifice and all you give each of us. Thank you for the beauty you created and letting us experience childbirth. Thank you for it all. Bless me to be more like you. Thank you, Amen. I'm so sick of being sick! Think I need my lungs tapped. Got to go to doctor on Tuesday. So, if I can hold on until then, I guess I will get that done. Trying to be stubborn and ignore it. That's not working.

October 28, 2019

Thank you Father for your sacrifice and all you've given. Thank you for strengthening me. Bless me to be more like you. Thank you and Amen. Getting worse but trying to hide it. Tomorrow I will probably get tapped. I'm not good. Going to get some rest.

October 29, 2019

Thank you father for allowing me another day. Thank you for your sacrifice and love. Bless me to be more like you. Thank you, Amen. Going to pulmonologists today. Probably going to tap my lungs again after a year and three months. I hope I get Dr. Day. We'll see. I'm draining though. Starting to feel much better today. Nope, got Dr. Meyer. He's okay. Going to sleep now.

October 30, 2019

Thank you Father for your sacrifice and all the love and support you've given me. Still not feeling good. I'm scared. My lung was tapped and still not breathing right. Think I caught a cold. Try to do trying to be normal and decorate for Halloween. But I must do it alone. Heaven and Gavin are too busy, and Tim is tired after work. I can't even get excited about it. My favorite holiday and I can't even enjoy it.

October 31, 2019
Thank you Father for all you've given. Thank you for allowing me to live another day. Bless me to be more like you. Thank you, Amen. Happy Birthday to my sister Judy. Feel even worse today! Hacked up some blood clots, but I'm going to keep an eye on it. If it gets worse, I'll call nurse. Going to sleep.

November 1, 2019
Thank you for another day. Thank you, Father, for all you've given us all. Bless us all to be more like you. Thank you and Amen. Happy B-day to my brother Don Juan! Still yucky! No more blood clots, but I'm convinced I'm suffering from a cold. Now not really eating.

November 2, 2019
Thank you Father for all you've given. Thank you for giving me life and for guiding me. Bless me Father to be more like you. Thank you, my debt to you is gladly paid. Amen. Still crappy, but a little better. Not eating much. So much mucus! Why? Now diarrhea starting. Fuck this!

November 3, 2019
Thank you Father for life! Thank you for all you've given everybody. Thank you for the

chance to live and experience life, love, and all the beauty you've created. Bless us all to be more like you. Father grant me patience and strength to face each day and all I must. Help me to love and show compassion, so I may share yours with others. Thank you. Amen. Happy Birthday to my Heavenly sister Teresa. Missed church, sad. Rough emotional day. Alone. Tim had to work. Heaven not home yet. Gavin at his Dad's. Mom worried about Judy. Donny worried about Judy. But I'm dying and nobody worries about me! Nice!

November 4, 2019
Thank you father for guiding me through each day. Bless me Father with patience to accept what I must and strength to withstand what I need. Thank you, Father, for all you've given. I'm sorry I failed you. Thank you for loving me. Amen.

November 5, 2019
Thank you Father for all you've given. For every day you create. For every night you carry me through. Thank you. Bless me father with more strength, faith, strength, courage, and patience. Bless me to be more like you. Thank you, Amen. Getting more nervous about Mayo. I just need it to good. Trying to do things today, but still a little sleepy. I'm fighting the rest. Got to do stuff while I can.

November 6, 2019
Thank you father for all you've given. Thank you for my family and all the people play praying for us. Bless them all. Thank you

for strength, patience, compassion, love, and caring me through this. I'm nothing without you. Amen. Yay! My new doors are in! The guy we hired Randy came and put them up and house numbers too! Thank you!

November 7, 2019

Thank you Father for loving me. For your sacrifice and carrying me through each day. Bless me to be more like you. Thank you, Amen.

November 8, 2019

Thank you Father for all you've given. I'm nothing without you. Thank you for letting me live. Bless me to be more like you. Thank you, Amen.

November 9, 2019

Thank you father for another day and all you've given. Thank you for carrying me daily through my journey. Bless me to more like you. Thank you, Amen. Getting ready for trip to Mayo. Still not as good as I'd like to be. Don't want them to put me back in hospital. I'm better than I was. So hopefully I just continue to get better by Monday. It'll be nice to get away for a bit though.

November 10, 2019

Thank you Father for all you've given. Thank you for caring me through each day. Father bless me to be more like you. Bless me with courage, strength, patience, and compassion. Thank you, Amen. We leave for Mayo today! So nervous. I pray it all goes well, but we'll see.

November 11, 2019

Thank you Father for another day. For all you've given and carrying me through each day. Bless me Father to be more like you. Thank you, Amen. Mayo appointment today. Wish me luck! Well, made it back. It was a good day minus my little freak out and Tim looking room keys. Forgetting where he put them. He's so funny. Tim took me shopping after appointments. That was fun. I just wish he didn't feel the need to buy me so much. Anyway, good day. Tim's amazing and I thank God so much for him. I don't think he feels it enough, but I do. Anyway, sometimes I'm a real anal bitch and I don't mean to be. Pray for tomorrow to be good.

November 12, 2019

Thank you Father for all you've given. For good news and life, itself. Bless me to be more like you. Thank you, Amen.

November 13, 2019

Thank you Father for all you've given me. Please heal this infection I have in my tube site. Thank you, Father. Started antibiotics again for infection. I pray it heels so they don't have to remove and put in another one. I love Dr. Frantz! He's amazing and I thank God for him. Glad they didn't keep me and I could be home.

This was her last visit to the Mayo hospital. She was scheduled to go in the spring of 2020, but the COVID-19 pandemic hit and forced many hospitals to cancel routine tests and routine follow-ups. It was okay though. Trips to the Mayo hospital were expensive, took a few days, and usually reported the same thing with her still dying of the disease, and we would need to tweak her medications.

November 14, 2019

Thank you Father for all you've given. For every day and night. For always caring me through all my life. I pray daily for tolerance, patience, and strength. Thank you. Bless me to be more like you. Thank you, Amen. Puking today.

November 15, 2019

Thank you Father for all you've given. For your love, shelter and sacrifice. Bless me to be more like you. Thank you, Amen. Puking again today!

November 16, 2019

Thank you Father for all you've given me and my family. For always rescuing me from problems or situations I chose. For always loving and guiding me. Even when I didn't listen. Thank you, Amen.

November 17, 2019

Thank you Father for all you've given. All you sacrifice. All you created and every day of my life. Keep me on your path you've chosen for me. Thank you, Amen.

November 18, 2019

Thank you Father for your sacrifice. For life and all you've given. Thank you for loving me and guiding me my whole life. Bless me to be more like you. Thank you, Amen.

November 19, 2019

Thank you Father for all you've given. For your sacrifice, love and guidance. Thank you for always being with me. Bless me to be more like you. Thank you, Amen.

November 20, 2019

Thank you father for all you've given me. Thank you for loving, guiding me, and strengthening me daily. Amen. Puking today! Worked so hard to make breakfast. Got it all eaten. Pills taken and then WHAM! Puked it all up! I missed taking my probiotic yesterday and I think that may be what did it. Don't do that again. At least I kept the orange down.

November 21, 2019

Thank you Father for all you've given. Please guide me through each day according to your will. Bless me with your strength, patience, and knowledge. Thank you. Amen.

November 22, 2019

Thank you Father for another day and all you give me. Bless me to walk the path I must. Thank you. Amen. Saw Dr. Condon today. Saw our friend Donny on the way out. That was great. He is struggling with diabetes. So happy I get to make turkey! Hope I can eat it! Dr. said I have thrush from antibiotics. So now I must take a mouthwash to get rid of it. Hope this is all worth it.

November 23, 2019

Thank you Father for all you've given. Thank you for another day. I'm nothing without you. Thank you, Amen. Family Thanksgiving today. Good day. No puking. Food all cooked good. No family fights. Took my 20 mg pill and I had no pain all day. Family came including Aunt Jesse and Uncle Gary came. It was just a good day. Thank you, Father, for that.

November 24, 2019

Thank you father for life. All life. Thank you for your sacrifice and all you've given. Bless me father to be more like you. Thank you, Amen. Tim must work today. Puking again today. Resting a lot today. Feeling sick again. Really praying this isn't getting worse. My niece Brittany and her babies are sick. The boys were starting to get colds. Hope they aren't getting sick. Really loved seeing everybody over weekend.

November 25, 2019

Well, thank you Father for all you've given. For protecting me and loving me. Thank you for all you've given me. I'm blessed. Please guide me Father on my journey. Bless me to be more like you. Thank you, Amen. Puking. Hope this doesn't keep going. Really tired of puking, shitting, and feeling like crap. I feel like maybe God's pissed at me or something. I must have been a horrible person in a past life to have to go through all the stuff I have in this life. I'm sorry. Sorry I was a shit. I don't remember it and I think I've been pretty good in this life. Who knows? I'm just going to keep begging for forgiveness.

November 26, 2019

Thank you father for all you've given. I'm sorry I fell short sometimes on my walk. I don't mean to. You know my heart, but I will try harder. Thank you again and bless me to walk straighter for you. Amen. Puking today. Diarrhea too. Tried not to be miserable today. No good. Slept on couch all day. Pretty worried now that I'm just going to keep getting sicker. I pray not, but it's looking sad. At least I'm not back in the hospital yet. The boys make me happy. Gavin seems to be getting better some. I honestly hope he takes after me and goes out and carves out his own path. I don't want him to be stuck in Dodge working as a delivery driver. Living like his dad. He can do so much more.

Savannah worried about all the kids. They were all under thirty and needing help and guidance at times. She knew she was running out of time, and as she got sicker, she knew she would not get to see them as they were older. She wanted them to be more established and more successful, but we both knew that our kids were going to be okay. I knew that I would continue to see them grow and develop and become more mature and more established as they grew older. We had talked, and although she worried about them, she knew they'd be okay.

November 27, 2019
Thank you Father for your sacrifice. I pray you forgive me for falling short of your will for me. That you forgive me for the wrong I've done and hold me in your arms when I'm called to you. Bless me Father according to your will. Thank you, Amen. Puking and diarrhea again today. No more antibiotics, but still got thrush meds.

November 28, 2019
Thank you Father for your sacrifice. For all you've given everybody and me personally. I'm nothing without you. Bless me Father to be more like you. Amen. Happy Thanksgiving and happy monthiversary for my husband Tim and I!

November 29, 2019

Thank you Father for all you sacrificed, given, created, all your love, and for your guidance. I am nothing without you. Bless me to be like you and all I do. Thank you, Amen.

November 30, 2019

Thank you Father for all you've given. I am nothing without you. Bless me to be more like you. Thank you, Amen. Happy birthday to my friend Dena! Some days I swear my mind is going. Seriously, I don't understand why I do things. I'm such an anal person and sometimes I can't let shit go anymore! Why do I have to be that way? Heaven's the same at times! How are we supposed to survive? Other people don't care, they just keep doing shit they know irritates you. Then when we can't take anymore, we're the bad one. Help, Lord!

December 1, 2019

Thank you Father for all you've given me. For your love and guidance. Thank you, Amen. Dry heaves today! Going to have Tim bring tree out of garage storage so I can decorate for Xmas. Tim helped Gavin get a car so Xmas will be tight. I hope my children all appreciate Tim. I think they forget sometimes. I always hear things like so-and-so helps this kid. Wish I had somebody to help me. We help we've all moved back home; we do free babysitting, we borrow money to all of them repeatedly and some never pay back, we've helped them all get cars. What more do we have to do? My God. We always do birthdays and Christmases for them all. Short of live your life, raise your kids and pay all your bills. That's it.

Want us to do more? Sorry, you have what you need.

December 2, 2019

Thank you Father for all you've given. For allowing me to rise each day to build more memories daily. Bless me to walk my path a little straighter, Thank you, Amen. Happy heavenly birthday Daddy Joe!

December 3, 2019

Thank you Father for another day. Thank you for all you've given me, I'm not worthy. You're amazing and I'm nothing without you. Bless me to be more like you. Thank you, Amen.

December 4, 2019

Thank you for every day. For your sacrifice, your love, your guidance, and for carrying me when needed. Bless me to be more like you. Thank you, Amen.

December 5, 2019

Thank you Father for each day. The many blessings you bestowed on us. For your sacrifice, love, and guidance. Bless me to be more like you, Amen. Happy birthday Emmett!!

December 6, 2019

Thank you Father for your sacrifice, love, shelter and granting me another day. Bless me to be more like you. Thank you, Amen. Started antibiotics tonight. Dr. says sinus infection or ear infection.

December 7, 2019

Thank you Father for all you've given. Bless me to be more like you. Can I pray healing Angels surround me cleanse my body of infection? Thank you, Amen. Starting antibiotics again. Have a cold or sinus infection going. So tired of being sick again, and again.

December 8, 2019

Thank you Father for all you've given. Thank you for loving me when no one else did. Bless me to walk straighter on my path and strengthen me so I need not to be carried. Thank you, Amen.

December 9, 2019

Thank you Father for all you've given and sacrificed. Thank you for each day, your love & support, and guidance. Bless me father with health, strength, love, and to be more like you. Thank you, Amen.

December 10, 2019

Thank you Father for your sacrifice, love, strength, guidance, knowledge and shelter. Thank you for blessing me daily, though I am unworthy. Bless me Father to be more like you. Thank you, Amen.

December 11, 2019

Thank you Father for all you've given. I appreciate your love and guidance and the strength you've given me. I wouldn't be here if not for you. Bless me to me more like you. God forgive me, please for my shortcomings. Thank you, Amen. Diarrhea and puking phlegm!

December 12, 2019

Thank you Father for all you've given. I appreciate each day and your guidance, strength, and love. Bless me to be more like you. Help me to be strong. Thank you, Amen. Puking again today!

December 13, 2019

Thank you Father for all you've given. Bless me with health today. Bless me to be more like you. Thank you, Father. Amen. Puking again! Last dose of the antibiotics today for now. Keegan's Christmas concert today. I really went want to go; I never miss it. God willing, I won't today.

We went to the Christmas concert. However, she never told me she was feeling poorly that day and many days. After I read her journal, I really understood how often she was sick but never told anyone. Oh my God, if I would have known she was this miserable, I might have taken more days off during her sickness. However, when I asked her daily before I went to work how she was feeling that day, she would always say she was doing okay and encouraged me to work.

December 14, 2019

Thank you Father for being with me daily and all you've given. I am nothing without you and I'm grateful for all. Bless me to be more like you. Thank you, Amen. Getting Lincoln today!

December 15, 2019

Thank you Father for all you've given. Bless me to be more like you in all I do. Thank you, Amen.

December 16, 2019

Thank you Father for all you've given. Bless me to be more like you. Strengthen my body and mind. Thank you, Amen. Hurt my arm. Going to have to go to Dr. today. They put me in a splint and sling so couldn't write more.

December 17, 2019

No entry.

December 18, 2019

No entry.

December 19, 2019

No entry.

December 20, 2019

Thank you Father for all blessings you've bestowed on me. Bless me to be more like you. Thank you, Amen. Been in a splint and sling since Monday. Got it removed today! In Ace bandage and sling for a bit. Couldn't write at all before. If my arm doesn't get better in a week, we will need to go back. Went to all the grandbabies' Christmas shows but Lincoln's. We don't know about when his is. His dad never tells us. Thank you, God, for letting me see the ones we did see. Going on date tonight *Star Wars* movie is out!

December 21, 2019

Thank you Father for all you've given me. Thank you for another beautiful day and your love & support. Bless me to be more like you. In Jesus name. Amen.

December 22, 2019

Thank you Father for all you've given me and the world! We are nothing without you. Bless us all to be more like you. In Jesus name. Thank you and Amen. I'm so damn emotional. It's stupid! Why do I always feel like this? If I say anything, it usually offends. Not meaning to. Just can't word things right for everybody. I'm always saying something that somebody is offended by. Used the wrong word or explained it in a way they didn't like. Or I apologize too much. Nobody cares if the things they say offend me and why is your way the only right way?

December 23, 2019

Thank you Father for all you've given me. I am nothing without you. Bless me to be more like you and forgive my shortcomings. Thank you. In Jesus name, Amen.

December 24, 2019

Thank you Father for all you've given me, I am nothing without you. Bless me to be more like you. Thank you, Amen.

December 25, 2019

Thank you Father for all you do, have done and do daily. Bless us all to be more like you.

December 26, 2019

Thank you Father for all you do have done and will do. Bless us all to be more like you. Grant me peace, strength, and serenity. Thank you, Father. Amen. In Estherville today.

December 27, 2019

Thank you Father for all you do, have given, and we'll give. We are we are and have nothing without you. Bless me to be more like you. Thank you, Amen. Going home today. Long ride home. Watched boys until their dad came. Got a dresser moved stuff around for dresser and getting ready for Marinia's visit. Really need help getting back on track with Tim. He takes care of me and I need to be more relaxed. Just get annoyed by his habits at times.

December 28, 2019

Thank you Father for all you do, gave, and will do. Bless us all to be more like you. Thank you, Amen. Happy monthiversary!

December 29, 2019

Thank you Father for all. I'm blessed beyond what I deserve. My life is only comfortable because of you. Bless my husband and I to continue our love and help us with tolerance of the other when it's super hard. Thank you, Father. Amen. Going to church today (sick or not). I think I have flu. Puking all day.

December 30, 2019

Thank you Father for all you've given. Thank you for carrying me through the flu. Bless me Father with tolerance, strength, and patience. Thank you. In Jesus name. Amen.

December 31, 2019

Thank you Father for all you do, I am nothing without you. Bless me to be more like you. Thank you, Amen.

Notice the decline in the last year. On New Year's Eve last year, she was bound and determined to go out. However, this year, she had no interest in going out and didn't even mention it in her journal a year later.

Chapter 5

Her Journal 2019—Coming to Accept the End

January 1, 2020

Thank you Father for all you've given me. For another day. Strengthen me Father, for I feel weak. Surround me in your love. Thank you, Amen. I am puking blood at times (I think). Hopefully not, but I'm trying to be strong. Help me. Please, somebody?

January 2, 2020

Thank you Father for all you do and have done. Bless me to be more like you. Thank you, Amen.

January 3, 2020

Thank you God for all you have given me. Bless me to be more like you and help my family tolerate me. Thank you, Amen.

January 4, 2020

Thank you Father for all you given me. Bless us all to be more like you. Thank you, Amen. Tim's sisters Pam and Susie are coming to visit!! I love Tim's family. They're awesome. Hopefully I can find room for them because Marinia, Justin,

Ilana, and Lincoln are here too. Cramped quarters, but we're getting it done, Thank God. Good visit. Probably talked Pam's ear off. We all had fun playing a video game you play with your cell phone. Well, I watched because boys needed a phone.

January 5, 2020

Thank you Father for all you've given the whole world and us. Thank you for all you do for us. Bless me to be more like you. Thank you, Amen.

January 6, 2020

Thank you Father for all you've given and all you will give in the days to come. Bless me and my family to be more like you. To follow the path, you chosen for us. Thank you, Amen.

January 7, 2020

Thank you Father for all you've given me. Bless me to walk the path you planned for me. Thank you, Amen.

January 8, 2020

Thank you Father for all you've given to me and all you do daily. I'm nothing without you. I am truly blessed by you. Bless me to be more like you, Thank you, Amen.

January 9, 2020

Thank you Father for all you've given me and all you give daily. Bless me to be more like you. Thank you, Amen. Neck is still hurting. It's the 3rd day! Nothing helps! Going to Dr. at 2:30 pm.

January 10, 2020

Thank you Father for always having my back. For all you've given and give daily. We all to you. Bless us all to be more like you and to travel the paths you've chosen for us. Thank you and Amen. Neck still hurting like hell. Taking the meds but this is killing me. I need some damn relief! Pot pills, patches, rubs, meds, nothing helps! It's partly because of stress too. My sickness has caused so much shit! My life is being destroyed a little every day. My marriage, my family, my self-worth, all of it being destroyed. I'm strong but who's that fucking strong? I love my kids, but they come and go with a quick spin when you don't give what they want, but my husband that messed me up. I need my husband. I know we are strong, but this is hard on us. He's so stressed. If I died today all his problems, go away. Bills would be all paid or mostly paid. Problem is I don't want to die yet!

I cry when I read these words because I would gladly would have had her live forever. I never saw her as a burden, and I wish she didn't see herself this way. Writing this book after she died, I can say earnestly that my problems did not disappear after she passed. I cry daily thinking of missing her. I know, working in hospice, that many patients express seeing themselves as a burden, but I have never heard that from family or spouse.

January 11, 2020

Thank you Father for all you've given and all you do daily. We have nothing without you. Bless us to be more like you and follow the paths you've chosen for us. Thank you, Amen. Neck still hurting, Meds starting to work on pain (I think or I'm tolerating it better). Hope the pain stops soon. I can't even function. Life still the same. My husband is a real asshole when he's hungry or stressed. My daughter is bitter and cold. Me I'm angry and emotional. Gavin seems the only chill one for now. Anyway, I'm just working on myself and praying for the rest. It is stressing. I must remember their stress is as bad as mine.

No entries from January 12 to February 4, 2020, a period in which she had the flu, shingles, dehydration, pain-medication changes, etc. She was sleeping most of the time and felt miserable. I don't think she had the energy to even write in her journal. This was the first time I was getting scared. I realized she was dying, but at this point, I was thinking it might be soon.

February 5, 2020

Thank you Father for being with me each day. For all you've given, give and will give. Bless me with strength, comfort, and peace while I'm going through this time. Thank you, Amen. Been really sick for a while now and now I have shingles. Pain!! I just scream in pain and cry but keep praying for it to end. Other than that, I'm doing awesome. My oxygen is at 98 or 99 for a while now. Just got to get through this. Life here is more peaceful. Thank you, God! Everybody getting along and pitching in. My boys are back too! I love these kids so much, all my grandbabies.

Besides all the illnesses and medication side effects, Savannah was also afflicted with shingles. Shingles was so intense for her that it was important to talk specifically about this. For those who are not aware, shingles is derived from the chicken pox virus many of us get exposed to when we were kids. However, as we get older or have a weakened immune system, they can come back in splotchy areas that penetrate to the nerves deep inside our skin and into the bones. Some people have mild flare-ups, while others can be severe. Savannah had them one time about nine months before she died. The first time she had it, it lasted about six weeks. She was miserable from shingles. It burned and itched for weeks. It was perhaps one of the precipitating events that led to her decline in the last year of her life. She had home health contact the doctor a couple of times, but creams and pain pills had little impact. I watched week after week as she suffered, and there was nothing I could do. When she had her side effects from the medications in the evening, it even got worse because when she had heat flashes, you could see the redness and burning in her skin get a darker red. She was beaten down after this outbreak, but eventually it slowly got better. Then about two or three weeks after she had thought it was over, she had another flare-up. I had read online that secondary outbreaks were not as common. I suggested it was side effects with the meds, but when we went to the doctor, he informed us that sometimes it can take months or even over a year, and some people are horrifically impacted by the shingles. After this, I was made aware that there are shingles vaccines after you turn fifty. I went and got my vaccine after she passed. Seeing her suffer like she did, I wanted to make sure others were aware of this complication that can occur, and it is completely avoidable. Savannah would be glad to know someone got vaccinated after reading these words.

February 6, 2020
Thank you Father for all you given and give daily. Thank you for walking with me through it all. Bless me to be more like you. Thank you, Amen. Happy Birthday to my Keegan Jo! Only three burning and itching attacks today! Boy are they intense and burn like hell! It almost feels like hellfire, I guess. Emmett's home with flu. Poor little guy. At least my energy is coming back! Thank God! Heaven's got stuff going on with her health too. Hope she's okay.

February 7, 2020

Thank you Father for getting me through each day and night. Guide me and bless me to be more like you. Thank you, Amen.

February 8, 2020

Thank you Father for carrying me through another day and night. For all you've given and give. Bless me to be more like you. Thank you, Amen. Going to Cedar Falls to get my pot pills and going to try to visit Tim's family. Yay! We got to see them! Met up with everybody at a restaurant. I love how they just all (that can come) show up and make you feel like family. His family is all I ever wished my family was. It's awesome that God put Tim in my life and gave me a family like everybody else should have. Thank you, Father!

February 9, 2020

Thank you Father for all you give and have given. You created all of it. Bless me Father to be more like you. Thank you, Amen.

February 10, 2020

Thank you Father for everything. Guide me and bless me to know and be strong. Thank you, Amen.

February 11, 2020

Thank you Father for all you've given. Bless us all to be more like you. Thank you, Amen.

February 12, 2020

Thank you Father for life given and all the many blessings I've received. Bless me to be more like you. Thank you, Amen.

February 13, 2020

Thank you Father for every moment of life given to me. Bless me to be more like you. Thank you, Amen. No school for kids today!! Happy birthday Lincoln! I wish we could see you, but we had you for a visit and that was Awesome. We love you so much buddy.

February 14, 2020

Thank you Father for all you've given to me. I am nothing without you. Bless me to be more like you. Thank you, amen.

February 15, 2020

Thank you Father for my life. Every day and every hour I owe to you. Bless me to be more like you. Thank you, Amen.

February 16, 2020

Thank you Father for life and the many other gifts you've given. Bless me to be more like you. Thank you, Amen.

February 17, 2020

Thank you Father for my life daily and all you've given me. I am blessed. Bless me to be more like you. Thank you, Amen. Today my cousin's husband died. I bawled because I can't imagine. He had cancer. He lived less than a year after being diagnosed. That's awful. I'm whining about my pain and discomfort, but it could be worse. I could die! Suck it up! God has a way of sending a message, huh? I pray I am as brave and strong as he was. Please send her comfort Lord. I wish we were close still. I miss her so much.

February 18, 2020

Thank you Father for all you given me. I'm blessed, truly. Bless me to be more diligent in my faith and to be more like you. Thank you, Amen.

February 19, 2020

Thank you Father for every day and all you've given. Bless me with strength, tolerance, and peace. Thank you. Amen. Sorry, I haven't written much in a while. I've been fighting the shingles still (2nd round). Been sleeping a lot and too miserable to write. The shingle I've discovered are one of the most painful things you can go through! I'm okay though. My oxygen is good, and my lungs are full of air and my color is better this time. They got pain med dosage under control. Thank God! My attitude is good. I'm calm and dealing with it (with a lot of pot pills). I'm doing better this time. Thank you so much Father. We prayed for relief and you did that.

Fairbury 20, 2020

Thank you Father for life itself and all you've given me and the world. We're nothing without you. Bless us all to be more like you. Thank you, Amen. I'm getting so anxious to have the shingles gone. God please let this be the end of shingles for me. It's getting closer, just got to take one day at a time.

February 21, 2020

Thank you Father for all you've given me and the world. Bless us all with humbleness, gratefulness, love and peace, patience, etc. Bless us all to be more like you. Thank you, Amen.

February 22, 2020

Thank you for all you've given me and the world. Bless me and my family to be more like you. Thank you, Amen. Tim is making me go out! I'm scared to go even though it is to DMV and store. Scared to catch something again. I went. I got pot license renewed and went to store. Then he said let's get me a bath. So, bath it is. Yes! Awesome bath! That felt amazing! Spending the rest of the evening doing what we do on weekends. Watching movies and playing games. Keegan came down. I love seeing my grandbabies. Hate that he calls himself fat!

February 23, 2020

Thank you Father for all you've done for me. Thank you for all you've given the world. Still have blisters on my neck and head. Shingles sucks! Tim and I are thinking about moving south would be great. I still have issues with wanting not to move. I will think on it. Anyway, everybody's good now. The kids are over colds, but Heaven has some stuff going on. She's going to have tests done. So, I'm praying. Please, bless her with health Father. Thank you, Amen.

February 24, 2020

Thank you Father! Thank you for all you've given me and the world. Bless us to be more like you. Thank you, Amen. I think I still have shingles! This crap needs to go away!! Anyway, I can't get down because my cousin's hubby had cancer and he didn't whine. He also died. So that says to me that I'm real lucky to still be here. Tim really wants to move South. I don't blame him, but I have babies here. I love seeing my baby's. It wouldn't be the same. I love my home. I love my garden. I get it. It's better for both of our health, but my babies are friends are all here. Still we do need to downsize and get these kids out on their own living their lives.

February 25, 2020
Thank you God for all you've given me. Thank you for all you've given the world. Bless me to be more like you. Thank you, Father. Amen. I'm making a vow... No more blank pages! I will do my very best to keep writing daily.

February 26, 2020
Thank you Father for all you've given me and the world. Thank you for life itself. Bless me to be more like you. Thank you, Amen.

February 27, 2020
Thank you Father for all you've given me and the world. I am truly blessed, and I owe that to you. Thank you. Bless me to be more like you. Thank you, Amen. Happy Birthday to my friend Missy!

February 28, 2020
No entry.

February 29, 2020
Thank you Father for another day and all you've given the world and me. Bless us all to be more like you Father. Thank you, Amen.

March 1, 2020
Thank you Father for all you've given me and the world. Thank you for protecting me, for

taking my pain, and all of it! Bless me to be more like you. Thank you. Amen. Happy Birthday to my brother Franky! Happy Heavenly Birthday!

March 2, 2020
Thank you Father for all you've given me and the world. Bless us all to be more like you. Thank you. Amen. No more pain pills until Friday! So, I'm praying and then I'm going to load up on pot pills. I want this shit gone! Other than that, I feel good.

March 3, 2020
Thank you Father for life and all you've given me. Thank you, Amen.

March 4, 2020
Thank you Father for all you've given and do for me. I am nothing without you. Bless me father to be more like you. Strengthen me. Thank you, Amen.

March 5, 2020
Thank you Father for life and all you've given me. Bless me to be more like you. Thank you, Amen.

March 6, 2020
Thank you Father for life and all you've given me. Bless me not to take it for granted and live each moment. Bless me with your strength, patience, faith, tolerance, and love. Thank you, Amen. Also please heal Raven (the little 2 yr. old with cancer). Thank you, Amen. We are leaving for Kansas City today. Tim has an interview on Monday.

Raven was a little kid she read about on Facebook. It bothered her that people younger than her were terminally ill or sick. She told me often that she would give up some of her remaining days just to give them longer lives. It doesn't work this day, but she prayed for children and others that she read about on Facebook. Here she was dying, and yet she felt badly for the people younger than her. She always cared more for others than herself. We had talked about moving south when we retired, and I had a job interview in Kansas City. It paid much more, but she was reluctant to move at this point, and I didn't blame her. I was offered the position later, but I decided to turn it down. I know she wanted to stay in our home. I'm glad we stayed where we were because she died where she wanted to…at the home she loved and surrounded by kids and grandkids.

March 7, 2020
Thank you Father for everything! Bless me not be so emotional today so Tim and I can get along and think clearly. Thank you, Amen.

March 8, 2020
Thank you Father for everything. I owe my life to you. Bless me to be strong, fearless, faithful, and full of your love. Thank you, Father. Amen.

March 9, 2020
Thank you Father for all you've given me. Bless me to be more like you. Father please guide me on what to do. Thank you, Amen. We're home! Got home last night. I love my home God gave me.

May 10, 2020
Thank you Father for all you've given me. Bless me to be a better person. Bless me to be more like you. Thank you, Father. Amen.

March 11, 2020

Thank you Father for all you've given me. I am nothing without you. Bless me to be more like you. Also, Father surround little Raven [two-year-old she read about on Facebook] with warring angels to kill the cancer killing the little angel. Thank you, Father. Amen.

March 12, 2020

Thank you Father for all you've given me. I am nothing without you. Bless me to be more like you. Thank you, Father. Amen.

March 13, 2020

Thank you Father for all you have given me. Thank you for all you've done for the world. Bless us all to be more like you. Thank you, Amen. Nurse came today. My oxygen was good. Lungs clear. Blood pressure best it's ever been. The coronavirus virus panic is so crazy! No toilet paper in stores and other stuff. It's ridiculous. Went to the movie "I Still Believe". What an AWESOME movie! Great tribute to guy's wife and God! So glad we were late to the other movie and went to that instead. Thank you for your story.

March 14, 2020

Thank you Father for every day you given me and all you taught me. Guide me to your will and bless me to be like you. Thank you, Amen.

March 15, 2020

Thank you Father for all you've given me and the world. Bless us to walk our paths as you've laid them out. Strengthen us. Guide us and bless us all to be more like you. Thank you,

Amen. Also, Father I forgot, protect us and shelter us from coronavirus. And if we must go, may we pass in your light. Thank you, Amen.

Mark 16, 2020

Thank you Father for all you've given. For your perfection, your love, and your security. Bless me with strength to bear the cross I must bear. Thank you. In Jesus's name I pray. Amen. We found out Heaven has ulcerative colitis and autoimmune disease. She's so depressed. I'm watching boys. Wish she not freak out until she knows more from her doctor.

March 17, 2020

Thank you Father for all you've given. Your son especially. Bless me to be as you…laid out for me. Thank you, Amen. Taking care of boys again. Heaven can't seem to wake up. She's so depressed again.

March 18, 2020

Thank you Father for all you've given me and world. Guide us to our paths. Bless us all to be more like you. Thank you, Amen. Happy B-day Mary! Heaven is sleeping in again. She says she was awake at 11. That pissed me off. Why didn't you get out of bed and take care of your boys then? WTF! We're going to battle. This his will not continue. Never mind her snippy little remarks every time I say anything. WTF? Get off your phone, take care of your kids, and stop being a shit to me. I did raise you, this is our home, and you don't pay rent on bills. So, stop. I'm your mom. You didn't wait 1½ hours for me to do something a mom should do. It's bullshit!

Heaven was really struggling with her health during this time. She was often sick to her stomach and had almost no energy. She often spent the day in bed. We didn't know how serious she was sick at the time, but Savannah was thinking it was more that she didn't want to get up at the time. After she got more information from the doctors and started taking medication for her health issues, she was back to normal for the most part and taking care of her kids.

March 19, 2020

Father I thank you for everything. I know nothing would be here, if not for you. Nobody would be here, if not for you. Father, we are all weak. Some hide their fears, but it comes out as anger. I'm asking that you strengthen us to unite and accept what we must. Bless me to be kind to others, to help others, and protect others. Most importantly bless us all with faith in you. Thank you. In Jesus's name, Amen.

March 20, 2020

Thank you Father for all you've given. For your son Jesus who washed me of my sins. Bless me to be more like you. Thank you. In Jesus's name, Amen. We don't have to move! Thank you, Father!

March 21, 2020

Thank you Father for all you given the world. You're an AWESOME Father! Thank you for blessing us with all the beauty of creation and life. Bless us all to be humble and to unite together as you planned. Thank you. In Jesus's name, Amen.

March 22, 2020

Thank you Father for all you did do and will do. We are all blessed to have you. Bless us to be more like you. Thank you. In Jesus's name, Amen.

March 23, 2020

Thank you Father for all you give, have given, and will give my family and I. Thank you for life and every lesson and blessing. I give all my praise to you. Bless me to be more like you. Also, I thank you Jesus for all you give, have given, and will give. In Jesus's name, Amen.

March 24, 2020

Thank you Father for all you've given me. Bless me with strength to deal with all that I must. Thank you. In Jesus's name, Amen.

March 25, 2020

Thank you Father for every day you've given your guidance, love, grace, and all of it. Thank you for all you've given and Jesus. Bless me to be more like you. I know you protect us, and I thank you. In Jesus's name, Amen.

March 26, 2020

Thank you Father for all you've given us. For being there for love, support, and lessons. Thank you for giving us Jesus. And him for loving us so much to save us. We are nothing without you. Guide us to be more like you. Thank you. In Jesus's name. Amen.

Mark 27, 2020

Thank you Father for all you've give, have given, and will give. We are nothing without you. Bless us to be more like you. Thank you, Amen.

March 28, 2020

Thank you Father for all you've given me and my family. Bless us to be more faithful and more like you. Thank you, Amen.

March 29, 2020

Thank you Father for all you've given the world. I pray we all become more grateful to you. Bless us all to be more like you. Thank you. In Jesus's name, Amen.

March 30, 2020

Thank you Father for all you've given. For being awesome and caring for us. Thank you. In Jesus's name, Amen.

March 31, 2020

Thank you Father for all you've given. You're awesome. I'm amazed by you. Bless me to be more like you. Thank you. In Jesus's name, Amen.

April 1, 2020

Thank you Father for all you given me. Bless us to be more like you. Protect us. Thank you. In Jesus's name, Amen. Happy April Fool's Day!

April 2, 2020

Thank you Father for each day. I know I'm only here by your grace. Thank you. In Jesus's name, Amen. I have a cold, sinus infection, or whatever. Something is not right. Hope and pray it's not Covid-19. I'm not going to be paranoid. Just go one day at a time. I have faith and I won't be fearful. Spring is coming and that's giving me hope. The world is getting crazy. People hoarding and it's like the zombie apocalypse! LOL

April 3, 2020

Thank you Father for all I have, all there is, and all I am. Bless me with strength and health to get through this cold. Bless us so we may survive this virus. Thank you, Father. In Jesus's name. Amen. If I do nothing, they get upset because I did not cook or clean their mess. I'm not your maid. I'm your mother! Offer some help to me when supper is being made. Don't just sit there when you're going to eat too! Or when it's is for your kids too. Don't expect me and my husband to pay for everything and do all. He works all day and you both sleep all day. They need to help more!

April 4, 2020

Thank you Father. Without you there is nothing. Guide me Father to your will for me. Thank you. In Jesus's name, Amen. You ever feel invisible? Maybe not invisible, but just taken for granted? Like I bust my butt doing as much as I can to keep everybody happy and me too but seems like nobody gives a shit! I clean it, they dirty it and leave me the mess. I wipe it, they spill and don't even wipe up. They need space. I make as much as I can, but they need more. Just seems like me matter what I do it's never enough. Like when I was little.

I noticed at this time that Savannah started getting upset over minor issues, things like putting the strainer in the sink, making sure the toilet seat was down, the cupboard doors were open and should be shut, the front porch light wasn't on at nights and it should be, etc. I thought at the time she was being very anal and frustrated over tiny things, but now I realize she was running out of energy and unable to take care of these things so much on her own. These things were never an issue before, but that was because she just did them and no one noticed. Now she just didn't have the energy to correct these things when she saw them. She figured we would just do them if she couldn't.

April 5, 2020

Thank you Father for all. You are the only reason I am here. Guide Father to your will for me. Thank you, Father. In Jesus's name, Amen. Oh my gosh, somebody help me! Hard to breathe, no fever, don't feel like my lungs are full of fluids, just phlegm. Doing breathing treatments, but this sinus needs to stop! It drains at night and when I wake, I hack up a lot of phlegm. I just need a break from being sick! Flu, shingles, shingles again, and now this! Fuck this! I'm going crazy.

April 6, 2020

Thank you Father for all you've given. I am nothing without you. Bless me with health Father. I am still fighting this cold. Thank you, Amen. P.S. I forgot to add also bless me with patience and love so I'm not so grumpy. Thank you. In Jesus's name, Amen. I need to come up with a hot drink I can drink. I don't like tea or coffee. Thinking maybe orange juice pineapple juice, ginger and cinnamon might work and some clove too. Yeah, that might be good. Really hard to breathe today.

April 7, 2020

Thank you Father for all you have given and all you give daily. I'm very grateful. Bless me to be a better person, more loving, and more tolerable. Bless me to be more like you. Thank you. In Jesus's name, Amen. Everybody's getting tired of quarantine, but I've been there for 2 years now. Now maybe they'll see how I feel. I doubt it. This cold is kicking my ass. So tired, can't breathe, getting scared. Going to pray a lot that it's not the damn virus! I don't want to die from a damn virus! I fought too long and too hard for that shit!

April 8, 2020

Thank you Father for all you've given everybody in the world. Thank you for all you give daily. We are nothing without you. Bless us all to be more like you. Bless us to be kind to one another and know that you are the one and only. Thank you. In Jesus's name, Amen. Happy 3rd Birthday to my great niece Jaynia. I can't believe you're 3! Easter's coming and the anniversary of the day they told me I have 2 yrs. to live. I'm approaching my 2nd year and I was told on Heaven's birthday (April 13). I pray I make it through all this cold and virus. I'm also getting angrier. Not meaning to, but I see my anger rear its ugly head more now. I pray for release, so I don't place it on anybody.

April 9, 2020

Thank you Father for getting me through another night. I know I don't exist without you.

You are awesome. Thank you. In Jesus's name, Amen. Feeling somewhat better. Waiting for diarrhea to pass. My lungs are better each day, but I can't wait until this is over. I want summer, well Spring first. We're all still in quarantine and going nuts. I wish Heaven would get up earlier and take boys outside so they can run. Hopefully she'll get back on track and start getting her shit together. I fear she just gets lazy here. She knows we will all take care of boys. I pray she sees this and changes.

April 10, 2020

Thank you Father for all you do. We have nothing without you. Bless us to be kinder to each other, tolerant of each other, and to love each other (even on days that it's hard to). Thank you. In Jesus's name, Amen. I will not give in to this sickness. I'm keeping busy as I can. Made breakfast again for Emmett, Gavin, and Kalem. I wish she'd get up. I'm cleaning fridge out today. Deep cleaning it. It's gross. I'm breathing better than I was. I feel good in the fact it's not fluid in lungs, but I have a lot of phlegm. Keep moving, that's what I'm doing.

April 11, 2020

Thank you Father for another day and all else you've given the world. I belong to you. I only trust in you. Bless me to do better at all in life and to be more like you. Thank you, Father. Amen.

April 12, 2020

Thank you Father and thank you Jesus for all you've given to me. Bless us to know and appreciate these gifts. Thank you is not enough. We owe all to you. Thank you. In Jesus's name, Amen. Happy Easter! He is risen.

April 13, 2020

Thank you Father for all you've given the world. We all owe all to you. Thank you for carrying me through another night. Bless me to be more like you. In Jesus's name, Amen. Happy Birthday Heaven (27)! Trying to make today as good as I can for her. She's up early! Amazed me.! She won't be tomorrow I bet.

April 14, 2020

Thank you Father for all you've given me. I owe my life to you and I am forever grateful to you for all. Still sick. Had a panic attack that I was dying. I know I'm dying, but that was just wrong. Tim continues to be awesome at worrying over me. I love him so much. Thank you, Father, for him. I know nobody else would stand by my side through all this. He's the best support. Yeah, he frustrates me, but I love him so much. He cares for me like no other as I do him. I think Heaven & Gavin are in denial that I'm dying. They're always asking, "You okay?" No, I'm dying and it's becoming obvious.

April 15, 2020

Thank you Father for all you've given me and the world. We're blessed beyond words to have you watch over us. Father, we ask that you keep us safe and help them find a cure for this virus. Bless us all to be healthy and recover from this. And if it is our time, that we go quickly and in peace knowing we will join you. Thank you

Father. Amen. Still sick or maybe it's progression of my disease. Who knows, but I'm still rough.

April 16, 2020

Thank you Father for all the blessings, lessons, and hope you're given me. Bless me with strength to get where I need to be for you Father. Thank you. In Jesus's name, Amen. Thank you for protecting my husband today when that semi almost ran him off the road.

April 17, 2020

Thank you Father for all you've given our family. We are all so blessed. I am grateful to you for blessing me with another day. Thank you. In Jesus's name, Amen.

April 18, 2020

Thank you Father for another day and all you blessed me with and my family. Bless me to be more like you. Thank you. In Jesus's name, Amen. Still not back to me. No diarrhea, but my breathing still needs help.

April 19, 2020

Thank you. Thank you. Father there are no words I can say to thank you enough for all you've given me. I am truly blessed. Father, each day you give me and bless me to be appreciative and grateful for all. Thank you. In Jesus's name, Amen. They're up today. Damn this phlegm. Feel crappy. Worried they may be right, that I may be dying. Can't seem to shake this shit. Praying harder than ever I make it through each night and day. We'll see.

April 20, 2020

Thank you Father for another day! Thank you for the many blessings in my life. I am truly blessed. You're an awesome Father. You have taught me many lessons. Thank you. Bless me to be more like you. In Jesus's name, Amen. It's been 2 years and 7 days since they told me I would only live 2 years! Starting to feel somewhat better.

She was very proud that she had outlived her prognosis of one to two years. From here on out, I noticed she was marking down the days she had exceeded her expected prognosis. She knew she was on borrowed time and noted the days she had gone beyond the two years in her journal daily now.

April 21, 2020

Thank you Father for another day and all the blessings I've been given. Bless me to be more like you and to be patient. Thank you. In Jesus's name, Amen. It's been 2 years and 8 days. Feeling better today. My color is good. Still coughing, but better. Got outside for some fresh air and much-needed sunshine! Thank you, Father! Oh my gosh beautiful day. Had Tim grill tonight. I love spring!

Again, she loved the sunshine. At this point, she would want to go outside, and it would take us about ten minutes to get her oxygen tanks and her walker to the door. Then she would be outside about five minutes, and then she would want to go back inside. She apologized for the time and effort it took but really appreciated it. Going outside for even a few minutes made a difference in her day. Even if it was a lot of work, it was worth it.

April 22, 2020

Thank you Father for loving me, blessing me with all that I am, and for the many blessings I receive daily. I am nothing without you. I owe all to you. Thank you. In Jesus's name, Amen. It's been 2 years and 9 days. Feel so much better today. Had virtual appointment with Jenny Condon (pulmonologist). That's cool! Better than going, I think. By end of night I was sick again!

April 23, 2020

Thank you Father for getting me through another night. Bless me to accept your will for me no matter what. Thank you. In Jesus's name, Amen. It's been 2 years and 10 days! Thank you, God! Sick again. I have a fever and I puked!

April 24, 2020

Thank you Father. Praise to you God for another day! I'm truly blessed to wake each day. Thank you. Bless me father to take each day one at a time. Thank you. In Jesus's name, Amen. It's been 2 years and 11 days! Puked again. Wish this shit would just leave my body. Fever seems to be gone.

April 25, 2020

Thank you Father for another day and all the blessings you've given. Bless me to be more understanding and a good wife to my husband. For some days I have hard time remembering how. Thank you. In Jesus's name. Amen. It's been 2 years and 12 days. P.S. my prayer was not being sarcastic. I truly mean it. It's hard to remember how he suffers too.

April 26, 2020

Thank you Father for another day and the many blessings I've received from you. You're awesome. I owe all to you. Bless me Father to be more like you. Thank you. In Jesus's name, Amen. It's been 2 years and 13 days.

April 27, 2020

Thank you Father for another day. Thank you for the many blessings myself and my family have received from you. We owe all to you. Bless us to know you better each day and to be more like you. It's been 2 years and 14 days.

April 28, 2020

Thank you Father for another day. I owe my whole life to you. You've blessed me in many ways. Thank you. Bless me to be more like you. Thank you. In Jesus's name, Amen. It's been 2 years and 15 days. Happy Monthiversary!

April 29, 2020

Thank you Father for another day & for the many blessings you've bestowed on our family. Bless us all to walk the path you've chosen for us. Thank you. In Jesus's name, Amen! It's been 2 years and 16 days.

April 30, 2020

Thank you Father for another day! For all you've given me. All you taught me. Bless me Father to be more like you. Thank you. In Jesus's name, Amen. It's been 2 years and 17 days.

May 1, 2020

Thank you Father for another day! Thank you for all you've given me. We are nothing without you. Bless me Father to be more like you. Thank you again, for all, In Jesus's name, Amen! It's been 2 years and 18 days! Happy Birthday Me! 51 years old. I never thought I'd make it this long. Thank you Father!! Glory be to God.

May 2, 2020

Thank you Father for another day and all you've given me and my family! Bless me more like you. In Jesus's name, Amen. It's been 2 years and 19 days. Feeling much better today! Not perfect, but better.

May 3, 2020

Thank you. Thank you. Thank you, Father, for giving me another day! Thank you for always watching over me. I am honorably blessed and forever grateful. Bless me to be as you've chosen for me. In Jesus's name, Amen. It's been 2 years and 20 days! Feeling a little better each day. I hope and pray it continues. Going outside today! Getting my flower beds under control! I'm so grateful to get some sun. Still no cure for virus. Still having a hard time breathing. Still have shits from meds but feeling some better.

May 4, 2020

Thank you Father for all you've given me. For always taking care of me and my family. We are truly blessed. Help us know you or find you for some. We owe all praise to you. Everything in Jesus's name we pray, Amen. It's been 2 years and 21 days! Feeling better each day! Thank you, Father.

May 5, 2020

Thank you Father for holding me in your arms in my time of need and daily. I'm amazed by your love. Bless me to see harder and more faithful now. Strengthen me to get through all I need to. Thank you. In Jesus's name I pray, Amen. It's been 2 years and 22 days! Happy Birthday Michaela. Shooting pains in left leg today. Kicking my butt!

May 6, 2020

Thank you Father for holding me close all night. I know I wouldn't have made it we're not for you. Bless me to know my place always is with you. Thank you for all you've given. In Jesus's name I pray. Amen. It's been 2 years and 23 days! Feeling better today, but we'll see how it goes.

May 7, 2020

Thank you Father for all you've given us. Bless me to never forget I owe all to you. In Jesus's name I pray, Amen. It's been 2 years and 24 days! Feeling so much better today! Still have some runs, but that I can handle, if my O2 keeps going up.

May 8, 2020

Thank you Father for all you've given us. Bless us know we owe all to you. Bless me, Father to be more like you. In Jesus's name I pray, Amen. It's been 2 years and 25 days. Still sick, but slightly better? Lungs feel great, but still coughing croup up.

May 9, 2020

Thank you Father for all you've given me. I am nothing without you. Bless me Father with patience and strength to get through what I must. Also bless my family to know that these decisions are mine and to accept them. Thank you. In Jesus's name I pray, Amen. It's been 2 years and 26 days. Still waiting and praying this illness ends. I'm so weak from fighting. My Mom and my sister Evelyn came to visit today! That was nice. We bought them lunch.

May 10, 2020

Thank you Father for holding me through the night. I'm nothing without you. Thank you for all you've given. In Jesus's name we pray, Amen. It's been 2 years and 27 days. Happy Mother's Day! Pretty bad today. I hate this!

May 11, 2020

Thank you Father for all you've given me and my family. We ask that you continue to watch over, shelter, protect, and bless us. We're nothing without you and your grace. Thank you. In Jesus's name I pray, Amen. It's been 2 years and 28 days! Feeling a little better today.

May 12, 2020

Thank you Lord for giving me each day and all the blessings I've received. I know I'm not worthy of it all, but I am deeply grateful. Bless me to know my faith and to be strong, coura-geous, and loving as you always have. Bless my family with the same. I thank you Father, in Jesus's name I pray, Amen. It's been 2 years and 29 days! Happy Birthday to my friend Arlyne. Feeling much better today. Hopefully it continues every day getting better. My son tells me I'm the strongest person he knows, but I feel so weak. I try to hide it, but I'm not doing so well this week. I'm broken and I am angry because I can't do anything about it.

I believe this was when I noticed the biggest changes in her. She was right, and she did try to hide it, but it was easier to see that she wasn't feeling good most days. Her suffering was much more noticeable. She cried more often, and she was no longer able to do chores she used to do. She no longer made the bed. We started getting paper plates and silverware so she didn't have dishes. She also took longer to recover when she got up and moved around. She basically lived on her purple couch now with occasional trips to the bathroom. Cooking was not as often. We started ordering meals online from a company that sold prepackaged healthy foods.

May 13, 2020
Thank you for allowing me to wake today. Today I pray for strength, peace, love, tolerance, and patience. I need it all besides the obvious. Help me know that I am still me and not succumbing to this damn disease. I am a loving, nurturing person, and I won't like to stay that way. Just less emotional. Thank you, Amen. It's been 2 years and 30 days.! I fear I'm dying. Not fear but accepted that I'm declining as they say. I'm sad, but still trying to be me. I don't want to change, be needy, or emotional. I hate that I'm a strain on Tim. He is not trying to show it, but he is stressed. I wish I could fix that, don't know how. Heaven exhausted again so she's down too.

Gavin is taking care of Dad's place, because they had a baby.

I was stressed, and about this time, I noticed how overweight and out of shape I had gotten. I was not taking care of myself, a big no-no for caregivers. During the last four months of her life, I decided I needed to get in shape and went on a diet and started working out early in the morning. This was not because I was anticipating she would die soon, but rather, I had really gotten out of shape sitting inside and watching TV all the time. I was worried that if I didn't improve my health, I might have a heart attack, and I wouldn't be able to take care of her. I learned the only time I could focus on myself was early in the morning. She was starting to sleep later, and I got up at 5:00 a.m. and went to the golf course by 6:00 a.m. If I had lawn work, I would do this instead. She had planted flowers but could no longer tend to them. This early morning time allowed me to destress and get ready for the day. I then went to work, but by this time, Heaven and Gavin were up and were there during the day. Probably the only reason I could go to work the last six months of her life was knowing if she needed anything that our adult kids were in the house.

May 14, 2020
Father watch over me today. Surround me with healing angels to heal whatever is your will. Whether it be emotional or physical and I thank you for all the blessings and lessons. Thank you will never be enough. In Jesus's name I pray, Amen. It's been 2 years and 31 days! Feeling a little better today. Nurse coming today. Please don't say I need tapped! It doesn't feel like that, but they always say that. Anyway, Heaven is still having issues so she's sleeping. Boys are up, Gavin's sleeping, Tim is off to work. Just me and the Indians and cat running about.

May 15, 2020

Thank you almighty Father for all you've given the world and the personal blessings and lessons I've received. We are truly undeserving. Bless us all to take time to thank you for all you've done and to praise your name. Thank you. In Jesus's name, Amen. It's been 2 years and 1 month and 1 day! I'm so grateful to be alive and to be a shelter for children and grandchildren. It's so beautiful out today, I hope I can get out in it.

May 16, 2020

Thank you again Father for all you've given me and the world. You've blessed me so much and I'm but a humble human who makes mistakes daily. Thank you. Bless me to appreciate all you've done and to praise you completely. In Jesus's name I pray, Amen. It's been 2 years and 1 month and 2 days. Another beautiful day, rain later, but sun is shining!

May 17, 2020

Thank you Father for allowing me to wake today. Thank you for all you've given for all and the many blessings I receive. Lessons I've learned. Bless me to be more like you. In Jesus's name, Amen. It's been 2 years, 1 month, and 3 days! Rainy today.

May 18, 2020

Thank you Father for teaching me, guiding me, protecting me, and loving me. I pray you continue to watch over me and get me through this journey. Thank you again. In Jesus's name I pray, Amen. It's been 2 years, 1 month, and 4 days! Cloudy still today. New nurse coming.

I feel okay but have been better. I'm just taking one day at a time, which is all I can. Trying not to let this control me. Well, that didn't work, but at least got dishes done. Hopefully, one day soon I will feel better.

May 19, 2020
Thank you Father for all you've given me and for all you've taught me. Bless me to be more like you. Thank you. In Jesus's name, Amen. It's been 2 years, 1 month, and 5 days! Feeling a lot better today. Hope the sun comes out. Well, didn't get to go out today! So frustrating that warmer weather hasn't come yet. Heaven is gone still. I worry about her and the boys. She doesn't know the choice she's making effects their lives. Some choices may lead them exactly where she doesn't want them going. She will figure it out. I hope soon.

May 20, 2020
Thank you Father for another day! I owe all to you. Only you have sheltered, taught, guided, and loved me unfailing. I praise your name. Thank you, Father. In Jesus's name I pray. Amen. It's been 2 years, 1 month, and 6 days! Gloomy again out today. Hope the sun comes soon. I need outdoor therapy! Everybody is gloomy, except Tim. He seems pretty chipper, then he seems grumpy. Maybe it's me.

May 21, 2020
Thank you Father for letting me live another day! Thank you for the many blessings and lessons taught. Bless me to know your way for me and to make me at peace with what I must face.

Thank you. In Jesus's name, Amen. It's been 2 years, 1 month, and 7 days!!

May 22, 2020

Thank you Father for allowing me another day to live, love, and honor you. Bless me to be patient, kind, loving, and wise today with myself and everyone around me. Thank you, Amen. It's been 2 years, 1 month, and 8 days!! Just need sun and this crap to go away.

May 23, 2020

Thank you Father for another day. I could never repay all you've given. I try to follow path that's proper, but I am human and fall short. I vow to keep kicking and getting back up and knowing you with protection of me. Just be patient I ask of you. I know I've no right to for I am but a peon. but I know you put me here to do more and that's all I want to do. Thank you again. In Jesus name, Amen. It's been 2 years, 1 month, and 9 days! In pain today. Getting a little scared too. I'm fighting, I'm strong, but it's getting harder. Finally got a bath again. Thank you, Father, for that and my husband. Legs are swelling. I need to exercise and get it gone.

About this time, we noticed her legs were starting to swell up during the day. This was water retention and signs that her heart was having a hard time circulating fully. She put them up on pillows to help reduce some of the swelling. They added more water pills to help her go pee more, but her legs were pretty much swollen the last four months of her life.

May 24, 2020

Thank you Father for all you've given me every day! I praise your name only; I owe all to you. Bless me to walk the path that has been chosen for me and defeat all I must face. Thank you. In Jesus's name I pray, Amen. It's been 2 years, 1 month, and 10 days! Feel crappy today, but lungs feel good. This damn coughing is kicking my ass! I'm going to golf today damn it!! Thank you, Father, I got to golf 4 holes! It felt so good to get out of the house! Felt good to whack some balls! I'm one armed, so I will hurt tomorrow, but I don't care, I love to golf! Didn't feel like going back in house, so we got home and pulled some weeds from flower beds. Should be real tired tonight.

May 25, 2020

Thank you Father for all you've done. I owe all to you. I praise only you. Bless me to be better at your will. Thank you. In Jesus's name, Amen. It's been 2 years, 1 month, and 11 days! Woke up at 7:30 a.m. coughing dry heaving, and shit, and back to bed. Up at 9:15, coughing, dry heaving, shitting. I need this to stop, I have shit to do!

May 26, 2020

Thank you Father for all you've give given. I owe all to you and praise only you. I owe all to you for the love, patience, mercy, grace, and beauty you've shown me. Thank you. Bless me to be more diligent in my faith, praise and walk. Thank you. In Jesus's name I pray, Amen. It's been 2 years, 1 month, and 12 days!

May 27, 2020

Thank you Father for all you've blessed the world with. Bless me father to appreciate all you've given me and to walk straighter on the path that lies before me and to stay faithful to you as always. Thank you. In Jesus name, Amen. It's been 2 years, 1 month, and 13 days! Starting to feel like I'm getting to the end of this crud!

May 28, 2020

Thank you Father for all you've given the world. Bless me to be faithful, honest, courageous, strong, and loving. Thank you. In Jesus's name, Amen. It's been 2 years, 1 month, and 2 weeks. Spent most of the day outside today! We weeded, built my pond, and enjoyed! So beautiful out! Forgot we trimmed some trees too! Thank you, Father, for giving me strength to work today!

May 29, 2020

Thank you for all you've given me and the rest of the world. Thank you for your guidance, love, patience, and teaching. You're awesome. I owe all to you. I praise you. Thank you. In Jesus's name I pray, Amen. It's been 2 years, 1 month, 2 weeks, and 1 day! I'm sore from yesterday! So, hoping to get outside again today. I'm so happy to have gotten so much done.! Thank you, Father! Coughed so hard something snapped in my side! Tim thinks I have broken a rib. Okay, I think Tim is right because can't breathe, cough, or move without my rib hurting. Fuck!

May 30, 2020

Thank you Father for allowing me another day! I praise your name. I owe all to you. Bless me Father with strength to get through this pain and today, with gladness in my heart, with courage to keep moving and mercy for others and love. Thank you. In Jesus's name I pray, Amen. It's been 2 years, 1 month, 2 weeks, and 2 days! Feel like shit again, but I don't care! Going to push myself anyway!

May 31, 2020

Thank you Father again for allowing me another day! I owe all to you. Trust in you and praise you alone. Thank you. Bless me to walk straighter on my path and be stronger and be more courageous in all I do. Thank you. In Jesus's name I pray, Amen. It's been 2 years, 1 month, 2 weeks, and 3 days! Think I broke my rib on Friday. This damn thing hurts. Every time I cough, laugh, move, breathe, it's all fucking hurts. Coughing is the most painful and I still have a cough going. Oh well, it will get better, I hope.

June 1, 2020

Thank you Father for blessing me with another beautiful day. I owe all to you. I praise your name. I am nothing without you. Thank you. In Jesus's name I pray, Amen. It's been 2 years, 1 month, 2 weeks, and 4 days! Started feel like I'm getting ready to drain or something. I'm very sleepy and sluggish and my feet are so swollen. Going to try to do something though.

June 2, 2020

Thank you Father for blessing me with another day. I am nothing, have nothing, without you. I owe all to you. I am yours. Bless me Father to strengthen my faith, courage, love, and walk straighter. Thank you. In Jesus's name I pray, Amen. It's been 2 years, 1 month, 2 weeks, and 5 days! Really sluggish today. Coughing a lot and it fucken hurts!! Going to rest a little.

June 3, 2020

Thank you Father for all you've given me. Thank you for all you given this this world. Bless us all to love more, appreciate more, to be more peaceful, and to be more faithful. Thank you. In Jesus's name, Amen. It's been 2 years, 1 month, 2 weeks, and 6 days! Diarrhea this morning. Ever since I made tacos that night. Maybe the home-made seasoning makes my lungs drain. Usual night, TV or movies, then bed at 11 p.m. I get tired early now. I'm so emotional! I thought I could become cold and distant to people, but I feel like they are to me and I get sad. Sometimes and cry about it when they're not around me. I got to stop. Damn drugs! I hate being so emotional, but I can't do anything about that!

June 4, 2020

Thank you Father for your love, patience, guidance, faith, and strength. Father, thank you for all you've created, but mostly I thank you for creating me so I may know love and the beauty of all you've given. Bless me to appreciate all I am, have, and can do. Thank you. In Jesus's name I pray, Amen. It's been 2 years, 1 month, and 3 weeks.! Feel like my lungs are draining. Diarrhea already this morning. Maybe I should have tacos homemade every week! My emotions are on a roller coaster today, but I will get through this. Good thing Tim's working and everybody here just hangs up stairs while I sit here alone.

June 5, 2020

Thank you Father for all you've given the entire world. For all the love, grace, and mercy you've shown. Bless us all to love each other and to be peaceful as you intended and faithful to you. Thank you, Father. In Jesus's name I pray, Amen. It's been 2 years, 1 month, 3 weeks, and 1 day! Feeling better but had dry heaves today and coughed up a lot of phlegm. Damn ribs still hurt. Hope this heals fast.

June 6, 2020

Thank you Father for giving me another day. I ask that you instill gladness in my heart and comfort my body for it's getting hard for me daily. I don't want to be grumpy because of pain and misery. Thank you. In Jesus's name I pray, Amen. It's been 2 years, 1 month, 3 weeks, and 2 days! Rough morning, but I'll get through it as best I can.

June 7, 2020

Thank you Father for another day! I thank you Jesus for saving us all. I praise your name only. Bless me to walk a straighter path and share your love. In Jesus's name I pray, Amen. It's been 2 years, 1 month, 3 weeks, and 3 days! Thank you for another day, blessed Lord! I don't feel the greatest and my feet are swelling, but I'm grateful to be here. Tim and I had a spat, but nothing big. I've adjusted, just like I always have.

June 8, 2020

Thank you Father. Thank you, Jesus. Thank you, Holy Spirit, for all you've given. I praise your name and I trust in you. I will follow no other. Bless me to walk a straighter path and stay me. In Jesus's name I pray, Amen. It's been 2 years, 1 month, 3 weeks, and 4 days! So far rough morning health wise and then personal wise. Had an argument with Heaven and I apologize for my part, but true Heaven like always, I get no apology from her. And she'll be pissy towards me until she sees fit. That girl has always been like that. She doesn't know it yet, but one day she'll figure it. You should care about people who love you too. I've always given to her because I felt guilty that I was such a stupid woman and didn't amount to much. I've always tried harder with her because of the way I grew up and she didn't have her dad and Gavin did. I just wanted to give my kids as much as I could. Love, home, and family. I tried the best I could. It's not easy. I still find myself helping, but it just never seems enough. I do not talk or say things right, I don't help enough. I should have done more. Short of giving her my car for free and staying at our home for free, I don't think that would be enough either. I'm trying guys! I sold my car to her because it was a good car. Not happy AC needs fixed. I will fix that. Let her live here. She has the biggest room and boys have a room, but not enough space, I cook for us all almost every night. She eats some, but she has health issues and now says can't eat any of the food. I try to accommodate her health issues. I have my own but not to no avail. I just don't know how to help her, I'm helpless. I'm thinking we should just sell this house and pay our debt and give the rest to the kids and just go be silent and far away until I pass. They couldn't say I didn't do for them. Hell, they can't now. We've always helped whether with money, babysitting, moving, a place to live, I'd say we've given our fair share. I love them all so much and that is more than I got. My emotions aren't weakness or manipulation. They were my pain, my heartbreak, my love, my happiness, my anger, my disappointment, my pride. Hope they see in the end how they very much I loved them all. This generation doesn't know how lucky they are at all. There are so many parents still taking care of adult children and sacrificing our space, lives, etc. We don't expect that of them. Hell, we've talked (Tim and I) we both agree that we've given and keep giving either it's babysitting. home, cars, money, etc. We gave that out of our own because our parents couldn't help us. There is no closeness anymore because we aren't supposed to ever stop. They only give when they have time, but we are to make time always. Nobody pays or has paid our bills for us. Nobody gives us a home, car, or makes time whenever we need it. Hell, and don't ask if anybody can go to the store. They can only do that on their time, but if you forget to buy diapers for your child we are to jump and get them. Better not get jumbo pack to save money or time for them, because you don't have a space for that. We won't get a thank you at all. Nobody went and got my baby's milk because I was sick and couldn't go to the store, I had to do it or at least pay. Nobody co-signed on a car for me, I had to get what I could afford. I just don't understand. We got nothing from our parents, and we respected, loved, honored, and did what we could for our parents. We gave all we can to our kids and for some it wasn't enough. The thing is they'll go through this too with their kids. I hope not, but I have a feeling they will as we did too. Our parents gave us more than they got growing up and so on and so on. Lesson learned.

As you can tell from this journal entry, she was becoming more frustrated with those around her. Heaven and Gavin were living with us at the time, and she often expressed frustration toward me and them. This truly was not who she was, but she was sick and miserable. Her emotions ranged from crying out loud to angry and bitter. She wrote much more than she voiced, and so I wasn't aware of these thoughts she had until she had passed away and I started reading the journals. In some ways, it seemed like she was disappointed with us all at times, and she was, but later you'll notice she was especially thankful for us in her life. You must consider we had four adults and two grandchildren living in a three-bedroom house. There was bound to be conflicts at times. I told the kids that it was a normal part of the declining process, and it really was. Consider when you have been sick and others are around you. You are more likely to be grouchy and moody. Now put yourself in her shoes, not feeling well for weeks and months and years. I'm surprised she didn't become angrier, but I guess that is why she used the diary. It was a way of letting her emotions run without voicing her thoughts. It wouldn't have mattered if she had. We loved her deeply, and we would have understood.

June 9, 2020
Thank you Father in Heaven above. Thank you, Jesus. Thank you, Holy Spirit. For all you've given. Thank you for saving me. Thank you for life itself and all you've taught me. I ask that you

please bless me to forgive completely and to love as you want us to love. Thank you, I believe it. I receive it. In Jesus's name I pray, Amen. 2 yrs., It's been 2 years, 1 month, 3 weeks, and 5 days! Well, hopefully today will go well. I had Tim get donuts for us all. I had a glazed one. Mmmm it was worth it. Kind of gloomy out so far, but it's okay. I feel all right. It could be worse. Still moving. Less than I used to but working on that.

June 10, 2020

Thank you Father, Jesus, Holy Spirit. Thank you for another day! Bless me please to be strong, courageous, and full of love today. Thank you. In Jesus's name I pray, Amen. It's been 2 years, 1 month, 3 weeks, and 6 days! Hardly any sleep last night. I feel weird, but I'm fighting. Feels like something's changing with me. Better or Worse, I don't know. I can only pray. I did a lot of going through stuff today. Oh my gosh! I kept everything my kids ever made me! It was good therapy for me.

June 11, 2020

Thank you almighty God. Thank you, Jesus. Thank you, Holy Spirit. For another day. I thank you for all you've given the world. Thank you for carrying me. Bless me today as I journey to be strong, loving, courageous, and get stuff done. Thank you. In Jesus name I pray, Amen. It's been 2 years, and 2 months! Feeling better today. It's crazy, but I feel like I can do more, I'm doing more. Thank you, Father. Starting to feel like me more. Still have pain, still trouble breathing, but I think it's going back to where I used to be. Before winter kicked my ass.

June 12, 2020

Thank you Father. Thank you, Jesus. Thank you, Holy Spirit. For all you've given. I praise your name and I trust in you alone. Bless me with strength, courage, tolerance, patience, kindness, and love and make my faith stronger. It's been 2 years, 2 months, and 1 day! Feeling somewhat better today. Hope and pray I get outside today. Tim and I agreed to watch kids for weekend for Heaven. They can't go to their dads because his woman may have been exposed to Covid-19 virus. We got outside. The boys had a blast. We planted flowers, they explored. They love getting outside so do I. Watched movie with the boys. Me and Tim had a fight. We're okay, he just makes me so mad sometimes. It's through and all is okay. Think me getting that pissed blew out some shit because I feel more me! LOL! What a thing. I tried M&Ms tonight... I so miss chocolate. At least I could eat some. Hopefully, we can take boys golfing tomorrow. Well I can't golf, but we can watch Tim. Maybe we'll get some yard games for in the yard and we can have Keegan come and we can cook out.

June 13, 2020

Thank you Father. Thank you, Jesus. Thank you, Holy Spirit. For allowing me another day and all you given me. Bless me to be patient, kind, loving, strong, and faithful in all I do today. Thank you. In Jesus's name, Amen. It's been 2 years, 2 months, and 2 days! Feeling better some today. Is still coughing, but I feel less weighted down. Like maybe I can walk outside without half dying. We'll see. We plan on wearing these boys out today! LOL or they will us! Took boys golfing. I didn't golf, but Emmett, Kalem, Keegan, and Tim did, and everybody had fun. On the way back home, we got kids ice cream! They are Happy Boys.

June 14, 2020

Thank you Father. Thank you, Jesus. Thank you, Holy Spirit. For all you've given and all you continue to do. I'm truly blessed to know you. Bless me to not feel despair today. I am weak and need strength, Thank you. In Jesus's name I pray, Amen. It's been 2 years, 2 months, and 3 days! Took boys outside. They played all day. We got yard work done. Well I couldn't do much. Then we grilled and then the boys roasted marshmallows. They are Tired Boys.

June 15, 2020

Thank you Father. Thank you, Holy Spirit. Thank you, Jesus. For all you've given. Thank you for saving me and blessing me with another day. Bless me please with strength to carry on today. Thank you. In Jesus's name I pray, Amen. It's been 2 years, 2 months, and 4 days!

June 16, 2020

Thank you Father. Thank you, Jesus. Thank you, Holy Spirit, Thank you for all you've sacrificed and done for me and the world. Bless me to praise you more daily, to do your work daily, and to love more. In Jesus's name I pray, Amen. It's been 2 years, 2 months, and 5 days! Diarrhea again today!! Think I'm draining. Holy cow! Felt pretty good all day, but then flushed all night. So again, I had little sleep! So tired but can't sleep.

June 17, 2020

Thank you Father. Thank you, Jesus. Thank you, Holy Spirit. For all you've given. We all are blessed. I am truly grateful for all you've done in my life. Bless me to take each day one day at a time and to appreciate all. Thank you. In Jesus's name, Amen. It's been 2 years, 2 months, and 6 days! I'm worried. Still not doing better and my feet are swelling up bad. Feel like something good is happening, but my body doesn't know and it's dragging along. That's the worst part. I'm fighting, but I don't know how long I can.

Something good was happening. God was making room in heaven for her in a few months. She told me that she was starting to feel strange, like something was happening to her. I immediately became scared because I saw her increased weakness and swelling legs every day. Also, I noticed at this time she would take breaks going to the restroom downstairs. She would walk about ten feet and then sit on a chair and catch her breath before she would go about another ten feet and take a break and catch her breath again. I knew she was declining, and I was scared. She believed in some ways she was getting better. Now I look back, and I do believe she was getting better spiritually. Her faith was rock solid, and seeing how much she trusted in God throughout made me realize that God was protecting her throughout the last two and a half years. God would call her to her heavenly home in a few months.

June 18, 2020

Thank you Father. Thank you, Jesus. Thank you, Holy Spirit. For another day! I owe all to you. I praise your name and I'm forever grateful to you. Bless me with your presence and fill me with your light, I thank you Father. In Jesus's name, Amen. It's been 2 years, 2 months, and 1 week!! Praise God I woke up today! I was scared then a calmness surrounded me, and I woke up! Hallelujah! I missed taking a bath (hot) up to my neck! Miss getting completely wet in the pool. I miss standing in the rain and squishing my toes in the mud! It rained today and it made me sad. Oh well, I'll get over it.

June 19, 2020

Thank you Father, Jesus, Holy Spirit for all you've done for me. I am forever grateful to you. Bless me according to your will. In Jesus's name I pray, Amen. It's been 2 years, 2 months, 1 week, and 1 day! Rough day again. Tim had a hospice nurse stop by to look at me because he feels I'm progressing. He thinks I have less than 6 months. How's that feel? Knowing my hubby thinks I'm checking out soon! I'm pissed! I understand, but wow!! Oh, well, I'll get over it. He deals with this shit daily. I shouldn't be surprised. Lord, help me forgive him for that and get through this. I still have hope. Thank you. In Jesus's name I pray, Amen. Happy Birthday Linda my sister!

I asked a colleague of mine to stop by from hospice, and she did an assessment. I did not want hospice ever, but working in hospice for six years, I also knew it was very good care she would receive, and the hospice team would be much more of a presence in the home than home health. The home health nurse came only once per week, and I knew hospice would have a nurse two or three times a week and a hospice aide stopping in about three times a week and a chaplain and a social worker would stop in once or twice a month. Besides, I knew that just because you were on hospice didn't mean you would die within six months. We often had patients live a year or two on hospice, and the additional support with her decline was what I was trying to get to her. In no way had I given up. I also did not know this visit bothered her so much until I read her journals later. She never told me that she was upset by the visit.

> *June 20, 2020*
> Thank you Father, Holy Spirit, and Jesus for all you've been, done, and given to me and the world. I am forever grateful to you. Bless me today with health, peace, and love. I thank you. In Jesus's name, Amen. It's been 2 years, 2 months, 1 week, and 2 days! Not doing so good breathing today. I'm considering going to the hospital to get x-ray to see if my kegs need tapped. I hate getting my kegs tapped here. You never know who is going to do it and if they'll hurt you. Oh well, what do you do? Die or get tapped? I will probably opt for tapping.

Occasionally (about every six to nine months) her lungs had too much fluid, and she would need to go get her lungs drained at the hospital. She hated these procedures, and I saw incredible pain anytime she had to undergo this procedure. In the last few months of her life, we started noticing fluid building up in her legs at first. They used more powerful diuretics, but there were consequences with those as well because they could cause kidney failure. In the last month of her life, she had fluid buildup around the lungs, and fluid was building up in her abdomen. The treatment team suggested she could have fluid drained off her abdomen, and she might need fluid drained off her lungs every week, all of which required needles with syringes inserted into her back or stomach areas and hoses and suction to suck the fluid out. The pain on her face when those procedures were done was gut-wrenching, and I felt powerless as I saw my loved one suffer. Finally, she had enough and refused any more. Her breathing was very difficult, and the fluid continued to build in her, but she was at peace with this decision. If you or a loved one are in this situation of medical procedures or medications constantly being adjusted or applied so it can prolong life, keep in mind there is a trade-off for everything. Medications have side effects. Medical procedures can be painful.

June 21, 2020

Thank you Father. Thank you, Holy Spirit. Thank you, Jesus. For another day and all that you've given to and for me. I am forever in your debt. Bless me to know always that you're with me. Bless me to live by you and not of myself. In Jesus's name I pray, Amen. It's been 2 years, 2 months, 1 week, and 3 days! Praise God. Hallelujah! Another day! Good day. Took Tim golfing and then bought him supper for Father's Day. He went to bed early and as we hugged goodnight, I started bawling because we haven't held each other that long in a while. I miss his touch. This damn disease has taken a lot from us. I'm going to try and take some back before I go. We both deserve that.

June 22, 2020

Thank you Father. Thank you, Holy Spirit. Thank you, Jesus. For all you've done to, for, and in me. I'm forever in your debt. You give all and I praise your name for it. Bless me to never forget all you are and all I have because of you. In Jesus's name, Amen. It's been 2 years, 2 months, 1 week, and 4 days! God is amazing! I'm so blessed to still be here. Gavin's work shut down because two girls (not sure if they're lying) said they have Covid-19. I told Gavin not to fear until they find out truth. I also reassured him that if he is positive, I won't fear for my Shepherd is with me. One thing I've known my whole life is God watches over me for some reason. Will try to stay strong no matter what.

Perhaps the biggest medical issue we faced other than her terminal disease was COVID-19. Although she never contracted it, it had a huge impact on our household in the initial few months of the pandemic. We used lots of Clorox wipes and sanitation products for our nightly medication mixes. Additionally, weekly we had to change her dressing on her pump infusion insertion site on her chest. Medication mixes and dressing changes required a sterile environment, and we were lucky she never got an infection around her tube site. Immediately we noticed a shortage of Clorox wipes when the pandemic hit. We used these daily to sterilize the surface we mixed medications on. Toilet paper was also in short supply for a while, and we had to resort to generic brands at times. Many would not think this was a big deal, but at times she had diarrhea, and the generic toilet paper was harsher on her skin. She got a few sores a few times and had to use medication around her bottom area at times. The biggest thing it affected was our ability to get out. Savannah was one of the high-risk populations that the virus targeted and would have caused her severe medical complications. I worked in health care, and I was wearing personal protective equipment (mask, gloves, etc.) early on. Gavin was still living at home, and there was a scare with coworkers testing positive there. Gavin expressed concern that if he got it, he would feel guilty if she got it too. Savannah reassured him and explained that if she were to get it, it would not be his fault but rather God's will. If she did go to the store, we made sure she had gloves on and a face mask. She noted how people were being careful and practicing social distancing but how in previous cold and flu seasons people had come up to her and hugged her, and yet they had been coughing and sneezing. She thought it was ironic that now people were being precautious, and yet previously they had not even thought of if she had gotten colds or flus. Those viral infections could have caused her severe problems besides. After a while, the news coverage on the news of COVID-19 was irritating to her. She laughed about getting "COVID, COVID, COVID," but never did. Ironically, I think I got exposed five days after her death at her funeral and celebration of life as the following week I tested positive, and it caused restrictions for me to only do telehealth or phone visits with patients until I got cleared by being negative of COVID-19 two weeks later. It is important to note, anyone with a terminal illness will need to be aware of any viral infections and not overlook the common flu or cold and be extra precautions with a weakened immune system.

June 23, 2020

Thank you Father, Holy Spirit, and Jesus for all you've given and done. I'm forever in your debt. I praise only you. Bless me to follow the path you've chosen for me and use me for your works. Thank you. In Jesus's name I pray, Amen. It's been 2 years, 2 months, 1 week, and 5 days!

June 24, 2020

Thank you Father, Holy Spirit, and Jesus for all you've given and done for us all. We truly know not how blessed we are. Bless me to walk in faith with you and to stand fast by your side. Bless me to be strong, yet soft. Bless me to be brave, yet meek. Bless me to be stern yet loving. Thank you. In Jesus's name I pray. Amen. It's been 2 years, 2 months, 1 week, and 6 days!

June 25, 2020

Thank you Father, Holy Spirit, and Jesus for all you've given me and the world. I praise you only. Bless me today with your love as always and calm my body. In Jesus's name I pray, Amen. It's been 2 years, 2 months, and 2 weeks! Feeling better. My friends Arlyne, Mary, and Alex all came to visit me today! Wonderful visit. I made them laugh a lot. Gavin's Covid-19 test was negative!

June 26, 2020

Thank you Father, Holy Spirit, and Jesus for all you've given and done for me. I'm truly blessed by your loved and honored. Bless me to honor you in every way. Thank you. In Jesus's name I pray, Amen. It's been 2 years, 2 months, 2 weeks, and 1 day! Happy Birthday to my nephew Lucas! Tim's family will be arriving today. Can't wait to see them. Love them so much. Tim's family has arrived! I love seeing them. They're awesome. They visited until about 10:30 or 11. We had a fire going. It is so nice to sit out and enjoy them and the beautiful night air. Lightning bugs and people setting off fireworks.

June 27, 2020

Thank you Father, Holy Spirit, Jesus for all you've given me. Bless me today with health, strength, and love. In Jesus's name I pray, Amen. It's been 2 years, 2 months, 2 weeks, and 2 days! Very nauseous today. Had a rough morning, but not stopping our cookout! Tim's family came, my brother Roy came. I love that they treated Roy good too. Not at all like my family. I made strawberry lemonade from scratch with Tim's sister Pam. It's awesome. Anyway, good food, good company, special memories.

June 28, 2020

Thank you Father, Holy Spirit, Jesus for all you've done for me and my family and friends. Bless us all today with open heart, loving arms, patience, and everlasting love. Thank you. In Jesus's name I pray, Amen. It's been 2 years, 2 months, 2 weeks, and 3 days! Nauseous again, but it'll pass. Tim's family stopped by to say bye. They're so good to me, I love them so much. Still having a rough go at it, but hopefully it'll pass. I'll be moving around more. It's too humid to get outside for me, but hopefully it will get less humid.

On hot days, she easily got exhausted quickly, and it would increase her thirst, which she was limited from drinking too much. If she was out in the heat for very long, she was fatigued when she was back inside. Even bug bites would cause extra itchiness and discomfort. Savannah often prayed under her breath at night for just one day she would feel good. It never happened, and each day, I saw her suffer with her latest setback or illness.

June 29, 2020

Thank you Father, Holy Spirit, and Jesus for all you've taught me. For blessing my life with a loving husband, children, and grandchildren. Thank you for every breath you've given me. Bless me to be strong in faith and follow the path you given. In Jesus name, Amen. It's been 2 years, 2 months, 2 weeks, and 4 days!

June 30, 2020

Thank you Father, Holy Spirit and Jesus for all you've given the world. For every breath I take, every beat of my heart. Bless me today to be faithful and all I do and to be humble, grateful, and loving as you were. Bless me with strength and courage to get through each day. Thank you in Jesus's name I pray, Amen. It's been 2 years, 2 months, 2 weeks, and 5 days!

July 1, 2020

Thank you Father, Holy Spirit, and Jesus for all you've given me. For all your blessings and lessons. I praise you only. You're an awesome Father. Bless me with comfort today. Thank you. In Jesus's name. Amen. It's been 2 years, 2 months, 2 weeks, and 6 days!

July 2, 2020

Thank you Father, Holy Spirit, and Jesus for all you've given and all you've done. Bless the world with peace, love for one another, and faith. Thank you. In Jesus's name I pray, Amen. It's been 2 years, 2 months, 3 weeks!

July 3, 2020

Thank you Father, Holy Spirit and Jesus for all you've given. Bless me to be a better person and more patient with people. Thank you. In Jesus's name, Amen. It's been 2 years, 2 months, 3 weeks, and 1 day.

July 4, 2020

Thank you Father, Holy Spirit, and Jesus for another day. For all you've given me, my family, and the world. Bless us all to fulfill the destiny you laid out for us according to your will. In Jesus's name I pray, Amen. It's been 2 years, 2 months, 3 weeks, and 2 days! I feel like crap today! Crap, utter crap!

July 5, 2020

Thank you Father, Holy Spirit, and Jesus for all you've given. Bless me to be faithful and praise only you. Bless me with tolerance and hope that you never give up on my faith in you. Thank you. In Jesus's name I pray, Amen. It's been 2 years, 2 months, 3 weeks, and 3 days! Tried to golf today. I was so fucking weak; I couldn't hit the ball. In my defense it was humid, but I had to try.

Flushing hard tonight. Really sick of this. I just wish I was doing good again.

July 6, 2020
Thank you Father, Holy Spirit, and Jesus for another day. For every breath, and every emotion. Thank you. I know I wouldn't be alive if not for you. I praise you only. Bless me to tolerate what I must today and fight negative emotions. Thank you. In Jesus's name I pray, Amen. It's been 2 years, 2 months, 3 weeks, and 4 days! Crap day, not well at all.

July 7, 2020
Thank you Father, Holy Spirit, and Jesus for all you've given me. Bless me to forgive, be tolerant, be loving, and faithful. Thank you again. In Jesus's name, Amen. It's been 2 years, 2 months, 3 weeks, and 5 days! Well, I overslept. Was up until 3:30 a.m. and then got up at 10:30 a.m. Shit myself and went from there. Did dishes after making bacon. Fell asleep after lunch for a bit. Got my purple walker today! Made supper felt better than yesterday, but still like shit. Flushing hard again tonight. Went through more shit in attic too.

The home health nurse ordered her a walker with a seat on it. This was after we told her she had to take breaks about every ten feet to catch her breath as she went to the bathroom. She didn't argue with the need for one at this point, and she used it daily. As she progressed, I noticed in the last three months she was no longer insisting on doing dishes and allowed us to use paper plates. We started buying TV dinners. She gave some of her half-finished projects away. Making the bed every day after she got up stopped. In fact, some days it took all the energy to get up out of bed. Dishes being washed were slowly replaced with paper plates. Taking a bath and washing her hair every week stretched to two or three weeks at a time. Cooking a meal every night was replaced with eating out more or getting those healthiest low-sodium TV dinners we could find. One of the last adjustments for her was allowing me and then eventually our kids on a couple of occasions to help her in the toilet and bath. This was very personal, but she knew at the end that we would need to help her, and she accepted it.

July 8, 2020

Thank you Father, Jesus and Holy Ghost for all you've given, taught, and commanded. Bless me to appreciate more and to be more diligent in my faith and on my path. Thank you. In Jesus's name I pray, Amen. It's been 2 years, 2 months, 3 weeks, 6 days! Feeling crappy again. Sometimes I wonder if I'm just making this worse by staying alive. I can't help that I fight this. I just love all that God has given me and will go when he says, but not a moment sooner!

July 9, 2020

Thank you Father, Holy Spirit, and Jesus for all you've given. All you taught, created, and your love. Bless me to know you're in control, not me. Give me strength to make that journey. In Jesus's name I pray, Amen. It's been 2 years, 2 months, and 4 weeks! Feeling much better so far today!

July 10, 2020

Thank you Father, Holy Spirit, and Jesus for all you've given. Every breath, every second, hour, and day. Thank you for all I have, all I am. I praise you. I am nothing without you. Bless me to never forget I owe all to you and I am because of you. Thank you. In Jesus's name I pray, Amen. It's been 2 years, 3 months, and 1 day! Blood work came back and I'm super dehydrated! Waiting for Mayo to call me back. More blood work next week. Moving around more today. Happy about that. Swelling in feet still off one cup one cup of water! This journey has cost so much. It's taking my freedom, my love life, my strength, and my body. I just need to remember it can't take my hubby, he's the best.

July 11, 2020
Thank you Father, Holy Spirit, and Jesus for all you've given. I'm so blessed to have your love. Bless me to always be faithful and grateful along my journey. Thank you. In Jesus's name I pray, Amen. It's been 2 years, 3 months, 2 days! Walked from our house to Michaela's and back tonight! We took a break at her house and when we got back! Of course, I was using a Rolls-Royce (Purple Rain), but kept Oxygen at 3 the whole way!

Her sense of humor helped her many days. I was shocked she accepted the walker as easily as she did. Working in hospice, I have seen many patients get walkers and then refuse to use them. She used hers, but she nicknamed it her Purple Rain Rolls-Royce. It allowed her to save face when she told her friends and family she now had a walker. She could laugh about it, but I didn't care what she called it. I was glad she used it.

July 12, 2020
Thank you Father for all you've given. Thank you for every breath, second, minute, hour, day, and all of it. I am forever grateful to you. Bless me to know you better. In Jesus's name

I pray, Amen. I am now 3 months and 3 days past my death sentence! Nausea is killing me! Then I threw up my bacon. Which really pissed me off! Tired of being sick. I need a break! Every time I eat, nauseous! Fuck that! I'm hungry!

Here she stopped counting the years and months from the day she was diagnosed with her terminal disease but instead only noted the months since she had outlived her initial prognosis of two years. Why? I'm not sure. I think it was getting harder for her to write in her journal. Sentences started to run on and on without punctuations. Her handwriting got sloppier and harder to read. I think she started noting just the days she lived past the two years at this point just because it was easier and took less writing.

July 13, 2020

Thank you Father for another day! Thank you for giving your son to save us all. Thank you for all you've created! Bless me to never forget who made it possible for me to be, every day. Thank you. In Jesus's name I pray, Amen. Now 3 months and 4 days! Just noticed a tree limb fell on our garage during storm. Wow! Well, it was a powerful storm.

July 14, 2020

Thank you Father for all you've given. We are so blessed to have your love. You're an awesome Father and I'm forever grateful to you. Bless me to know as long (to never forget) as I trust in you, all will be well. You've never let us down. We've always had what we needed and more. Thank you. In Jesus's name I pray, Amen. Now 3 months and 5 days! Well things seem bleak, but I will continue to have faith in my Father. We may have to sell our home and rest, but we will have each other and our Father. We'll be alright.

July 15, 2020

Thank you Father for all you've given. Thank you for watching over me and guiding me. Bless me to know your guidance and to act on it. Thank you. In Jesus's name I pray, Amen. Now 3 months and 6 days!

July 16, 2020

Thank you Father for all you've given. For your grace, love, and guidance. Bless me to be more faithful in you. In Jesus's name, Amen. Now 3 months and 1 week.

July 17, 2020

Thank you Father for all you've given me. Bless me to be stronger in faith and act on your word. Thank you. In Jesus's name I pray. Now 3 months, 1 week, and 1 day! Gavin moved into his own place! I'm so happy for him. Hopefully will remain responsible and doesn't have trouble staying on his own. All I wanted was for him to be happy, independent, successful and better than his father or I. Thank you Father.

July 18, 2020

Thank you Father for all and another day! What am amazing Father you are! Bless me to be strong and faithful knowing all is right in you. In Jesus's name I pray, Amen. 3 months, 1 week, and 2 days! Feel like shit!!

July 19, 2020

Thank you almighty Father for all you've given. I am blessed, truly blessed to know you. Bless me this day to be even more knowledgeable in you. More patient, more tolerant, more loving. and strengthen me for my journey. Thank you. In Jesus's name I pray, Amen. Now 3 months, 1 week, and 3 days. Vomited this morning. Don't know why. I did my inhaler and then started puking. At least I haven't eaten yet!

July 20, 2020

Thank you Father for all you have given and will give. I am blessed and honored with your love. Bless me to remember it's a journey already chosen and help me do my best to honor you. Thank you. In Jesus's name I pray, Amen. Now 3 months, 1 week, and 4 days! Rough day so far. Hopefully, I'll get to feeling better.

July 21, 2020

Thank you Lord for all you've given. Bless me to know you better. In Jesus name I pray, Amen. Now 3 months, 1 week, and 5 days! Feeling rough still. Praying nonstop. I just want to feel better and be as much of myself as I can be.

July 22, 2020

Thank you Father for all you've given, the blessings, and all of it. Bless me to know you better and to always be grateful for all you do. In Jesus's name I pray, Amen. Now 3 months, 1 week, and 6 days! Starting to feel better. Not sleeping well at night. Flushing hard in evenings. Still praying.

July 23, 2020

Thank you Father for all you've given. For always being there for me and loving me. Bless me to remember all and appreciate all you do. Thank you, in Jesus's name I pray, Amen. Now 3 months and 2 weeks!

July 24, 2020

Thank you Father for all you've given. For letting me wake each day to live another. For everything I am, all I have, and it's all because of you. Bless me to never forget this. In Jesus's name, Amen. Now 3 months, 2 weeks, and 1 day!

July 25, 2020

Thank you Father for another day. Thank you for all I am and all I have. I owe all to you. Bless me to stay close to you through all each day. In Jesus's name, Amen. Now 3 months, 2 weeks, and 2 days! I feel much better this morning. Still sore, still nauseous, but I'm alive and it could be worse. Just really tired this and not being able to sleep at night.

July 26, 2020

Thank you Father for all you've given me. Today I asked you to cleanse my heart and make me pure again. I owe all to you. Thank you, Father. In Jesus's name I pray, Amen. Now 3 months, 2 weeks, and 3 days! Rough day again! Slept off and on all day. Can't seem to stay awake. I'm back and forth with the diarrhea still. When where the hell is it all coming from!? Still swelling in my feet. I wish I could get up and be active.

July 27, 2020

Thank you Father for all you've given me. Thank you for watching over me and waking me daily. Thank you for my family, all we have, and all I am. I owe all to you. Cleanse my heart and purify me so I may know you better. Help me stay on the path to know you. Thank you. In Jesus's name I pray, Amen. Now 3 months, 2 weeks, and 4 days! Rough day again. Do not feel well at all.

July 28, 2020

Thank you Father for all you've given me. Thank you for always having my back every day, no matter what. I praise your name and owe all to you. Bless me to never forget and to be more faithful. In Jesus's name I pray, Amen. Now 3 months, 2 weeks, and 5 days! Feeling a little better today. I pray it stays that way. I got up early today! Stayed awake all but maybe 10 minutes. Well, Tim and I still can't discuss anything about bills or my flushing. He and I agree to disagree. Hate it when he says, "I don't listen", because all I do is listen. He's always too busy to talk or talks to me like I'm his patient, but whatever. I'm tired of fighting.

As for counseling, I am a social worker and believe in the power of counseling. Savannah accepted a social worker when she elected a hospice, but I had suggested it several times before this. She always argued against it because she lived with one. Sometimes she got frustrated with me and would say, "I'm not one of your patients." And she was right. I always thought it would have been good for her to vent her feelings and frustrations without me present. But I think she did this with her journal.

July 29, 2020

Thank you Father for all you've given. Thank you for continuing to bless me daily. I am forever in your debt. I owe all to you. Today I ask that you help me to love, even when it's hard, and remain faithful to you. Thank you. In Jesus's name I pray, Amen. Now 3 months, 2 weeks, and 6 days! Feel better but didn't sleep well. Up early 7:30 a m.

July 30, 2020

Thank you Father for another day! Thank you for always having me in your arms. I am nothing without you. Bless me to always remember this. Thank you. In Jesus's name, Amen. Now 3 months and 3 weeks! Feeling a little better today. Please keep going. Hopefully, better each day.

July 31, 2020

Thank you Father all you give. Thank you for blessing me each day. Bless me to know you better. Thank you. In Jesus's name I pray, Amen. 3 months, 3 wks., 1 day! Getting X-ray done to see if I need tapped. Don't want to, but oh well. Well, got my right lung tapped! It's never that one. Life's changed a lot. Tim and I are not the same anymore. He says it's not, but I say a lot has changed because we haven't had sex in a long time. Every time we have a bad fight, he makes the comment, "I know we don't have sex, but you don't need to be my mother." Or it's don't touch because we don't have sex and it's too hard for him because he gets worked up. Hello! I don't even masturbate because I feel like shit. So, it should be me who gets worked up. I'm done, you want sex... If I shit while doing so, or pee, or vomit or am uncomfortable...you got it. I've always been a pincushion for a man. They don't even put effort in it anymore. Years together now and I can't find your spot, but please notice me even if your health is bad. Even when we can't have sex, but I'll still love you. However, I won't try to your ideas, but you must follow mine. I must be in control of all. Here have it. I'm beat. I'll be a good little girl from now on. Oh God, forgive me and help me to be able forgive also. Amen.

To me, I was just being a smart-ass because she started becoming more anal about simple things like putting the toilet lid down. I sarcastically said something along the lines that I knew we didn't have sex anymore, but she didn't need to be my mother. I had no idea that comment cut her emotionally like it did. I regret making that comment now. Perhaps the most difficult topic for most couples is the idea of sexual intimacy. Making love, which was healthy throughout our marriage, went from several times a week to once every couple of weeks when she got out of the hospital to once a month to several months, and then the last year, we made love once nine months before she died. We talked about this as well. I admitted I had brought it up a few times out of frustration but never pressured her to have sex. I felt terrible about it later, but it is a normal desire for a couple in love. I understood, and I dealt with it by masturbation occasionally, but she couldn't even do that for release because it caused her heart rate to rise and caused her to have difficulty breathing. I understood, but she felt terrible about this and apologized often for this. Reading her journals, she had often wanted to make love but worried she might have incontinence issues. The thing is for any couple facing this is to talk about it. We talked about everything, including this. If you truly love each other, you can face lack of sexual intimacy together. She even went as far as to give me half-nude photos of when she was younger to help me visualize her instead of anyone else. However, because of my own religious beliefs, I practiced a period of celibacy and self-restraint before she died and after she died. I'm not saying others would need to do this, but for me, I am glad I did. The key is to talk about it as a couple.

August 1, 2020

Thank you Father for all you've given me. Bless me with patience and love. For it's becoming difficult to find these things in my heart. Bless me with your light. So, I can give the ones around me joy and happiness until I'm gone. So, they'll not be sorry for being in my life. Now 3 months, 3 weeks, 2 days!

August 2, 2020

Thank you Father for all you've given. Thank you for your love and patience for me. Bless me to know that all is possible through you. In Jesus's name I pray. Amen. Now 3 months, 3 weeks, 3 days! Feeling better today. My belly and feet are still swelling. My tummy hurts so bad at night. I can't get comfy, so I'm not sleeping well. Shit myself again and it pissed me off. I hate this!

August 3, 2020

Thank you Father for all you've given me. I am not worthy. Bless me to know my path. Bless me to be faithful to you always and to love even when it's tough to. Thank you. In Jesus's name I pray, Amen. 3 months, 3 weeks, 4 days! Nurse came. Our friend Dawn came and visited. Gavin came. I had good visits. Tim and I continue to disagree. He sees everything I say as a correction. I make suggestions or ask him to do something and he blows up. He says he doesn't need a mom. I'm just asking him to do some things to be considerate of me, like I would for him. He's so set in his ways, but at one time he did these things, but has since stopped. I've decided to just quit caring. He can live like a fucking bachelor. If that's what he wants, and I will be silent. Because I love him and willing to sacrifice my wants for him.

August 4, 2020

Thank you Father for all you've given me and my family daily. We owe all to you. Bless us all to remember that and to honor you daily. Thank you. In Jesus's name I pray, Amen. 3 months, 3 weeks, 5 days!

August 5, 2020

Happy Birthday Aunt Joyce! Thank you, Father, for all you've given me and my family. Thank you for love, patience, discipline, and support. I owe all to you. Thank you and bless me to know you better and to honor you. In Jesus's name I pray. Amen. 3 months, 3 weeks, 6 days!

August 6, 2020

Thank you Father for all you've given. Thank you for patience, love, guidance, and protection. Bless me to know you better and to not forget all you've given. Thank you. In Jesus's name I pray, Amen. 3 months, 4 weeks! Feeling shitty, but I'm alive! Found out Marinia, Justin, and Lincoln and Ilana are all coming next week! Super excited, but also dreading it. Heaven is already having a gloom going about it. Like she's any easier to handle. Some of the shit she does. LOL, Girls. Never could get these two to bond.

August 7, 2020

Thank you Father for all you are love, patience, guidance, support, and shelter. Thank you for always watching over me. I owe all to you. Bless me to never forget this. In Jesus's name I pray, Amen. 4 months, 1 day! Feel slightly good today. Enjoying it while I can. Going to try to get stuff done as much as I can. Tim's taking all my Goodwill stuff to Goodwill, so house is getting a little less cluttered. Was doing okay, but not now. This flushing shit is pissing me off! Feet still swelling. Still have runs. Belly still blowing up. I hurt. No drugs are working. I wish it would just stop! Saw Heaven for 5 minutes then she was gone. Still no Gavin.

August 8, 2020

Thank you Father for all you given me. Bless me to never forget I am nothing without you and that all is achievable through you. Thank you. In Jesus's name I pray, Amen. 4 months & 2 days! Puked! Hate puking! Gavin says he's going to visit, but I'm not holding my breath. Tim is getting room ready for Marinia and them. He's so busy always. Wish he'd relax sometimes. Felt crappy all day and it's not stopping for night. Good luck to me and a lot of prayers.

August 9, 2020

Thank you God for all you do, have done, and give daily. I am nothing without you. I owe all to you. Bless me to be closer to you and stronger for my journey. Thank you, in Jesus's name I pray, Amen. 4 months, 3 days!

August 10, 2020

Thank you Father for all you given me. For the many blessings you've bestowed upon us all. Bless us all to know that we're nothing without you and only through you are all things possible. Thank you. In Jesus's name I pray, Amen. 4 months, 4 days! Marinia and family arrived!!

August 11, 2020

Thank you Father for all you've given me. I praise your name for each day. I owe all to you. Bless me to know you better and to be able stronger in my faith in you. In Jesus's name I pray, Amen. 4 months and 5 days!

August 12, 2020

Thank you Father for all you do. I have nothing without you. I owe all to you. Bless me to remember this always. Thank you. In Jesus's name I pray, Amen. 4 months, 6 days!

August 13, 2020

Thank you Father for all you've given me. Bless me to know all things are possible through you. In Jesus's name we pray, Amen. 4 months, 1 week.

August 14, 2020

Thank you Father for all you've blessed me with. Bless me to know you better and praise you alone. In Jesus's name, Amen. 4 months, 1 week, 1 day! Had an x-ray today then blood draws.

August 15, 2020

Thank you Father for all you've given me. Bless me know you better. In Jesus's name, Amen.

4 months, 1 week, 2 days. Tim's sister Pam came to visit. Start new med today. Feel shitty!

August 16, 2020

Thank you Father for all you given me. Bless me with patience, strength, and stronger faith. Thank you. In Jesus's name, Amen. 4 months, 2 week, 3 days!

August 17, 2020

Thank you Father for all you've given. I owe all to you. Bless me to know you better. In Jesus's name I pray. Amen. 4 months, 2 weeks, 4 days! Second day of new med. I feel weird, but O2 is up. Marinia and Justin left for Colorado today.

August 18, 2020

Thank you Father for carrying me through all this diarrhea and blessing me with feeling better. Bless me to be closer to you and more faithful. In Jesus's name I pray, Amen. 4 months, 2 weeks, 5 days.

August 19, 2020

Thank you Father for all I have and all I am. I owe everything to you. Bless me to know you better and to be more like you in all I say and do. Thank you. In Jesus's name, Amen. 4 months, 2 weeks, 6 days! Found out today that Drs. are pushing for me to go on hospice. So I got to think about that. They say there's not really a point to continuing. Strange, I'm used to people leaving me and underestimating me, but when Dr. do… I'm numb. I don't know.

I had called the doctor beforehand and asked her to discuss the hospice option with her. I knew she was suffering daily now, but she was a fighter. I knew she did not want to go on hospice a couple of months ago when the hospice nurse had visited her. After visiting with the doctor, the next day, we signed up for hospice. As much as she loved life, it was obvious she was getting tired near the end. Besides having shortness of breath with any movement, she had many side effects with the medications. With a weakened immune system, she had constant battles with colds, flus, sniffles, and other illnesses. Finally, the right heart failure and the pulmonary hypertension worsened, and she started retaining fluid in her lungs, legs, and abdomen. She fought so hard for so long, but she mentioned to me several times in the last three months she didn't know how long she could keep fighting. Thank God we involved hospice in the last month of her life. They really helped make sure she didn't suffer. I hope doctors who read this realize how important they are to patients when it comes to end-of-life decisions. If her doctor had not had this discussion, I know she would have continued to fight even if she suffered more. However, having a doctor explain to her that she didn't need to keep fighting and she could get more relief with hospice helped her and us tremendously.

August 20, 2020
Thank you Father for all you given me. I owe all to you, all! Bless me to be closer to you. Bless others by the love you've shown me. To be a light in the darkness and help them as you've helped me. In Jesus's name I pray, Amen. 4 months, 3 weeks!

August 21, 2020
Thank you Father for all you've given me. I owe all to you. Bless me to be closer you and know you better. In Jesus's name I pray, Amen. 4 months, 3 weeks, 1 day. On hospice now. Feel like shit today.

August 22, 2020

Thank you Father for all you do, have done. Thank you for your love. Bless me to know you better and be more faithful in you. In Jesus's name I pray, Amen. 4 months, 3 weeks, 2 days! Little better today maybe. My brother Roy and my nephew Devon came today. Tim's family came today including Suzy, Charity, Ashley, and Myra came to visit too.

Once we told family and friends she had elected a hospice, we started getting a flood of visitors. She loved having company. I often worried it was too many visitors at times as she was short of breath now even with just a conversation. However, she enjoyed company, and I knew many of those people needed to say their goodbyes. She had a huge impact on people throughout her life. I was amazed by family and friends who shared stories about how she had helped them in life. Here she had thought she was a failure, but the steady stream of loved ones and those who gave her credit for being a positive influence in their lives made her realize how she was an important person to many. I already knew she was my everything, but hearing from all these people in the last few weeks of her life made me realize just how beautiful and special she was to many people.

August 23, 2020

Thank you Father for all you've given. I'm especially appreciative of the family I've been given from Tim and his siblings. Thank you for filling all my needs. Always bless me to remember all I owe you. In Jesus's name I pray, Amen. 4 months, 3 weeks, 3 days! Lots of my family visiting. Mom, Evelyn, Brittany, Judy, Adela, Anna, Jaynia, Roy, Dallas, and Trinity.

August 24, 2020

Thank you Father for all you've given me. I gave my life to you. Bless me to remember all is possible through you. In Jesus's name I pray, Amen. 4 months, 3 weeks, 4 days!

August 25, 2020

Thank you Father for all you've given. Bless us to get through my journey and remain faithful to you and not be swayed. In Jesus's name, Amen! 4 months, 3 weeks, 5 days!

August 26, 2020

Thank you Father for all you've given me. Bless me to be closer to you and to know you better. In Jesus's name I pray, Amen. 4 months, 3 weeks, 6 days! My friend Dawn came to visit! My friend Lace video chatted. Nurse Jenny came. Then my friend Mackenzie came. My brother Roy video chatted. I'm so emotional! Gavin came before work. Awesome day! Feel a little better today. I'm so blessed!

August 27, 2020

Thank you for all you do, have given. Bless me to remember to be faithful to you and strengthen me to handle my journey. In Jesus's name I pray, Amen. 4 months, 4 weeks. Busy day. Kindred Aide Kim came, washed my hair! Then Tim's entire office showed up with lunch, cake, cookies, roses and two presents. A special photo and a beautiful butterfly window decoration and a tree ornament. I cried as did Tim. Heaven knew about it! It was just very sweet. It was awesome that they came and hung out with us and did all that. Then our friend Jerri stopped in and visited. I love her so much! Tim's sister Pam called. Then our friend Sherry called and made me cry. Wonderful day. Thank you, Father, for blessing with all these people. Gavin called me today too. I'm so blessed!

August 28, 2020

Thank you Father for allowing me to have another day! I owe all to you. Bless me to remember all things are possible in you. In Jesus's name I pray, Amen. 4 months, 4 weeks, 1 day! Happy Anniversary! I surprised him today! I purchased my card for him last year and hid it. Today Heaven helped me plot to get a gift for him! I'm stoked. He's planning dinner on porch tonight. He's so tired. I need to feel good to do this and I'm doing my best. Thank you, Father for helping me.

August 29, 2020

Thank you Father for all you've given me. Bless me to never forget I am nothing without you. In Jesus's name I pray, Amen. 4 months, 4 weeks, 2 days! Tim's brother Wally and his wife Michelle are coming. My friend Niki's coming. Great visits. Fighting this hard, but I feel you lurking at my door. Go away! I need some good days, please. When my Father calls, I will go, but please, I beg you.

She knew death was coming. She wanted to make sure she got to say goodbye to everyone first. Here she was dying, and yet she was worried about missing someone that wanted to talk to her. She was still trying to give to others whatever advice she had or to just let them know she loved them. She was an amazing woman when it came to how she cared for others over herself.

August 30, 2020

Thank you Father for life and all you've given me. In Jesus's name I pray, Amen. 4 months, 4 weeks, 3 days! My friend Dena is coming today. Tim's sister Pam is coming today! My niece Tiffany and kids came. I'm getting worse. Face reality. I'm dying. Forgive me. I'm weak. I see your misery with each day, that kills me. Wish I could do better. I love you all.

August 31, 2020

Thank you Father for all you've given me. I owe all to you. I'm nothing without you. Bless me to never forget that. In Jesus's name I pray. Amen. 5 months, 3 days! Very yucky. Very sleepy. Scared to sleep every night for fear of not waking up. Praying. Praying. Praying. Just need a couple good days with my family.

September 1, 2020

Thank you Father for another day. I owe all to you. I'm nothing without you. Bless me to never forget I owe all to you. In Jesus's name I pray, Amen. 5 months, 4 days. Days are getting hard. I'm dying, I feel it. I don't want to, but I can feel it. It's hard to be strong and brave for them, but I fear we need to prepare. Really going to push to get stuff done. Not much energy as of these days.

September 2, 2020

Thank you Father for another day. I owe all to you. Bless me to be strong and not complain even though I'm in pain or miserable. Focus on peace, faith, and being with you. In Jesus's name I pray, Amen. 5 months, 5 days! Doing better today, not a lot better, but better. Days are rough, but nights are the worst. I've had so much diarrhea for days. My stomach is swollen, legs and feet swollen. Shit myself 2 times today. Right through my pad. Heaven and Tim have done so much for me and it's going to get worse. I hate this, but what do I do? My meds aren't working for me and it's becoming obvious. I must decide soon. Do I continue fighting and put them through more? Or do I just say I am done with my meds, dope me up and help me die peacefully? I'm going to pray more on it. I need to make decisions and finish what I can. It will be soon that I decide. And I feel I need to have a discussion with all my kids. I can handle all the other decisions, but this is hell. Father and I need your help. God please help guide me in my choices and help my family to understand the needs I must choose and why. In Jesus's name I pray, Amen. PS thank you Father for the walk Tim and I took. The sun was beautiful! I cooked supper with some help, but I did it. Thank you. I'm sorry you all must do simple daily chores for me. I'm sorry you must help clean me up, when I shit myself. Or when you see me in pain, how it hurts you. I'm sorry you're losing sleep because I can't sleep. I'm sorry I'm too sick and weak to cuddle or make love to you. I wish most of all I could change that and that I'm dying. I'm sorry I won't be there to witness the beauty of your life changes…love, graduation, birthdays, birth of children, happiness, heartbreak. But I'm there, know that I'm going to be watching. Always and forever and forever + 1 day. Savannah.

In the last few weeks, she often apologized for leaving me and told the kids and grandkids often she loved them. She had a list of things she had wanted to get done, and those started to be completed. She told us all she didn't think she would live another two weeks, but she was not panicked, but rather, she spoke these words calmly and in a matter-of-fact tone. She had come to peace with it and was no longer panicked or saddened by the idea.

September 3, 2020

Thank you Father for all you've given. For your patience with my stubbornness. I owe all to you alone. Bless me, my family, and friends to remember where we all owe our praise to. In Jesus's name I pray, Amen. 5 months 6 days!! Overslept today! Like major. Still filling up, harder to sleep comfortably.

September 4, 2020

Thank you Father for all you've given me. Bless me to never doubt or take your love for granted. In Jesus's name I pray, Amen. 5 months, 1 week! Still getting worse. Still swollen. Feet have some mottling (right foot by big toe). Trying to breathe is hard today. Stomach is so tight it hurts. Got to get shit done. Tim and I made our hand statue. Now just to get the rest done. Marinia and Ilana will be coming soon. She wants to be here to help while I'm dying. Gavin came by today. Had a good talk and cry with him. I just want him to be okay.

Marinia was living in Colorado, and when I told her that Savannah had elected to go on a hospice, she immediately wanted to fly home and help. Knowing that a hospice was a prognosis of six months or less and sometimes patients live for months or years on hospice, I reassured her that I would let her know when she was closer to dying. I could tell she wanted to make sure she was home and have an opportunity to help and visit before she died. A couple of weeks later, I told her that Savannah was declining quickly, and if she wanted to come home, she should do so. Marinia made it home and got to visit and express her feelings for Savannah. Michaela was starting to visit several times a week but told me she didn't think she could be there when she died. She cried as she told me, but I noticed she came back almost every day and was present when she passed. I'm glad she was able to visit and be a part of her last days as I think she would have felt guilty and had remorse if she hadn't had. Gavin had moved out two months before she died, but he was stopping in several times a week. Gavin was the one with the idea to do a plaster hand mold with her. We bought additional kits because Savannah wanted to do this with all the children. Even in the last week of life, she wanted hand molds done with me and the kids. We got those done as one of her last crafts she did. A couple of nights before she passed, she was in a hospital bed that the hospice had provided, and she was sleeping more but still able to engage in short conversations with others. Gavin curled up with her and cried and held her. He had got to tell her how much he loved her and was going to miss her. I saw this, and I took pictures because it was so sweet and beautiful to see this grown boy in his twenties in top physical condition (as he worked out a lot) cuddled up on her like a little boy. After this, Gavin left to go to work, and I went into the other room. I came back, and Heaven, too, crawled up beside her momma and was talking to her. Heaven was crying as she, too, had a very intimate moment to say her goodbyes as well. Each of those moments were a realization that their mother/stepmother was no longer going to be there in their lives. Savannah knew they needed to be around her near the end and loved them all in a way that allowed them to let go.

September 5, 2020
Thank you Father for all you've given me.
I owe all to you and I'm nothing without you.

Bless me to know you're with me always. In Jesus's name I pray, Amen. 5 months, 1 week, 1 day! Preparing for my end. Getting all my shit in order before I enter eternal sleep. This is rough. I have a hospital bed in my living room now.

September 6, 2020
   No entry.

September 7, 2020
   Thank you Father for all you've given me. Bless me to always remember I owe all to you. Thank you. In Jesus's name I pray, Amen. 5 months, 1 week, 2 days! They did my hair today!

September 8, 2020
   Thank you Father for another day and all you've done for my family and I. Thank you for the opportunity to be able to say good-byes, when I know a lot of people don't get that. Bless me to remember today and every day. I owe all to you. In Jesus name I pray, Amen. 5 months, 1 wk, 3 days!

Her last journal article was September 8, 2020. She died six days later on September 14, 2020.

On September 9, 2020, I noticed that day that she started having air hunger. Air hunger is often associated with COPD patients. This is when the person can't breathe, and they panic from fear of suffocating. I myself had air hunger one time when I had a flare-up with my asthma, and I had forgotten to bring my inhaler. They tell you to remain calm and breath through your nose and breath out with your mouth. It's not easily done when you can't breathe. In my case, I called an ambulance, and they gave me a nebulizer treatment before I could catch my breath. In Savannah's case, she pointed out she was panicking because she felt like the fluid in her stomach was going to burst. Inhalers and nebulizers can cause shakiness and nervousness but relieved her symptoms for a while. Near the end, only Ativan and morphine brought her relief, but they caused her to sleep a lot. Savannah did not like medications and, by the end, discontinued most of her medications and opted for just the comfort medications that made her sleep most of the time.

On September 10, 2020, she was having difficulty staying awake for very long. But she managed to finish the last of the plaster hand molds with the kids. We talked after the kids had gone to bed. We talked about the idea of being cremated, and eventually both our ashes would be dumped into the Grand Canyon. It was one of the most beautiful places we had visited together, and we wanted to be together underneath that beautiful sky with all those stars to look at. We discussed what she wanted to do for a celebration of life, and she even picked out music she wanted played. Then she fell asleep again. At this point, I was giving her comfort medications about every four hours. These medications did relieve the pressure she was feeling with the fluids building up inside her, but she slept most of the time now.

On September 11, 2020, she had slept most of the day. However, there were items like pictures of her niece's parents that she made sure were put in a small box, and we mailed to them. We had everything figured out except pictures she had from childhood. She had pictures of a guy and his sisters back in elementary school. Their families were good friends, and they lived next door to them when they were kids. She knew his name and had held onto the pictures for over thirty years on the off chance she would run into the family again in the future. Yet when we looked online, we could not find him on Facebook. We did find his brother online, and I contacted him through Facebook but got no response. I looked again and found another relative (maybe a nephew) and contacted him on Facebook. He got back to me and told me the guy we're looking for was his uncle, and he died a few years ago. I told her, and she said, "Oh, dang. I always wanted to get him those pictures. Does he have family that wants them?" I contacted the nephew on Facebook again, and he indicated he did not. However, his daughters might, and he gave me their names to look up on Facebook. I did not contact them right away as we had visitors that day, and I was trying to hold myself together for the kids' sake. I tried to remain calm and cool because I wanted to reassure our children she was going to be okay and not have pain. Inside I was scared to death and wanted to cry. The love of my life was dying.

On September 12, 2020, she had slept most of the day. She had a cowboy hat and a wooden coffee table that she had gotten from her friends (Dena and Russ), who lived in Wisconsin. She made sure she got on Facebook video chat with them and made me swear that I would get these items to them after she had passed away. It was kind of humorous because the cowboy hat I was not sure where it was. We had moved a couple of times, and kids had moved in and out a few times. She thought it was up in a cupboard area in a sack. But I looked and could not find it anywhere. So she made me agree to buy them a new hat if I couldn't find it. She was insistent, and they agreed that would be good enough if I couldn't find it. I did deliver the table and the hat a month after she had passed, but it was not in the cupboard, and it was not in a sack. However, when I delivered it, they confirmed it was the hat. She had held onto the hat for twenty years.

On September 13, 2020, she had slept most of the day. However, I remember having one conversation with her between her many naps. Previously, we had talked about how patients sometimes said things out of frustration and/or confusion as the terminal illness caused continued weakness and confusion in the mind. The night before she died, we talked briefly. She recalled our conversations about this and wanted to know if she had said anything hurtful to me or the kids. I assured her she had not, and she smiled at me and told me she loved me and asked, "I just don't want to hurt any of you." Then she fell back to sleep. At that moment, I cried, and I knew she was going to die. Even as she was dying, she thought of others and didn't want to hurt anyone. My last conversation with her was how she wanted to make sure we knew she loved us, and I feel her love yet today.

On September 14, 2020, it was morning. I gave her pain medication. It was a liquid that I used drops under the tongue, and normally she made faces and disliked the taste. This time, she did not wake up and showed little reaction to the taste. I kissed her, and her lips were cold to the touch, and she continued to sleep. I knew then it would be soon, and I cried inside. My beautiful flower was fading away and had no warmth of life. By this time, Savannah was sleeping all the time and not very coherent if she did wake up. Trying to make sure I followed her wishes, I looked up the daughters of her friend from childhood on Facebook and contacted them on Sunday. One daughter responded and said she would love to have pictures of her dad when he was a kid. I got her address and leaned over to tell Savannah we finally found some family to give the pictures to. She was sleeping. However, twenty minutes later, I looked over at her, and I noticed she was not breathing. She had passed but not before everything on her list had been completed. It was like she knew everything she wanted done got done. She slipped away without any suffering or pain. It truly was a sign of who she was as a person. She was on her deathbed, yet her concerns and last wishes were about making sure others were okay and things had been returned to those they belonged to. She was about giving rather than what others owed her. She was beautiful like this, and I am so glad all the little items she wanted done got completed. It would have made her happy!

When she did pass away, it was like she just slipped away into permanent sleep. My beautiful Snow White slept, and no kiss could bring her back. As a caregiver, you never want the love of your life to die, but after a while, you do not want to see them suffer either. It is a very normal, odd position to be in. You want them to live, but you hope they don't suffer, which means you start to accept death as the only alternative. I still sometimes am torn up about these feelings, but I also know she went as peacefully as anyone could, and I do find comfort in that.

Chapter 6

Immediate Aftermath and Celebration of Life

When she passed, the kids and I were in a momentary state of shock. The woman that brought us all together as a family had died. We cried without talking much. Each of us struggled in our own way, but we all felt the loss of something gigantic in our lives. Of course, we reassured each other and were thankful she did not suffer. She went very peacefully. I called the hospice nurse. The hospice nurse came and confirmed she had passed. We stepped outside as the funeral home arrived and got her loaded up. We stepped outside and stood in disbelief. The best way I can describe it was it was like we would be okay for a few minutes at a time and then suddenly a panic attack to the point we couldn't even hardly breath. The woman we all loved was gone forever. What did this mean now? What were we as a family now? We all had the next few days off, and we went to the funeral home the next day. The funeral planning helped us stay focused and not completely fall apart. I tried to be calm and in control as the kids and I went to the funeral home. I think they were trying to do the same for me. Of course, as we sat there and tried to write out an obituary, I started breaking down. How do you put volumes of good things you knew about this person into a few short paragraphs?

Savannah and I hadn't discussed her funeral until the very end. It was depressing to think about and an easy discussion to avoid. Working in hospice, I knew it was something that needed to be done, but I didn't want to deal with it either. We had done a life review book together in the hospital because we're not sure if she was going to make it out of the hospital, so some of her past and family were written down so I could look at this. She did suggest getting a local funeral home called about a week before she died. A representative came to our house and gave us a planning guide. We had talked about being cremated as we both did not like being buried in the ground. We also talked about me being cremated in the future and having our ashes dumped in the Grand Canyon someday. This was a beautiful scenery when we had gone on our honeymoon celebration a year after our marriage. We both thought it would be beautiful there, and we could look up to the sky at night and see the stars together that way. Still, we had to decide on a service or not, whether to display the body or not, a reception or celebration of life afterward, pictures and memories we wanted to display, an obituary, and other little details. Some of this were decided after she had died by me with input from the kids. I am glad we had a general understanding of what she wanted from her as it made it a lot easier for us as a family. It turned out very much the way she would have wanted it. Hopefully, discussing these final preparations will help families as they, too, will need to make these decisions themselves.

First, we had to decide on burial or cremation. We had discussed this before she died, and we both liked the idea of cremation and having our ashes spread at one of our favorite places we had visited. We had life insurance and could afford burial, but we personally did not want burial. It is important to note for those who have not decided and are worried about costs that burials generally run $5,000 to $7,000 more than cremation in our area. It was never about the money. We both hated the idea of being in a box in the ground. Even though we had decided on cremation, we also had to decide to display the body before cremation or just have pictures at the funeral. Having her body displayed before cremation was an additional $2,000 because of embalming, renting a coffin, etc. She thought about displaying her body for her aunt who lived out of state in case she was coming, but otherwise she did not care because it was silly in her opinion to keep her body around for a few extra days when she was dead already. She died, and initially her aunt had sent a message that she might not make it to funeral because she was older and had health issues of her own. That made the decision easy for us at that point, so we opted for immediate cremation, and we would just display pictures. However, that was our decision. Those in similar circumstances may decide on burial or actual display of body before cremation. It is important to note though that it should be your decision and not necessarily an entire family decision. Savannah and I had made the decision for cremation and not displaying the body. This was not opened to our four children, not because we didn't value their opinion but because we were the soul mates and they had their own life to worry about. Besides, we paid the funeral bill ourselves without help from the kids. It was our personal choice and our financial right to decide. And we did not ask her mom or siblings or extended family for their opinion. We loved our families and extended families; however, trying to seek input from all these additional people is just asking for potential conflict. More people also mean more opinions. Savannah and I both agreed we could try listen to everybody and try to make everybody happy, but someone would have had bad feelings eventually. We knew we couldn't please everyone, so we just made our decision ourselves. It avoided lots of headache. Now if only kids are involved or there are no surviving immediate family members, then it might need to be a group decision. And if one is paying for the funeral, don't be surprised that they may want to make the decisions on the funeral. If it boils down to group decision, then just realize the more people you have involved, the more complicated it can be.

She was pretty much conscious up until the last two days, and at that point, the outcome was already determined. Sometimes couples don't want to discuss this, but I'm glad we did. One thing to remember is that one medical power of attorney is enough with a backup. Sometimes I've seen people list several children, and then they all must come to an agreement on what course to take. This can lead to disagreements and hard feelings. As for the financial power of attorney, it is important to know that this is to allow for someone to financially speak on your behalf, but sometimes banks and other financial institutions don't always recognize this, or it takes extra steps to get things done financially if they are not able to speak for themselves. To save on any hassles or questions, I was added to her financial accounts when we got out of the hospital. That way, I didn't have to bring my "financial power of attorney" paperwork every time I went to the bank. I also got my living will completed at the same time, and it's a good idea for anyone over fifty to do this as you never know when medical issues could become an issue. Heart attacks and other medical issues are more prevalent with people over fifty. It is much better to have clear directions for your family what you want done and who you want to speak on your behalf. I chose for mine my oldest daughter, Michaela, and then Heaven as the second medical and financial power of attorney. Living wills help prevent disagreements between family members when it comes to medical and financial decisions that may need to be made.

We had some of the most open talks any couple could ever have. We discussed dying, the kids, what she would miss out on, and my future without her. We even talked about me dating and meeting someone else eventually. Have you had that talk with your significant other? How many couples have had that talk? She wanted the kids and I to be happy. She did not want us to mourn forever or be depressed. I knew what I had with her would never be replicated, but I agreed that I was a social person, and I would get lonely, and perhaps I would date or even live with someone again. However, at this point, I highly doubt I would ever marry again. For the kids, she wanted the kids to be okay but did not want me to give them cash or assets. However, I did not want to be collecting money on the kids after she had died. So I paid off some few small loans we had cosigned with the kids and transferred a house and car that had been paid off previously to the kids. The house I still lived in remained in my name. All totaled, it was probably $60,000 of property and cars and payments I just wiped the slate clean. She thought we had done enough for our kids and did not want them to take advantage of me financially. But I explained to her that I did not want to be in the position of trying to collect money from our kids monthly. I had a good job, and life insurance paid everything off and most of our bills. To me, I was okay with this, and I was not in the mood to be the bad guy and try to collect money from the kids every month after she died. She finally agreed, and we told kids that was the only financial help we would be doing. To me, it was worth it. If we did not have life insurance, this would not have happened. As for me moving on…I'm happy, but not ready to have a relationship anytime soon. I will eventually, but I need my time to grieve.

The day after we had visited the funeral home, we were still in a daze. Oscar, her nephew, had come up from Texas and stopped in to offer his condolences. I suggested that he come over and eat with us that night. Oscar was kind of a shy kid, but she always enjoyed his company. I thought it might be a good distraction for us to visit with him. He came over later with his sister and her baby. I grilled food and started a fire in the firepit. We slowly sat there and drank a few beers, but we didn't say much. Oscar started talking about memories he had of her when they were kids. Soon our children were also sharing their favorite memories with her. We laughed and cried some too, but I noticed we were talking again. We needed Oscar to break the silence of grief. We had a wonderful talk that night as a family and enjoyed the fire, sipping on some beers. It almost felt like she was in our circle listening in and laughing at times with us. The kids also agreed they felt her presence that night. We needed it, and like the true, caring person she was, she comforted us all that night. Talking about her life took a little of the sting out of her death. We all agreed that night that Savannah would not want us crying our lives away after she had died. That was why we felt her that night. We were laughing and living, and that was what she wanted for us.

Looking back, I am so glad we had taken steps to plan for end-of-life decisions. Life insurance was something I thought was cheap, but I had gotten more in case I had died. I wanted to make sure she and the kids would be taken care of if I had died. But in getting it for me, we got it on her too. Term life was relatively inexpensive but really helped us to have some breathing room financially to allow me to take time off as she approached death. It also made me less stressed financially after she died, and I only had one income. We still had bills, including hospital bills, but communication with creditors and medical bills is the key. Most will work with you and arrange for manageable payments. You must understand this and talk with them. Ignoring these bills will only make them worse later. The living will and will we had finalized the first time she went into the hospital. We were not sure she was going to make it out of the hospital at first. She did not want to be kept alive with machines and thankfully was able to articulate her own medical care clear up until the last few days. A will helped us transfer real estate and assets over to me after she had died. I also had a will done that designated my kids as equal benefactors after I pass away. It is important to consider having life insurance, living wills, and wills developed ahead of time. It prevented a lot of anxiety and worry as she got sicker. We focused more on our time together rather than trying to figure out what needed to happen medically or financially.

We discussed lots of things about what life would be after she was gone. She grew up poor and had collected and held onto many things throughout the years. She wanted to know if our kids wanted pictures and other items from the house. She was disappointed when boxes of pictures and school papers and memories from the kids growing up were not wanted. Gavin and Heaven looked through items but kept very few things. It is important to understand generational and societal changes when it comes to keeping pictures. Nowadays, pictures are kept on online social platforms like Facebook. Even I noticed we took more pictures early on in our marriage, but we did take lots of pictures and posted them online with Facebook. And I happen to agree with our kids that this is a much easier and safer way to keep pictures. Physical pictures kept in scrapbooks and boxes are exposed to weather changes and exposure to elements in attics, basements, garages, and other storage areas often utilized to store them. And you need space for these items, but storing pictures online is easy and less time consuming, and you don't have to worry about them fading over time. As for passing down trinkets or old memories from one generation to another, this, too, is not practiced as much anymore. She kept dishes that she thought the kids might want, but in this modern era of break and replace with cheap replacement dishes or other items, passing on such items is just not very feasible anymore. Savannah knew that I was not going to do a lot of cooking on my own. She also knew I was not interested in keeping all the furniture. The kids took some items from the kitchen and some furniture items, but not nearly as much as she thought they would. So don't be surprised if your kids and grandkids don't want all the items you kept for them. The digital world and order on demand and shipped to your door have replaced scrapbooks and heirlooms being passed down. Don't be upset by their lack of interest. Just keep in mind these ideas have shifted even in our lifetime. After she had passed, the kids all had great memories I knew they would have in their hearts forever, and to me, that is more important than anything I keep for them.

Savannah had postponed thinking about dying and what she wanted to do with her stuff for the first year. However, eventually she started having me get boxes out of the attic and from the basement and started going through things. Pictures went to the kids. Her art desk and paintings were to go to the kids. Dishes and kitchen appliances and gadgets were offered to the kids first. Often these items were traditionally offered to the kids first and then opened to other family members and then donated. The kids did not want many of her clothes. They did ask for an item or two, but otherwise in these were donated to other family members and what was left over went to the YWCA. She would have liked knowing the clothes were going to be used by those that appreciated them or were going to use them. So much of what she wanted to give away went to the kids or others that would use them.

Working in hospice, I was aware how many people express their last wants and needs, such as having a steak for their last meal or seeing a family member one final time. However, it is much more than this. Most times, they are wanting to know they will be remembered and honored. Savannah wanted to discuss our family and how we would do after she was gone. These were not easy conversations to have. It would be easy to avoid talking about her death and life afterward. However, she was the one that was strong and initiated these conversations. She wanted us to love life as she had loved life. She wanted to know she was in our heart and souls and would guide us in life afterward. She did not want us to suffer watching her die or to suffer in grief afterward. In the many years of providing social work services to others in hospice, I have never known a person dying to want their family to suffer and grieve indefinitely. Savannah talked about what she wanted to give to the kids, not because of the material worth attached to such items but more for a positive memory or something to bring comfort to them later in life. She talked about returning items to friends and family. She talked about me dating again someday and continuing to live and find happiness in life. These last wishes meant more to her than any last meal or visit from a family member. Knowing her husband and kids and family and friends were going to be okay and would be happy again brought her comfort in the end.

On the last week of her life, Savannah and I talked about the details for the service. She wanted convenience and decided to do a service at the funeral home instead of a showing there and then move to a service to a church. Many of the family members were from out of town or elderly, and we figured we would lose people in the transfer. We discussed pictures she would want displayed, and that was easy. Her most prized pictures were on the wall in our house. She wanted all of those displayed. I called the funeral home, and they transferred all these pictures onto a DVD with music. About a week out, she had not selected the music she wanted at the viewing, but I finally got her to come up with a list of songs she wanted. After she had died, as I was getting pictures together, I found her goodbye speech she had written. In fact, she wrote her own farewell speech to be read at her funeral.

Dear family and friends,

I'm sorry I wasn't strong enough to keep fighting. It gets hard. Please know that I'm so happy to have had each one of you in my life at whatever point you were. I'm grateful to God for each of you. I'm human, I made mistakes and some bad choices in life, but also some good. My only regret is I didn't live as freely as I could have. I didn't have enough time with all of you. And I wish I could have given more to you all.

I loved with all my heart, as much as I could, and deeply as I could. My family and friends meant the world to me and I tried to never forget any of you. My rock in life was my faith and my husband, Tim Heller, my children (all four), grandchildren. I was truly blessed to have each of them.

I just want you all to know that I'm at peace with this. I fought as long as I could.

Today, I hope that you will all celebrate my life and not mourn. You can cry (I would've), but smile, sing, dance, laugh, eat while you do so. And please somebody have a damn drink for me! Mountain Dew and peach schnapps or do my favorite shot French Kiss. I will be there. Sing a song for me. Dance like nobody's watching. Enjoy your food for me. Golf some holes for me. Be kind to each other and hug one another for me. I love you all and like I said I wish I could have given more. Take care of each other and enjoy life for me because we're all not promised tomorrow.

Well, that's it, see you soon.

PS can somebody please pray that I get a purple halo and wings instead of horns?! Thank you.

I read it at the service. Of course, I had to stop and cry a few times because it was her goodbye to everyone. We talked about a celebration of life afterward. She had insisted she wanted to have a party. She wanted food and music and karaoke (as she was an avid karaoke singer) and dancing. We talked about catering food in but decided against this because we had done this at previous events like our wedding renewals and we had food left over. Besides, we're not sure how many people would show up because of the COVID-19 pandemic. She came up with the idea of a potluck. She always loved potlucks because people brought a variety of food and their own tableware. It meant easy cleanup and less hassle for us afterward. It also meant we would be prepared for a few people showing up or hundreds of people because it would be expected they bring a dish. This was a brilliant idea as we had more people than we expected and could not have predicted how much food to be catered. But now we had plenty of food, and they took food and cleaned up after themselves afterward. Many of our family get-togethers were like this, and it worked out well. She indicated people could cry, but she wanted them to enjoy food and dance or sing and remember her as a happy person. This event could not be at the funeral home, but we were both members of the Moose Lodge in town, and they were more than willing to host it. I gave out drink tickets, and we all toasted her during the evening. People did eat, laugh, sing, and dance. She would have been happy. It was what she wanted.

Chapter 7

Impressions and Thoughts After Reading Her Journal

When I first started reading her journals after the celebration-of-life event, I was amazed how she was able to capture her feelings in her journal for that period. I first noted how her faith was so important to her. Every day, she was thankful. Every day. She thanked God for helping her daily and most often referred to God as her Father. She really had been through a lot in life, and she strongly believed her Father had led her out of difficult situations. And I noticed she was not begging for a cure, but rather she wanted God to help her through each day. We prayed nightly together, but in her journals, you can truly see how personal and close her relationship with God was. My faith has also increased since her death. Although I am a man of science and educated well, the idea of it all being an accident and matter of chance, I'm not arguing that some things were not allowed to develop and change through time, and I don't ascribe to the belief that the world was created in seven days. Seven ages or eras maybe, but it is also important to note that many liberties have been taken by translations of the Bible over time. Having faith in our life helped us cope tremendously. It gives me hope that I will see her again. A love like ours will not be stopped by death, space, or time.

Another thing that becomes clear reading the journal is that it was abundantly clear that she suffered tremendous daily, but it was not always from the terminal illness. The daily side effects included everything from dry mouth to severe nausea and temperature swings, breathing difficulties, etc. Regular illnesses including the flu and cold were severe struggles for her. Besides regular illnesses, she was easily fatigued and often affected by the weather outside that day. One of Savannah's roughest health issues was two bouts of shingles. Shingles was perhaps the biggest physical ailment that caused her to decline rapidly in her last year. Savannah wanted to make sure others knew there was a vaccine for this virus that many people currently have in their system now. The biggest potential health crisis in her last year of life was the COVID-19 pandemic. Although she never got COVID-19, it caused a huge change in our social behaviors and limited contact with others. Seeing the suffering she went through and watching her get sick and tired of being sick and tired eventually allowed for me to come to accept death. It hurt us to watch her feel so bad all the time. We often felt powerless to help her. We hated the idea of losing her, but eventually we came to understand that her death was an end to the suffering. It is an ironic concept that loved ones eventually come to realize.

Reading through her journals over the past two years of her life, it was evident she suffered a lot more than she let on. She loved life and never wanted to give up. Her zest for life was evident, and each day in her journal, she thanked God for another day. However, simple tasks like getting out of bed or going to the bathroom or taking a bath became increasingly more difficult. Near the end, she would walk to the bathroom with a walker, and I would walk with her because she was so weak, and I worried she would fall. She would return to the sofa (where she stayed about ninety percent of the time) very winded. She would say, "Walking to the bathroom is like running a marathon." At the very end, she was just tired. She never gave up even when she refused any more treatment and just opted to pain medications when she had pain or was having difficulty breathing. She never gave up, but she needed to rest. Fighting a battle to live daily wore on her, and as a caregiver, you realize death is not as scary as seeing your loved one anguishing in pain and suffering. Rest and peace become more of a desire than the daily struggle to live. In the end, she was happy with her decisions, and she went peacefully. I believe it was the right decision for her. It is your decision. It is not your doctor's decision. It is not your spouse's decision or your family's decision. If you are a loved one and they no longer can speak for themselves, then put yourself in their shoes. Would they want to go through all the extra medications and/or procedures if the result is the same? Knowing how much she suffered helped me come to grips with her dying. I don't know how she did it. If it had been me, I think I would have given up and just taken the comfort medications early on. I am glad she is no longer suffering. For me as a caregiver, this was the hardest part for me. I watched her suffer daily, and there was nothing I could do about it. That sense of powerlessness with an illness bothered me the most because I would have done anything to help her. I often asked God to allow me to take her sickness, but the only relief she got was when she had passed away. My faith allows me to see her in heaven without pain and suffering, and I am thankful.

Chapter 8

Dealing with Grief

I remember telling people that I worked with in hospice about dying and grief and their own belief system (most often their own ideas of God and heaven). I explained that when our loved ones die, there is no idea of time in eternity. So twenty or thirty years of separation is like a split second. They will be in heaven reaching back their hand for us, and in eternity, we would be with them in a split second. It is only us on earth that will think time is a long time until we are reunited. I often used this analogy to bring comfort to help families know their loved ones will not be alone and we would reunite someday. I hold onto this and look forward to the day I can hold her hand again. We had plans to grow old together. Our business we had started was doing well for a first-year startup. We had met expenses and made a slight profit. We were hoping to build it, and eventually I could quit my regular job and work the bar/events center with her. We got along so good we didn't mind working together and living together. Most couples needed some space, but we didn't. If we traveled, we traveled together. If we went out, we went out together. We had traveled every couple of years. We had traveled out west and had made trips to Florida. We traveled to Graceland with my sister and her mom one time before she got sick. We started the business together, and we were planning on going to Mexico before she got sick. Our goal was to work hard and travel and do things together while we watched our kids and grandkids grow and become who they were going to be. Even after she got sick, we talked about renting a vacation home with the kids and grandkids along the beach somewhere, but when we investigated it, she wasn't sure she could make the trip. We talked about all this, and it made us cry at times as we had wanted to grow old together and die in each other's arms. One of our favorite movies was *The Notebook*, but it was not to be. However, we did realize we had been the perfect soul mates for each other, and the decade we spent together was the most glorious period in our lives. We had faith that God had brought us together to experience true happiness even if it was not for as long as we wanted here in this life. However, we knew we would reunite after death, and our souls would truly unite once we met after this life. This knowledge helped me several times in my grief. Many felt sorry for what we were going through, but we felt sorry for them because our love and commitment was rare, and most people never experience what we had.

I went back to work a week later and got COVID-19 after she died. I isolated from family and friends for forty days as a religious expression of my grief. This was a time I really focused on finishing the book. I cried daily for months, and I still cry often, but I also know she wanted us to be happy. I started texting our kids every night a short prayer and an excerpt from her journal every night. Sometimes they comment to everyone on our group text. I started doing this for two reasons. One was to let the kids know that I, too, was grieving with them and they were never alone. I encouraged them to call or text me if they needed anything. They are slowly moving forward in life, while I continue to be stuck in my grief at times. The other reason I texted them daily was that Savannah and I used to text each other daily little sweet notes or words of love for each other. Altogether, we had texted each other for a total of 3,552 days in a row, almost ten years of texting somebody that you loved them and were thinking of each other. The nightly texting has brought me more comfort than I think the kids get from me. LOL.

Days blended into weeks, and weeks turned into months. Then in November, I got a request from one of her friends to see if I could send her some of Savannah's ashes. I really struggled with this. I did not want to give up any of her ash. I remember I opened her ashes and rubbed my fingers through it. I cried uncontrollably for a while.

I cried tears of hurt and tears of joy, thinking about how we were perfect for each other. It gets easier with time. I miss her every day. I miss calling or texting her daily and just completely alone and just seeing if she needed anything on the way home I could get with her. I miss venting to her about life or work or kids or politics or anything. Sometimes I talk to her in my room at night and tell her I miss her, that I love her still. However, to lose a soul mate is not something I will ever get through or get over. There is simply no way to ever fill that hole she left. I knew grief hurt, and I had felt loss before with my parents both passing before she did. We really saw the world in a very similar passion. My emotions are still raw. I've visited friends, and I've returned to doing karaoke every weekend at the bar we met. Writing the book has helped tremendously as well, especially on Thanksgiving and Christmas. I told the kids I was not going to do Thanksgiving or Christmas, but rather I was going to the park and write our story. Both days, I felt completely alone and cried hard by myself as I read her words over and over. Yet I found comfort in her words. It feels like I'm honoring her, and perhaps maybe someone can be inspired or helped by our story. How glorious would that be? Out of our suffering, we can provide insight and even hope to others.

The story continues, and my love for her has not diminished. I still carry our wedding bands on a necklace she bought for me. The only things I can add to this book is hoping God touches you and your loved ones as he has mine. Death is part of our existence. Not one of us will escape it. Maybe this is the time to talk over this with your family. Do you have life insurance? Do you have a will, a living will, and power of attorneys in place? If not, maybe you should? We did not expect that illness, and I never thought I'd be writing a book about our experiences together as she battled a terminal disease. I wish I could better explain how great of a wife, mother, and grandmother she was. She made everyone around her feel better even while she was dying. She loved life and God. Like I explained, it was impossible to write an obituary and put everything in a few paragraphs. Same goes for this book. As I wrote it, I recalled thousands of conversations and little moments that I could not include in this book. I feel a sense of accomplishment, and it has helped me come to accept her death and more importantly my life without her. We will meet again. This I'm sure of. I pray for all of you that someday you will experience a love like we had. I am deeply saddened she is no longer with us, but I feel very blessed we had our time together. She was a blessing to me and all those around her. Thank you for everything, babe, and I will love you forever and a day. Amen.

About the Author

Tim Heller is a licensed master-level social worker in the state of Iowa. Tim has over twenty-five years in the human services and social work fields. Tim held a wide variety of jobs, ranging from helping troubled kids to teaching college courses to medical social work. Tim is currently a full-time social worker for hospice for over seven years. Tim and his wife, Savannah, were informed of her terminal diagnosis in April 2019. The couple discussed writing the book together, and initial writings were together. However, as the terminal disease took hold, Savannah started journaling daily. After Savannah passed away in September 2020, Tim finished the book and included her journal entries. The couple intended for this book be a resource and a comfort to other couples and families facing terminal illnesses.

CPSIA information can be obtained
at www.ICGtesting.com
Printed in the USA
BVHW081515281221
625047BV00003B/126

9 781662 454544